THE MEMOIRS OF
LAETITIA HORSEPOLE

THE MEMOIRS OF LAETITIA HORSEPOLE, BY HERSELF

{edited by}
JOHN FULLER

Chatto & Windus
LONDON

Published by Chatto & Windus 2001

2 4 6 8 10 9 7 5 3 1

Copyright © John Fuller 2001

John Fuller has asserted his right under the Copyright, Designs and Patents
Act 1988 to be identified as the author of this work

First published in Great Britain in 2001 by
Chatto & Windus
Random House, 20 Vauxhall Bridge Road,
London SW1V 2SA

Random House Australia (Pty) Limited
20 Alfred Street, Milsons Point, Sydney,
New South Wales 2061, Australia

Random House New Zealand Limited
18 Poland Road, Glenfield,
Auckland 10, New Zealand

Random House (Pty) Limited
Endulini, 5A Jubilee Road, Parktown 2193, South Africa

The Random House Group Limited Reg. No. 954009
www.randomhouse.co.uk

A CIP catalogue record for this book
is available from the British Library

ISBN 07011 72053
Papers used by Random House are natural,
recyclable products made from wood grown in sustainable forests;
the manufacturing processes conform to the environmental
regulations of the country of origin

Printed and bound in Great Britain by
Mackays of Chatham plc, Chatham, Kent

Contents

Preface

The odd story of the discovery of this manuscript is fully in keeping with the character of the memoirs contained in it. These conceal within an elegant structure a passionate self-exposure, which yields its surprising secrets without any fanfare, almost at a whim. I am not an art historian, and would have hesitated before taking on the editing of the manuscript myself, were it not for two things. First of all, the memoirs, though written by a painter and containing much about her practice and theory of art, are principally the intimate revelations of an individual, and their interest is a literary one. Second, my wife and I not only discovered the manuscript ourselves, but realised when we did so that it had been unwittingly in the possession of the family for nearly thirty-five years. It seemed natural, therefore, having deciphered and transcribed the memoirs, to see to their publication myself. There was, of course, no problem about copyright, since Horsepole had no heirs. In dealing with the MS I have benefited from the advice of Dr Christiania Whitehead, of the University of Warwick, who gave freely of her time and expertise.

In 1966 Philip Hendy, my wife's stepfather and formerly Director of the National Gallery, bought for £1200 from Ciancimino Ltd, of the King's Road, London, a large inlaid cabinet. The cabinet was then described, and always known in the family, as the 'Venetian Cabinet', although in a recent inspection by Christie's it was placed no more specifically than north Italian. It consists of an early sixteenth-century set of twenty-six visible drawers in an architectural design, with cornices, pillars, turrets and bronze statues in four niches, the whole mounted on a plainer eighteenth-century base, with a cupboard. There is a small door in the centre of the architectural façade, with four sprung metal latches, a pair on each side of the interior. The latches release the statues, behind which are four further sets of drawers, eighteen in number. One of the right-hand latches was broken, and had been ever since its purchase. After my mother-in-law's death in 1993, when my wife inherited the cabinet, I made every effort to find a way to reconnect the latch with the hidden spring that releases the front right-hand statue, but the mechanism was concealed in the solid interior wooden structure, and was inaccessible. It was not until we contacted a firm of antiquarian restorers in 1997 that this front set of four drawers could be opened. In the second and third of these drawers (which measure approximately two by nine inches) were two tightly rolled sheafs of paper, eighty-two sheets in all, covered with handwriting in a sometimes barely legible faded brown ink. This untitled manuscript, which I have ventured to call *The Memoirs of Laetitia Horsepole, by herself* (being the sort of title that the memoirs might have been given if they had been published at the time, which as far as I can discover was not the case) may or may not have been placed in the cabinet by the author, and may or may not be complete. Written in 1820, they may or may not have been read by the intended recipient (Shelley), but it seems likely that they would not have been written at all unless a wider audience had been ultimately envisaged. There was no question, therefore, of omitting any of the material, as being of too intimate a character, though it is fair to say that some of the sexual remarks go well beyond what was thought proper for public consumption at the time. In fact, the manuscript is reproduced exactly as it stands, in spelling, punctuation and capitalisation, save for one or two silent corrections of evident slips of the pen (clear misspellings, repeated words, and so on) and one or two guesses at words. I have tried to keep my notes to the minimum.

This is not the place for an enquiry into the relative obscurity of Laetitia Horsepole's reputation, but any reader of these memoirs may well wonder why she is not better known. Like Gainsborough, she was a protégée of Francis Hayman, and for much of her life she was a professional working portraitist. She was a founding member of the Royal Academy at a surprisingly early age, and though she does not appear in Zoffany's group portrait, neither of course do Mary Moser or Angelica Kauffmann. Her best-known painting, 'The Untrusting Slave', has been compared by Berenson in its fresh and unstudied handling of paint to Hogarth's 'Shrimp Girl', and her late Italian work has attracted the attention of historians of Romantic painting. And yet her work seems widely dispersed (much of it untraced) and little discussed. She receives only a few sentences in Germaine Greer's *The Obstacle Race: The Fortunes of Women Painters and Their Work* (1979), for example. She is not mentioned at all in M. M. Betham's *A Biographical Dictionary of the Celebrated Women of Every Age and Country* (1804), but this was perhaps a calculated political snub. Modern reference books, such as *A Dictionary of Women Artists*, ed. Delia Gaze, 2 vols (1997), supply the bare outlines of her English period. There is no individual study of her work, or catalogue raisonné, so that my clearly inadequate list of paintings and drawings in Appendix D is simply an assembling of what is most obviously known, together with a few items that I have been able to chase up myself. I must leave it to those better qualified to take up the search.

The answer to this puzzle is perhaps twofold, and the *Memoirs* will help us to understand why. First, it is clear that Horsepole's sojourn in Madagascar was, in professional terms, a gross interruption of her career. The loss of her work completed during this period (not least the pioneering drawing of over one-third of Madagascar's recorded species of orchid) is itself an irreparable hiatus in the *œuvre*, and it seems from her own account that it took her some time to resume her painting seriously in England, distracted as she was by political activity. Joseph Farington (see Appendix C) was not alone in believing her career to be over, despite her great originality. The other reason for her obscurity would appear to be her extreme prickliness and disinclination to ingratiate herself with those in a position to advance her career. And of course her virtual disappearance to Italy and eventual seclusion with the eccentric Conte Chiavari did not help matters.

Shelley's celebrated discovery of her at the age of ninety, painting 'with the brush held in her gnarl'd fist eight or more inches from the tip, and more paint dropping to the furnishings of her ruin'd Palazzo than reach the canvas' (*The Letters of Percy Bysshe Shelley*, ed. Frederick L. Jones, 1964, II, p.224), has left us with the image of a memorable grotesque, incidental to his travels in northern Italy. Horsepole's memoirs, by contrast, suggest a profound sympathy of thought and feeling between the two. There are ideas in her writing which may very well have influenced Shelley, and Horsepole herself in her obsession with the *Æpyornis maximus* of Madagascar can now be shown to be a likely inspiration for his poem 'The Witch of Atlas' (see Appendix B). It seems all the more extraordinary, therefore, that she should have been old enough to have also inspired a poem by Swift (see Appendix A). Our impression is that she was a visionary born somewhat before her time, capable both of painting a landscape entirely in blue and inventing a version of the animated cartoon (see p. 189).

The memoirs, however, despite their insistent philosophising and their reflections on colour theory or the difficulties inherent in pictorial representation, are above all a dramatic adventure. They are cast in the five acts of a drama (perhaps like Walpole's *The Castle of Otranto*), reflecting her tempestuous involvement with the five 'husbands' of her life. There are many reflections on the vagaries of love and the erotic relationship, and there is, of course, for the first time a revelation of what actually happened to her in Madagascar.

1

Cumq; opere in proprio soleat se pingere Pictor,
(Prolem adeo sibi ferre parem Natura suevit)
Proderit imprimis Pictori γνωθι σεαυτον*

I took my first Breath in the World somewhat in the forepart of the Morning of the seventh day of August 1730,
in the City of Bristol, where my Father was a Ship's-
Surgeon. My Father has been cold in the Earth these
eighty-five years, & yet it does not seem so long a Time
as the eighty-five Minutes that I have been staring at this
Sentence I have written which so describes him. For this I
blame you, Percy,† for I write under your Encouragement
& Instruction, & as much to please you as to please myself
or any other Reader. For you are my Tormentor, are you
not? And will not take a No for an Answer, nor any thing
but a full account of my Life, & of my own pursuit of the
Invisible?—The Invisible you have a Greed for which is
all-consuming & purposeful as the Greed of most young
men of your age & breeding for Brandy or Horse-Flesh,

---

*The chapter headings are from Du Fresnoy, evidently inserted at a late stage in the
MS's composition. I shall give in each case Dryden's translation: 'Since every Painter
paints himself in his own Works (so much is Nature accustom'd to produce her own
Likeness) 'tis advantageous to him, to know himself.' (*The Art of Painting by C. A. Du
Fresnoy . . . Translated into English . . . by Mr. Dryden*, 2nd edn (1716), p. 64.
†Percy Bysshe Shelley. For an account of their relationship, see the Preface, p. x, and
Appendix B.

or for the Flesh of their own kind for the matter of that. I must take it as a spiritual Compliment then, of the greatest Distinction, that your Attention to my Being & to my Achievement, such as they are, can have nothing of the Flesh about them. For indeed, were you to be in Possession of my Years, and I of yours, your Interest in me would be looked upon with Aversion & Contempt, as it were a senile Debauch. Your every Insight the World would take as flattery, your Visits and Gifts the vain Hope of a Roué.

Even now, your Birthday Fishs lie in a Bowl on the Table in front of me. It is not an Hour since Giovanni brought them, smiling hiddeously & twisting his hat in tribute, so that the Terrace before him where he bowed & scraped was littered with his votive Straw. Dear Giovanni,—he is your wordless Messenger, Speech eludes him as it eludes the Blessed, for whom Knowledge must be the thing itself & not that Name which Men in Society give to it so that it may be ignored or destroyd. He is the perfect Carrier of Fishs, & belongs in a Parable.

I did pretend, having writt the first Sentence of my Life, that your Fishs distracted me from writing the second, et sequitur. Like everything in the World that occurs, the Fishs too set in motion a Series of Events that had not come into Being without them. It would be allowing too great a Dignity of Moment to call them Events, for like the Patriarchs in the Pentateuch their living Power has already been reduced to the meer Causality of a Chronicle, viz. Giovanni's bowing Exit begat the clink of the Garden Latch—the clink of the Garden Latch begat the appearance of Maria, to her Elbows in Flour, curious to know my early Visitor—the Appearance of Maria, begat in me a powerfull desire to drink Coffee—this

Desire begat its Satisfaction—the Satisfaction begat the Contemplation of the Dish.

—Does the Contessa wish for the Pesce to be frightened in Oil or to be bullied into a Soup? says the good Maria, taking up the Dish.

—Leave them on the Table, is my reply. —I may wish to paint them. You may take away the Coffee Pot.

Thus was I left at once with the Hour of my Birth imperfectly remembered, & with the Fishs, the Hour of whose Death I may never know, although before Sun-rise they were doubtless happy still in their watery World.

In your desire for my Life, Percy, you have given me a Voice, & you have given me a bowl of Fishs with which I may perpetuate that same Life. If you send Giovanni every Day perhaps you will keep an ancient Woman alive long enough for her life to be written down, but for the moment your Gift of a Voice is more like the Gift of the Fishs than you could imagine, for both are suffocated.

I have never thought the Power of Words to be as great as the Representacion of those Things which they name in their visual Splendour, but for once this Belief is defeated. The Creatures lie in their Dish—wet still, with the Gleam of their Home upon them, in Colours that cry to me to be matchd with Pigments,—and yet the few simple Words of my Sentence, without Form or Colour as they are, stir in me a greater Cry, that know their Being in my Heart. The 'seventh Day of August' possess the Solemnity & Radiance I have experienced on every anniversary of my natal Day—the 'City of Bristol', though unlike this Genoese coast as two marine Environments might be, is a phrase chargd with the Freshness & Delight of my origins—and 'Father' is a word whose incomparable Significance every Reader will in an instant recognise.

On this day of your Gift, Percy, itself a seventh Day of August, so a suitable day for Retrospection as you observd, my ninetieth & surely in all rational Expectacion the Last or nearly the Last of such, I hold in my Hand the Instrument whose true Power I had not suspected until now. Consider—I may paint the Vista of London, say from the Vantage of the Observatory as on several occasions I have done, with a Basket of Paper & Colours and a days Refreshment,—and the City lies before me, girded by the Thames where a hundred Sails reflect the light of the Sun, which calls them to their Voyages. You will look on the paper & know it for London & a great Port. The Brush has playd its Part in picturing the World. The Brush may also play its Part in picturing the Likeness of my Father (would that I had his Likeness before me now!), but to you it would be nothing but the Portrait of a Man with a certain Chin and Bearing who might or might not be the Father of some body. See now how the despisd Pen does it! With the Pen I write 'Father' & the Word conjures out of Invisibility the very Idea of Father, & may be your Father as well as mine. The Word allows you to share my Father in the Memory of yours, & to do so in an Instant, without the grinding of Pigment or the labour of Imitation. For as you have often told me, your Face reddening with Excitement in the expounding of it, Ideas partake of the Invisible & may make it manifest in Language. This is true in its essence, Percy, as I now see, for I acknowledge that my Brush, whatever strange things it may in my life have painted, things never before lookd upon by human Eye, it has never delineated such a Thing as 'the seventh Day of August' nor ever will.

What (asked the Madwoman) are the Colours of the Invisible? Why (replied the Sage) they are the Colours of

Eternity. And would not Eternity, taking Colour—like a chaste Nymph pursued by some cloven-footed Appetite —risk being devourd by Time? Nay, it is Eternity which is jealous of Time, for Eternity desires Motion & Change as a raging Prisoner desires his Freedom. Then (said the Madwoman) Eternity is as mad as I am, for I would live for ever, which is impossible, & Eternity would die, which is impossible also. However (said the Sage) the case is provd, since the Radiance of Eternity is broken into the Colours of the visible World, with infinite Variation and Eagerness.* Why then (said the Madwoman) the World is Eternity's mistake, & I am right to have turned from the painting of the World to the painting of Eternity. Indeed (replied the Sage), although your wherewithal be the same Colours of the World & not the Colours of the Invisible—therefore your Task is impossible. Indeed (agreed the Madwoman) & that is why I am mad.

Do not take this little Dialogue to mean that I wish that I had been a Poet & not a Painter. As well to wish that I had been a Husband & not a Wife. Being born to our Conditions, we choose them at our Peril. Said the Stoick, I accept my Death. Said God to the Stoick, there is no other Course before thee.

In all this Heat & with the attention of Flies, five Fishs in an earthen ware Dish will not outlast their leisurely Contemplation. For a time, their Colours are upon them in all the freshness and Gaiety appropriate to the Elements they are parted from, like Revellers in the dawn Streets after the Carnival. But soon they will put off their Masques and accept their eternal Sleep. Look there at the

---

*It is likely that Shelley was remembering this passage in 'Adonaïs', lines 462-3: 'Life, like a dome of many-coloured glass, / Stains the white radiance of Eternity.' The poem was written in June of the following year.

splayed Gills, like the skirts of Roman Armour! The Lustre of the Eye, like a Pool of Ink. The Design of blue on the Belly, like the Tangle of Veins in the Calfs of the Legs or the dimpled hammering of worked Steel! These are the Colours of Vivacity & of Attack, now inert in the Air which has choakd them. God has painted them in such Colours to shield our Eyes from weeping for them. We weep only for the pale Memories of these Feelings we have outlived. Take them away, Maria! I have better things to paint, and less visible.

Yet, the Significance of their Number does not escape me. As in Affairs of the Heart there is a Language of Flowers, so there may be a Language of Fishs. Your Gift is like Giovanni's Presentacion of it, wordless—but like his Manner, it is eloquent. I am not unmindful of that Occasion a month ago when you came with your friends to the Villa to meet at my Invitation the good Admiral Parker & his comfortable Wife, come for the Experiments with the Scafandro at Genoa.* It was then that you discoverd how little you knew about me, but I did not think that you would care one way or another. The Company was navigating one of Maria's bullied Soups, each as it were with his own little Boat & the Oar stroking the surface, each smiling & taking his time, breaking Bread into it as if expecting Fishs to rise and nibble at it.

Ld B†—This is very good Soup. Lady Parker, is this not an excellent Soup?

Lady P—Indeed, it is an excellent Soup.

Ld B—It is what you might call a Painter's Soup, an allegorical Soup. Look what I have found in it (showing a Prawn)—the birth of Venus!

---

*The experiment with the diving-suit is described on p. 194.
†Byron.

Lady P—?

Ld B—Or rather, considering its lapsed Appearance, the Death of Adonis.

Lady P—??

Admiral—(deaf) I believe that they call it here a Gamba.

Laet—(rescuing) The Representacion of classical Divinities is now out of Fashion, & it is some time since the Emperors of our day wished to appear as Gods.

PS—The Gods had too many shameful Secrets.

Ld B—Rather, our Emperors have too few. The governing of the modern World is a damned dull Business. Their only Secrets are straightforward affairs of State.

PS—The Earth itself has enough Secrets. But Contessa, would you paint an Adonis?

Laet—Only if you would sit for the Part.

Ld B—And only if the Part would stand for it, I dare say.

Laet—But I would rather attempt the Portrait of a Trade Wind.

Ld B—Which would never stay still for you.

Laet—The Stillness is necessary, I grant you, but the Stillness is in here, in the Head. Find the Subject in your Head and see it clearly. Then it will stay still for you.

Admiral—I have sat for Mrs Horsepole. As did my Father before me. I trust that we sat still enough, hey? Still enough for a good Likeness?

Ld B—As still as the sleeping Holofernes, when Judith bore off *his* Likeness.

Admiral—Mrs Horsepole's Portraits grace many of the Walls of the Admiralty. Large as Life. You have only to look up & there are all these Fellows that you once knew, dead now of course, staring down at you.

Ld B—I will do so on the very next Occasion that I am there.

Admiral—(unperturbed) The first, of course, was James Horsepole, then First Secretary. A gentle and magnanimous Soul. I playd Cock Horse at his knee many a time.

Ld B—?

PS—Then I suppose, Contessa, that it was your first Husband who obtaind these Commissions for you?

Laet—My first Husband, Sir, was a drunken Villain, who did nothing at all for me save leave me lame in the left Leg with a heated smoothing-Iron. His name was Crowther. James Horsepole may have been First Secretary & my first naval Portrait, but he was my second Husband.

PS—Forgive me. New Neighbours hear something of each other which early Friendship finds sufficient for a time, but which Curiosity gets the better of. May I ask when you met your third Husband and came to the Palazzo Chiavari?

Laet—I must disappoint you again. The Count was in fact my fifth Husband. I may be less old than you think, looking as I do like the Sibylla of Cumae, but I am older than I should be. God has forgotten me, & now I shall have to count my Husbands on a second Hand.

Ld B—On that other Hand, Contessa, after five of them you will have seen through the Stratagems of Husbands perfectly, & shall have no need to know any more.

Laet—You are gracious, my Lord, but I find Men impossible to divine & could never have enough of them.

Ld B—Is that so, Contessa? I am delighted to hear it.

Do you agree, Lady Parker? Have you, too, not had enough?

Lady P—Quite enough, I assure you. It was delicious.

Thankfully, though Lady Parker was not as deaf as her Husband, she had learnd to rely on *his* Deafness to assist her in Obliviousness to awkward Situacions. Her Instinct for social Safety would have made her an excellent Wife to an Ambassador. I rang for a Dish of Eels, & the Subject of Conversation was changd. Your Friends, Percy, would not be so interesting, nor perhaps your Friends your Friends indeed, if they observd the Proprieties, taking either less Vino Grigio before Dinner or Pleasure in teasing.

I did not then know that you did not eat living or once-living Creatures, preferring not to look guiltily in their Faces. You were polite to a Neighbour who had provided you with a Dinner, but I noticed that you did not take the Eels, nor the Osso Bucco neither. Well, Percy, I am sure that a Knuckle of Veal would not outstare you into Remorse, & the Bone of it might even make you laugh, as when the Count was wont to place it at his Eye like a Monocle to fright Maria into dropping a Tureen. Nor will Eels, once being stunnd & skinnd & made to lie still in a green Sauce, come alive once again simply by being ignored. However, my other Guests made up for your Deficiency of animal Appetite, & I admird your moral Position, though not your Constitution.

And what of you? Of my Morals you knew nothing, though curious about Husbands. As for my Constitution, what Interest may a Stripling (though a Poet) take in a Crone of my advanced Years, an ancient English Oak, throttled with Ivy & disfigured with Lichens, transplanted to a Mediterranean Littoral where the Cypresses grow gratefully straight up into the blue Air like dark green Smoak?

But you had some Intuition then of the Length & strange Experience of my Life, & before that Visit was over had privately urged me to write down my Remembrances of it for Posterity. But I had no Posterity was my objection. Your Face then perfectly expressed an unvoiced Exclamation.—What, five Husbands & no Children! Your Smile returning upon my Smile was a Sign then that no Posterity of the Blood may guarantee a Kinship of Feeling. Were you my own Great-Great-Grandson I could not at that moment have known you better, an Adonis indeed, for whom Progeny were the meerest Ballast in Love's voyage, with a Bill of Lading to be signed for, an Impediment to Exploration. We are both free Spirits, Percy, but you bear your Youth like the flight of a Bird. I recognise your Restlessness as you recognise my Experience.

Five Husbands. Five Fishs. A sign that a Multitude hungry for Truth may be fed from such a Life, were it to be written down, & were to be, as mine has been, a Life in itself eager to find that Truth.

Five Husbands. Five Acts of a Drama. A Sequence of Adventures and Resolutions with some Thing at the Core most unhusbandlike—Innocence, Intuitions, Inquisition, Injustice, Inspiration, which to call it thus were a pretty Play upon its Heroine who must be calld first upon the Scene. But (to continue this Metaphor, which seems the less appropriate the longer I contrive it) what Actress was ever a grammatical First Person? I, I, I, I, I, is the monstrous Egotism of Memoirs, where Drama is lost in the rush of Recollection. But the Role in Drama is ever a She, which the Audience may consider a moral Case, acting only when put to it by Circumstance, casting aside the Trivialities of an Existence, conscious of the clear & distinct Stages, whereby she is brought to Felicity or to Grief, as the separate Stroaks that forge a Soul.

Your own Metaphor, Percy, is I dare to say that of *angling* for Husbands. But that I never did. Unlike the ambitious Miss of this Century, I did not seek, but was sought. Men were accidental to me, my Quest lay elsewhere.

Let me return to my Beginning, which I had lost sight of. I took my first Breath in this World somewhat in the Forepart of the Morning of the seventh Day of August 1730 in the City of Bristol, where my Father was a Ship's-Surgeon. His own Father was a Doctor, as was my Mother's, and I fancy that my Parents were brought together on a Whim of their Families or as the subject of a Paper in Natural Philosophy to be communicated to the Royal Society, as 'A Common House-Sparrow brought to Mate with a Fulmar Petrel, with an Account of their Domestick Habits & the Features of their Young', for there was nothing in their Characters to suggest an accord in Nature, nor a common Purpose in Kind. My Mother was happy directing her Kitchen and happier in talking. She was a Creature of one Place and Precedent, and household Œconomy was the Horizon of her Curiosity.

The greatest Wonder of her Life was the Loss of a Needle one Morning & the missing of Church for the sake of finding it on the Grounds that some where in Scripture (she could not say where) was a Parable on the Virtue of discovering lost Needles that would otherwise be damned. The Wonder of finding it in a Pye she had baked that morning, & my Father producing it silently &

solemnly from his Mouth at Table, was perhaps no great matter, but it was a Tale she frequently told as evidence of some Divine Wisdom, the Nature of which I did not understand, being a Child, nor have understood since, though the Tale is as familiar to me as the idea of Pye itself.

My Father was a man of few words and of much quiet Humour. I remember riding on his Back through the Fields behind our House, where the Grasses were as tall as I was, and with a single stout Grass with dry Ears like Wheat changing his direction by prodding at his Cheeks. Indeed, I thought his Face a kind of Toy, for he could produce his Tongue from it by pressing his Nose, & this Tongue would move to the right or to the left according as to which Ear he twisted, & at the very same Speed as the twisting, whereupon with another pressing of the Nose it would disappear. If I had no Switch of Grass I might always be allowed to control the direction of my Mount by twisting his Ears myself. And I never knew whether one day instead of a Tongue a lost needle might not be produced.

It was my Father who read to me the Stories of the Arabian Nights, which I never tired of hearing. My Mother had Stories, too, but they were mostly of a moral kind about the Wickedness & Misfortunes of Children, or about the things her Sisters had done years before, or about significant Episodes of domestick Life (like the said Needle). I enjoyd these Stories indeed, & would shock my Aunts with their reveald Secrets, but the Stories I loved concerned Sultans and Genies and magick Wishes. The Adventures of Sindbad were my favourite of these, & because my Father was so continuingly away at Sea I naturally associated these Adventures with him. If a Father could be a Horse, or possess a mechanicall Face, why could he not also be Sindbad the Sailor, whose Exploits had been printed in a Book? When I was told that my Father had been carried off by a Fever at sea, & would never return, I could not help but imagine that he was meerly in the Power of some Spell which I might, when I was older, discover for myself & release him by my Efforts. To be carried off by a Fever to my childish Ears was as corporeal a Capture as that of Sindbad by the great Roc which carried him off. The word Fever itself grew Wings in my imaginacion, & so strong was this Identity that when I later learnd from my Grandfather the real Nature of my Father's Labours at Sea, which was to identify, with their Symptoms & Cures, all the various Fevers which are peculiar to Sailors on their Voyages, & to write them up with minute Descriptions in a compendious Dictionary of such Fevers for the better medical Treatment of their Victims, I could only hope for the posthumous Publication of this Dictionary as a fully illustrated Work, with each mortal Illness accompanied by small Plates of its distinctive graven Pinions, the tiny featherd Joints numbered, their rapacious Articulation fully explaind.

My Mother did not long survive him, a fact that I ascribe to her sentimental Sparrow-Nature, or perhaps a Touch of the Dove. I find it strange that she could not continue in Widowhood for more than a few Months, whereas for me it has been an intermittent condition of Life for seventy Years. Perhaps I became habituated to Loss from an early Age, & was forced to conclude that Death was a necessary Preparation for any subsequent Stage of Life. After my Mother was interred, beneath a Stone which at the same time recorded the Death of my

Father, who had been buried at Sea, I was taken to live near Dublin, where my paternal Grandfather was a Physician. It was from him that I learnd the History of my Father & of his Ambitions untimely cut short, from him that I discovered that first strange Fact that affects a Child with the force of Mystery much greater, on reflection, than the Mystery of Genies in Bottles, which is that her Father himself had a Father and was therefore once a Child.

There is some thing of a Parable in this, for the Genie appears in response to a Wish, producing a Bottle from which, when rubbd, a Genie may appear to do the poor Fisherman's bidding. The Wish for Wishes is perpetual, for Poverty is never satisfied. Like Adam in the Garden, whose was the first Wish, for a Mate, the wish for further Wishes is never ended, & so the Generations continue, rubbing Bottles, from which fresh Genies spring. Perhaps it takes an old Woman with an empty Bottle to see this so clearly.

Are you, Percy, such a Bottle-Rubber? You keep your Wife & Family at Pisa while you follow your Addiction to the Invisible, although I suspect that other Addictions are in question, for though your Peregrinations are a Quest for a suitable Villa (you say) this Quest is never satisfied. I would say your Quest is rather for Beauty, which may have little to do with Generation, or the loyalty of Bed-Mates, & perhaps the Shaddow of Greek Ideals is upon you, as it evidently is upon your Friend the lame Lord. Together you sit on the Terrace of the Villa for hours on end in Symposium, but your Eyes are upon the View before you of Giovanni's son swimming from the Rocks. That young Hyacinth! In his unblemished Body he contains all that we might wish from our physical

Life. In him you may imagine yourself perfected, fulfilled, unlamed, at home after long Wandering, or what you will. He is the innocent local Deity of this Shore, & is the effortless Image of all that wilful Bottle-rubbing would accomplish.

The fertile Sea is his Element, into whose motherly lapping he loves to insert his lithe Body. He rises from the Waters not cold & defeated in what must always be an unequal Struggle, but triumphant, as from an act of Generation in which his whole person has performed the part of the membrum virile—or, indeed has mimicked in its soundless Explorations the Embryo itself which it would engender. This Ocean-Charade is the preserve of male Enthusiasm & of male Vanity, evidently also a matter of posing upon rocks. It has little to do with Reality. I wonder that Leander, after his great Performance, had any interest in Hero in that way, having exhausted his vital energy in salt Water? The generative Parts of a Woman smell of the Sea for this reason, to tempt Men to the Voyage. Or else they might meerly admire themselves.

I hear that Bathing has become fashionable in England, & that it is the Regent's Pleasure to mount small retiring Rooms on Wheels and to have them drawn to the Water's Edge. I cannot think this a good Idea. The Climate is unfavourable, & you cannot turn the Protean Encounter into a Tea-Party. It is the kind of thing that my maternal Aunts, if they had lived today, & not in Bristol but in Brighton, would have readily undertaken, deafening the Waves with Gossip & the Pounce of Quadrille.

If I had not been claimed by my Connell Grandfather & taken off to Dublin, I might readily have been absorbed into the kindly world of my Bristol Aunts, where I would have remain an Object of Pity, put to plain-Work and the understanding of Puddings. But as a Connell I rapidly became not a Monument to the loss of my Mother but a living Heir to my Father—not an Image of Grief but a Promise of the Future. I dare say that at the Age of six I had not much Idea of what any One might expect of me, but I was ready enough to pursue my own Ends. I had drawn Heads & Figures before I could write, and would by no means desist from this Practice because I had been transported. My Grandfather, discovering me one day copying the Plates of a Medical Book in his Library & therefore spoiling the Margins, neither rebuked me nor found the activity inappropriate to my Age and Sex, for he soon supplied me with drawing Materials of my own & showed me how to make Coppies in proportion by making Squares on tracing Paper.

This, of necessity, must be performed in the Library, but when I could do so, I would gather up my Plans & Drawings & take them to my Summer-House in the garden, for there I kept an Academy of Poppets, deceased Stag-Beetles, jars of ants, Shells, & other Creatures living & deceased, including a Mouse in a Bird-Cage which the Gardener had made up with further strands of Wire to prevent its escaping. These Creatures served a dual Purpose, both as the Objects of Investigation & Delineation, & as a Critickal Society which pronounced upon the Results. This Summer-House was an old Pleasaunce, a stone Gazebo become roofless & entangled with Thorn & Elder. My Grandfather told me that in his own Father's time it was frequently the scene of summer Parties, & he showed me the stone Cavity in the floor which was designed for keeping the Wine cool. There was a zinc Bucket, now decayd, for carrying in the Bottles, which my Grandfather told me was but one

Example of many such polite Engines brought over to impress and to subjugate a barbarous People. He had the Roof patchd for me, & the undergrowth cleard. I planted Turnsoles* & used the upturned Wine Bucket as a shelter for my Menagerie.

This World was an Arcadia to me, for the warm Days seemd everlasting, & there was nothing to interfere with my Wishes. I learnd much from my Grandfather, & from Katherine, their last unmarried Daughter, but it did not seem like Instruction. Katherine, indeed, did not seem like an Aunt at all, for she regarded my affairs as being of no concern to her, never noticed when my Hair was unbrushd & seemed to have no serious plans for my Improvement. It was often remarked that I resembled her, but it did not occur to me to notice that she resembled my Father, still less to ask for Rides on her Back. I was too old for such Requirements, although still too young to see myself as a Rival to my Dublin Aunt for the affections of my Grandparents. In Age she was nearer a Mother than a Sister, but she claimed the responsibility or Devotion of neither. Her Dealings with me were always perfectly fair—distant without coldness, rational without argument, liberal without indulgence. Her Dress was plain, her Manner silent. She would tell me things if I needed to know them, not because they were good for me. If there were any Possession of hers that I might make better use of, it were immediately mine,—though with equal Justice she might as wordlessly take it back.

My Arcadia was therefore a kind of Commonwealth, a Representation of that ideal State where Man's Happiness is secured, not through the immediate Gratification of his

*Sunflowers

17

every Wish, but the rather through his not perceiving himself to have Wishes at all. Were Humanity to be without Anxiety in respect of Property or Desire, all social Intercourse would be harmonious. I have learnd much about the Obduracy of the Passions, & know that sometimes they are not to be reasoned with. Our Childhood is given to us at a time when our Innocence may teach us what we seek in Life, a Garden-State where Thorns may be pruned & all Creatures converse the one with the other,—where Duty entails Understanding, & Reason may reveal the secrets of the World. In this exercise of childish Confidence, my Academy was paramount, & all the Voices mine.

Laet—Shall the Dean preside?

All—Yes.

Mouse—Is it not my turn to preside?

Stag-Beetle—You cannot preside. You turn your Back too frequently on the Proceedings, & you are too dirty.

Mouse—But I would like to preside. Let me preside.

Laet—(kindly) You may preside to-morrow.

Stag-Beetle—Count yourself fortunate. You are much indulged here.

All—Continue, continue.

Chinaman (sc. Dean)—Will the Academy please come to order. I will not tolerate this Chatter, for it brings on my Head-Akes.

Laet—Please, your Deanship, will you look upon these Drawings?

Chinaman—With pleasure, my Child. Why, these Drawings are very tiny! How shall I see them clearly without my Spectacles?

Laet—I shall hold them very close to your Eyes.

Chinaman—That is much better. These are very satisfactory Drawings. These are Drawings that a Man may take an Interest in.

Wax Doll—They are all her own Work, and she is but seven Years old.

Chinaman—Tell me about this one. I cannot see if it is the Representation of a Fish or a Bird.

Stag-Beetle—Or a Stag-Beetle.

Mouse—If it were a Stag-Beetle it would have Horns. I have never in my Life seen a Fish or a Bird with Horns.

Laet—It is a Fever, Sir.

Chinaman—A Fever! No body has ever presented me with the Portrait of a Fever. This is very commendable, Child.

All—Huzzah!

It will be evident from this small Example of the Proceedings of my Academy, that my Grandfather had taken pride in showing some of my juvenile Work to his Friends, & that one of them, a Dr. Delaney, had taken it upon himself to show them to the Dean of St. Patrick's, Dr. Swift.* I remember being in his Garden, & being sat upon his Knee, which exceedingly terrified me, because he groand mightily & breathd like a pair of Bellows, & scarcely left off groaning to speak. I think my Drawings of Fevers gave him Pleasure, for I was taken off by his Housekeeper & given some Comfits of Quinces, some of which I ate there in a kind of Parlour, which was the filthiest Place I had ever seen, & the Rest I was to take home to my Creatures.

The Chinaman who played the part of the Dean was in

---

*Swift's poem on the subject, 'To Letty Connell, on her Pictures', was one of the last that he wrote. See Appendix A.

my eyes the most distinguished of my Company, though he was but a poor Fisherman in a blue Boat beneath a Willow, turning his Back on two blue Swallows that swooped to him. He was a Fragment of a Plate broke by Dorcas, for which she had been scolded, for it was not mendable. I was told that I might cut my Fingers upon it, but I begged with such Reason and Feeling that my Desire for it was eventually granted. To me he was less a Fisherman than the King of China himself, & I thought of him as in a kind of Loneliness and Agony in such a tiny Kingdom, stopping so abruptly at its Edges. Besides which, he was for ever turned from the Birds that hovered behind him, & a Crack wandered down over the Glaze of the Porcelain into his Head like a black Lightning, & it was my Fancy that this gave him a severe Chinese Head-Ake. When my Grandfather told me some years later that Dr. Swift had died, I buried my Chinaman in the Garden.

This Question of the difference between Fishs and Birds is a fine one, or rather, every Observer has noted the Similarities,—that Scales, like Feathers, grow like a kind of Plating or Armour,—that Fins, like Wings, assist their Propulsion through their proper Element,—that both tend to move together in Shoals or Flocks. But consider further. Their several Elements (Water, Air) afford them the Flexibility and Buoyancy which the Articulation of these Parts ensures. It is therefore perhaps no wonder that they take Joy together in those Movements which daily Foraging or seasonal Migration require. Their Life is a full inhabiting of these Elements, both in points of the Compass & in their Depth or Height. But Creatures of the Earth, however, are solitary and bald, rising their way through their heavy inimical Medium,—the blind naked Mole & the slow Worm, whose Struggles are arduous and whose Tribes make no surging Patterns. The Whale that carried off Jonah, or the Roc that carried off Sindbad, might, I thought, almost be forgiven for considering a man to be little more than a pitiable insect. And when my Grandfather came to read to me Dr. Swift's Brobdingnag, my opinion was confirmed, for Gulliver's views there appear largely contemptible, and he, too, is seized by a Bird. The Dean knew his Arabian Nights well, you can be sure, although at the time I was inclind to think it a meer co-incidence, for Gulliver's Fortunes are set out with all the small Circumstances of Truth that partly confirmd for me my Vision of my Father's Death. The Sea is not Man's Element, nor the Air, & he is foolish to trust himself to it. And yet he does so, out of the urge to explore the Globe. The Sea must be fathomd. It is mapped, as the Land is,—& as the Air will be, in dirigible Balloons.

But what of the fourth Element, fire? You may neither stand on it nor fly in it, though Milton represents Satan as achieving a fine swimming Stroak within it, such as reveals a familiarity with the Art to rival that of the bronzed Hyancinth, who casts himself off any Rock into the turbulent Sea with the Confidence that in that strange supplicant Motion of his Arms he will be strongly born up & conveyed in whatever Direction he pleases. If he were an Angel he might swim in Fire if he wished, yet Moths are drawn to it to their Destruction & the Sallamander is but a sleepy Solitary of Fire as the paddling Mole is of Earth. I was convinced by my juvenile Fancies and Researches that the true Denizens of Fire live in massed populations like Fishs & Birds, & flock together in instinctive purposes as they do, changing direction apparently at Whim. It was put to debate in the Garden-Parliament.

Chinaman—Order, order.

Stag-Beetle—Mouse is dead, but it was not my fault.

Laet—You need not worry. Aunt Kate says that it was no-one's fault.

Stag-Beetle—Then No-one must be brought before the Academy & arraigned for her Carelessness.

Chinaman—Had he been fed regularly?

Laet—Yes, indeed.

Chinaman—And his Water-Dish filled?

Laet—Yes.

Chinaman—Then he died of natural Mortality, & there is nothing that can be done about it.

Stag-Beetle—We must set about doing Nothing immediately. Something must be done, after all.

Spring-heeled Jack—There must be a Funeral, with Daisy-Cakes and dancing.

Laet—Aunt Kate looked closely at him when he was shaking, & declared that he had a Fever.

Chinaman—I see.

Wax Doll—Did you not yourself have a Fever last Whitsuntide, & could eat nothing for four Days?

Laet—Yes.

Chinaman—Were you not hot? Did you not feel as though you were consumed by Fire?

Laet—I did feel so.

Chinaman—Let me see the drawings of the fever once more. (The drawings produced.) It seems to me that these Creatures either come in Darkness when we can not see them, or else they are naturally invisible.

Stag-Beetle—It will be difficult to bring them to Justice if they are invisible.

Chinaman—We are powerless against them. They are numberless and unseen, & their long Claws sink deep into their Prey. Their mightiest Foe, the Hero Captain Joseph Connell, who knew more about them than any Man living, was powerless to escape their Attentions. Who knows where they will strike next?

Spring-heeled Jack—Bring on the Daisy-Cakes.

The Obsequies were performed, & soon the Mouse's Cage was empty. It was to be filled by a merry Family of Sailors made from Cloaths-Pegs, with white painted Heads, blue Caps and rosy Cheeks, but the Death of the Mouse was a signal Reminder to me that happy States and happy Places have little permanence in this World.

I was not, I think, conscious of a close Parallell to our Vacation of the Bristol House, for I was myself as happy in Dublin as any Cloaths-Peg Sailor, but to be impressed by Mortality so directly in a Creature I had fed and tended is a different matter from the demise of Parents. It is a more trivial Affair, but more closely observed. My Bristol Aunts had cared for my Mother in her illness, & kept me distant out of delicasy,—my Father's Death was meer Report. I do not remember a precise Moment when I ceased to believe in my Heart that he might suddenly return, in torn and salt-stained Cloathing, with Marvels to relate. Perhaps I have never ceased to believe it. Even now, as I sit here in the Shade of my little Italian Cupola at a wooden Table with Ink, Pens, Paper, & a Cup of wild Herbs drying in the Breeze, I would not think it entirely strange to see him at a Distance climbing over the Rocks, drenchd & in Raggs, but in a kind of Triumph at having discoverd my Whereabouts after so long. What we believe most deeply in our Hearts has no Reason,—he would be 120 years old.

But as I write these Words, my story of Five Fishs, although it is barely begun, I feel myself transported across

Time as across a navigable Sea, glittering in the morning Sun. While the Pen moves I am again a Child, and this Cupola, with its orange Lillies filling the Arch that frames a blue Horizon with fishing Boats, becomes the Dublin Gazebo itself. At one end of the Table are my little Trophies of Shells & Stones—my Sketch-Book—closer to me, the Bowl of Fishs—the Sprays & feathery Wisps of Herbs, Fennel, Thyme, Thistles & pale Grasses, plucked in an idle Moment—this Paper, with its Words coming into existence only as I write them, barely considered before the Ink descends & is drawn into the Fibres of the Surface in the linked Shapes we recognise as written Language. These are my Toys now, & I give them Animation as I did then.

I have sought such Places in my Life as Images of the Eden we have never possessed. Here we may retreat and assume our Innocence again, though we have changed our Shape & grown into other Fashions. It has been a Fashion itself to indulge in such Resorts, as in Landskips where you could not wander far before knocking your Head against an Ivied Tower or ruind Temple, where an old God lamented the decline of his Cult or still hopefully pursued a local Nymph or two who had strayd from their Flocks. I never liked such Fancies myself in Painting, for the Confusion they breed in the Onlooker, who will not know if he be in Berkshire or in Thrace. The Italian Painters are to blame for this, for their Bethlehems are all imagind among the wooded Hills of Tuscany. A Satyr or two there might come all the more amiss, but the Painter is carried away and will put in what he pleases.

In every Eden there is a Serpent, and in every Eden will occur a fatal human Mistake. Our very Bodies are an Image of the Eden we have lost, for their Perfection is brief. The Fevers watch & wait like Cormorants. Teeth loosen, Limbs thicken, Skin thins, Hair fades. I am remembering now my own Body as it was when it was still as the Fruit is, proceeding as Nature has designed towards its Ripeness. The Shape fills out, swelling & soft,—the Skin acquires Colour,—its Downiness is enticing to the Touch. The Form is characteristick of its Kind, grown to accommodate the Mechanisms for generating and perpetuating those Characteristicks. Nature has her Purposes, & will dictate our Future to us as though it were a simple Errand to be undertaken.

Nature—Now see here, Letty, you must leave your Play now. I want you to go & purchase a twinkling Eye, a handsome Leg, a gay Manner.

Laet—But how may I do that? How shall I pay for such things?

Nature—You shall show what you have, which is Currency enough, viz. a Temple finely built, with two Windows filtering orient Light beneath Romanesque Arches & two ante-Chapels half hidden in their Hangings, where Music plays,—an Oratory of red Velvet, where Wishes kneel in Reverence,—Incense over all, and damask Frescoes.

Laet—I am already gone.

But in truth I was not vain, & cared more for the Architecture of real Churches than the Sight of my own face in a looking-Glass. I drew them, indeed, from the Life & from Books, & would have sooner sketched a Pulpit than heard a Compliment, sooner transcribd a Memorial-Stone than a Sonnet, sooner traced a brass Crusader with coloured Wax than touchd a living Man. Or so I thought, but my Mistress had the better of me there & had, as it were, implanted my Errand in a Dream

25

of which, waking, I was hardly yet aware. Men, as I have since learnd, have their own Errands very much in mind, & are about them all Day long, without pause. Even Men perfectly satisfied in their Wives may be found to have Errands with their Cooks and Parlour-Maids, or even with the Wives of their Friends,—while to have successfully run one Errand is no Excuse for being sent straight upon a Second. I have sometimes wondered how they find any time to follow their Professions. A man may be at Change,* or entering a Committee, or negociating a Bond, & all the time he will be planning his Errands, regretting their Failure or Interruption, & calculating his Opportunities for furthering them.

When Dorcas first did my Hair, I felt as though I were carrying a good Part of myself on my Head for a Wager & must pay a Forfeit if it fell off. To dance at the same time seemed impossible. I was still not used to waddling like a Goose at the time of my Flowing, for the Thickness of the Towels there. The Life of a Woman promised to be a continual Impediment to any Freedom of Movement.

At my first Dance, which was given by Sir Henry Whybrow of Stonecastle on the Christmas after my fifteenth Birthday, I was handed about by several perspiring young Men, sometimes to the Accompaniment of Violins and sometimes not. But in all Cases I was clearly perceived to be not so much a Person as a Property. Ownership was noted in little Cards on Ribbands, & I was taken to the Lemonade as consciensciously as good Farmers water their Cattle. I must have protested to my Aunt Kate, for I remember her

---

*The Royal Exchange.

taking me into the Parlour, sitting me down before her & telling me that it was my Duty, & that I must expect to find a Husband. I did not ask her why she had not found One for herself. Perhaps she had got lost on her Errand & had forgot what it was. I did not see why I should run it for her.

Some of the perspiring young Men had been little Boys with whom I had collected Snails in the Church-yard after the Service. One was a Cousin who had once chased me into a Tree, but had been too fat or frightened to follow. I could not think what made them so solemn now, or why I should be solemn in their Company. In fact, I did not think overmuch of any of it, but I was nonetheless all the time being prepared for my Mistake.

My drawing-Master was Signor Canistrelli, an architectural Painter whose search for a European Capital, where the civick Vistas had not yet been exhaustively transferrd to Canvas, had brought him some years earlier to Dublin.* The Patronage he had expected was not forthcoming, & he sought Employment in such polite Society as there was, giving Instruction to the Daughters of Merchants and Surgeons in the Representation of Reality on plane Surfaces in both Pencill & in Ink & Wash. I did not flatter myself that my Grandfather had sought him out as a Consequence of recognising any Aptitude that I had for Drawing, but it was true that I had continued to cover any Paper that I could find with the Images that came readily to the end of my Pencill, & I did

---

*Luigi Canistrelli (c.1711–98) was a Venetian pupil of Jacopo Amigoni, and a friend of Canaletto (who himself visited London in 1746). Amigoni, who worked in England as a history painter between 1729 and 1739, had made his fortune there. His encouragement of Canistrelli did not apparently have the same success. As will be clear from the *Memoirs*, Canistrelli was the designer of the Palazzo Chiavari.

not think it at all out of the way that yet another Gentleman in an old-fashiond Wig should be sent to admire them. And that, perhaps, as I conceivd it, would be an end to it. However, it was not to be. The Days of my bringing my childish Successes and childish Sorrows to my little Garden-Academy were over. The great World had begun to trawl for me with its Nets, & I did not yet know if I were big enough to be caught.

Hour after Hour I argued with Sig. Canistrelli. At our first Meeting I had untied the strings of my Portfolio with all the Confidence of one who, while not used to receiving constant Praise, had been able to get plenty of it when it was needed & had moreover been so left to her own Devices that every Thing she did seemed unquestionably the Thing to do. Sig. Canistrelli thought otherwise, & began by ruling Lines across my Churches to demonstrate my faulty Perspectives. I thought this an Outrage, to be sure.

Laet—Why, you have spoiled it, Sir.

Can—Nay, the Lines are there so that you may improve it. They will see less of a Wall the further away it is.

Laet—I know that.

Can—But only in strict Proportion to the Angle of look-ing, & every Line must obey that Angle, even the thickness of a Buttress, or the wing of a bird flying above it.

Laet—You have cancelled it out like an Error in Calculation. I do not think that St. Patrick would be well pleased.

Can—St. Patrick would surely encourage us to overcome our Faults.

Laet—Yet I am sure he knew nothing of your Perspective.

Can—There are Rules of Drawing as there are Rules of Building. Your Church if it were built would fall down within half an Hour.

Laet—Then I will not draw Churches. I will draw God. God is omnipresent and can not therefore be seen only from a Distance. He can therefore have no Perspective, & could not even begin to fall down.

I am sure that I was flushd with Indignation, & quite intollerable in my Pride, my Language and my Conceits to a Man as patient & kind as Sig. Canistrelli. But he meerly smiled, & agreed—as far as you may conceive such a Man agreeing with a Proposition of that kind. Having been ready, in spirit at least, to stamp my Foot in a genteel sort of way on the Turkey Carpet (where it might have given off a perfectly acceptable sort of Thudd, like a vigorous Dance-Step) I was discomfitted by the Smile.

Yes, Percy, a spoiled Miss might have gone into the Sulks at all this, but although I had Ideas of my own, & held them with the Firmness of relative Ignorance, I was not in fact spoiled any more than my Drawing was spoiled. I was able to feel my own ruled Line as an interesting Direction, a Sign-Post profitable to follow. So I smiled back at Sig. Canistrelli, whereupon Dame Nature pointed out to me a Dimple on his own smiling Face which seemed strange to observe in a Man who would never again see thirty-five, & I did not know if it seemed fetching or not. Thereafter we might have our Arguments without fear of either Insult or Offence. I became not a docile but a responsive Pupil, & Grandfather was willing to continue to pay for our Debates. Having largely neglected to provide me with Play-Mates during the ten Years of my Dublin Life (saving the presence of the Cook's little Boy & Dr. King's Great-Niece, who came occasionally, & the fat coward Cousin, whom I detested) he now felt that he owed me some Attention and Expense. He had forgotten, perhaps, the Freedom of his Library, which had long been mine & which, with his unthinking Commentary & Guidance, had been a sufficient Education in most of the Respects in which a Girl might ever expect to get one, & a rather better one in some ways than any girl did get. I did not know this at the time, & was not surprised that I never found my Aunt Kate reading a Book. I presumed that at her Age she had read them all already.

It was at this time, coming with great clumsy Leaps and Bounds into my own Womanhood, that I first realised that my Aunt was of an Age not quite beyond Marriage. As a Child I had received her Attention as from one who was settled for ever in the single Life. She seemed old to me then, as a Woman of twenty may well do, and appeared to have no Attachments. But I would not have expected any Confidences from her. She was easy & gracious with Men, so did not appear to repel them, & at Card-Parties at Stonecastle, or at Bellville, was ready to converse & even to sing. Attention was paid to her, & sometimes she laughed, which she did not often do at home. As a child I had had little Opportunity to observe her in this social Role, & soon I began to view her Instructions to me about my Duty in finding a Husband in a more general Light. This, in short, was what all Women must do, & if there was a Point at which a Woman was compelled to retire, defeated, from the Field, then my Aunt Kate could not, in all Honesty, be said to have reached it.

Going out with her at last into Society taught me this. I realised that it was one of the ways in which Perspective could guide the Eye more securely to a Perception of the Truth. Alas! Our perceiving the Truth does not mean that we are always guided by it. My new Understanding of my Aunt's Position gave me, though I only partly sensed it, a certain Power over her. Though I had been for ten Years something like a Pupil, a Daughter or a Sister to her, albeit as the Result of practical Considerations & without Excess of Emotion, of which she showed little, now I found myself with great Surprise to be something of a Rivall.

Does not this all sound like a Novel, Percy? Are you not excited? Is there not some Romance in the Air?

I conceive that we are addicted in this Age to Fiction because we no longer truly believe in Fortune. That is as it may be, & I do not deny that there should be better things to believe in (electro-Magnetism, for example, or Freedom from Slavery), but in the Days when we all believed in Fortune, we had something convenient to rest our Hopes in, & to blame. Now that our Fortunes are in our own Hands, & our several Futures entirely our own Responsibility, we find we are so disappointed in them, even disgusted by them, that we turn eagerly to read of the Lives of others, Men & Women who never existed, meer Phantoms of the Scribbler's idle Brain. The Excitement, & the Interest, that we should experience in the Fulfillment of our own Projects is quite transferrd to the turning of a printed Page, where the Fulfillment has already been accomplished.

This is quite *not* like Life indeed, which to those living it is never finished till they be unconscious, when of course they will not know that it is finished. Whereas, in your Novel, the Reader may, if he wishes, begin at the End, with the opening of the Miser's Will or the brilliant

Marriage,—or he may read where he will,—or read it all once again,—whereupon the Machinery of Fortune is once more perfectly on Display, like the waxen Revolutionaries of Madame Tussaud, not the Life itself, but an Idea of it, preservd for us as a Substitute for our own, which has no historical Importance, and very little Story, either.

But I promised you a Drama, & something like my Hamartia follows.

Its Beginnings were at what now might be called a Picknick during that following Summer. I had long wanted to draw a Vista of the old Abbey, and it was for this Reason that the Party settled upon it as an Object of the Visit. The Visit itself, however, was a Part of a long Series of pleasurable Excursions and Gatherings proposed by Sir Henry for the delight of his Friends and Neighbours. He had a Nephew staying with him, the Son of an older Sister who had married well into the Trading of Silks. The Crowthers were established in Cheapside, where the Nephew, Peregrine Crowther, had recently inherited the great Family Business after the Death of his Father, Remorse Crowther. It is now quite forgotten, I think, but such was the early Success of this Business, though the Father brought nothing to it but his own Energy & Acumen, that before Queen Anne was quite dead indeed, if you wished to buy a certain kind of Shang-Tung you would think of buying 'Crowther', & that a certain Kind of Morning-Gown made of it, with a hidden tye at its waist was therefore known as a 'Crowther'.

It was clear enough to those who wished to talk of it that Crowther's Wealth exceeded Sir Henry's, for Sir Henry's Irish estates supported his Recreations, but little else, while the Crowther Fleets were ever in the China

Seas or rounding the Cape, laden with future Profit. To be in Trade could in those days be spoken of with Contempt by those whose Family Names were attached to the Farms and Villages which sustain them with Tribute, & amongst which they dwelt, in ancient Houses. But I did not see how the Deficiency of great Estates might devalue any Person, & was not brought up to believe that it did. The Connells had no Land, but devoted themselves to the Profession of Physick. To me, it is evident that a Person had better be known for what he has accomplished than for what he possesses, or for his Name. Why should it be better to be named for a Castle than for a silk Morning-Gown? My drawing-Master had the Name of a biscuit, after all, and there was no telling how he got it. Should I have taken Pride in my once having been introduced by Sir Henry to old Lord Stonecastle? Should I have been amused at being taught by a Biscuit?

At the Pick-nick I was first aware that Sir Henry and my Aunt Kate were walking together alone, and that this may have signified some Thing beyond polite Digression and Conversation. I was made aware of it because Mr. Crowther brought it to my Attention. I was sketching the foreground to my Abbey, & introducing into it some Figures.

Crow—Are these to be Shepherds?

Laet—Mr. Crowther! You startled me.

Crow—I had no intention of doing so.

Laet—I thought that you & Grandfather were finishing a Bottle of Wine together.

Crow—The Wine is finished, & your Grandfather is asleep. Your Grandmother is conversing with Miss Driscoll, & your Aunt is walking with my Uncle Henry.

Laet—Therefore you have come to bother me, Mr. Crowther.

Crow—I wish you would not call me Mr. Crowther.

Laet—Peregrine.

Crow—When my Parents baptised me, they clearly had Christian Purposes for me. I do not much like the name. You may call me Perry, as Henry does.

Laet—Perry, then. But it sounds like something from a Bottle.

Crow—It is indeed something from a Bottle, & therefore more suitable, as I am no Pilgrim. You should put some Pilgrims into your view of the Abbey.

Laet—Perhaps these are Pilgrims.

Crow—No, Letty. They are not exhausted enough to be Pilgrims, and they are too idle to be Shepherds. They must be a Sketching Party.

Laet—Then if it is your Pleasure, let them be so, Sir.

Crow—My Pleasure? You are very liberal, Letty. Are you concerned for my Pleasure?

Laet—Not at all, in fact.

Crow—Nor for the Pleasure of your Sketching Party, either. They carry themselves with a deuced stiff Air, I would say. You could send them packing, could you not? Since you have put them there you could remove them. Why do you not introduce a Silenus chasing a Dryad in their place? You have your Models yonder, at the edge of the Field.

Laet—Why, Sir, do you mean Sir Henry & my Aunt Katherine?

Crow—Why, Miss, I do. Are they not perfect? The one has Arms and Hands, the other a timid Manner. They would sit for you perfectly without being told what Myth it was they sat for.

Laet—I dislike Myths. They are not true.

Crow—Is that so? But they were true once.

Laet—Never.

Crow—Or may turn out to be true?

He knew very well that I could interpret his Insinuations in the Direction he intended, & I could see that this was his Pleasure. And if the chasing of Dryads were on his Mind, there was a closer Example that occurred to me, than Sir Henry and my Aunt. I did not at first think that there was any more Truth in that Case than in the Myth itself, but the Atmosphere of that Moment of the Afternoon, with Sleep and Wine casting their Influences, the thick Grasses quite still in the Meadow & Butterflies the only Motion, quite soon made me heady with new Speculation, not only about the Attentions he supposed to be paid to my Aunt, but about the Attentions he appeared to be paying to me.

So are all young Girls taken with Flirtation.

It was evident to all Eyes that Peregrine Crowther was a finer Fish to catch than Sir Henry Whybrow, and I wondered why my Aunt had waited for him to enter upon the Scene before raising Speculation about her Relationship with Sir Henry. I ventured as much one day to my Grandfather, who laughed drily, and let me know in no uncertain terms that the Courtship, such as it was, had been set in Motion many Years ago, & though intermittently revived had somewhat, like Polkas after Midnight, lost its Momentum. I was sorry for that, & wondered how I should know so little of it. It was as dull and familiar as a Law of Nature, said my Grandfather, & as little observed by those who had the sense to be living their own Lives. The amatory Nature of Sir Henry was (said my Grandfather) as sleepy & unpredictable as a half-extinct Volcanoe. You might pasture your Flocks in safety on its grassy Slopes, until alerted by a subterranean Rumble. Katherine had heard enough Rumbles in her time to be assured that a serious Eruption was unlikely. In any case (continued my Grandfather) she was half-extinct herself,—and it was quite likely that the Rumbles would soon be emitted in another Quarter. And he stared at me pointedly, until we both broke out in Laughter.

I had no Intention of being wooed by Sir Henry Whybrow. Though good-naturd, he was loud & heavy, not much more than an elderly Version of the plump Boys who handed me round at Dances, though with larger Estates. But now that he had been pointed out to me in the role of a Lover, I could not help interpreting his customary Politeness to me as the sign of Attention to my Person. I was ignorant of the Rules of Conduct in these Cases, & as little able to recognise real Affection as a blind Man to describe Colours. But it seemed at that Time as though Half the World was paying Court to the other Half, & as a girl of the Age I then was, it affected me, as though there were a Season for Love. I put it to my drawing-Master, when showing him my Portrait-Sketches (which had now begun to replace Buildings in my Studies).

Laet—I wish you would tell me, Sir, when you look upon these Faces, if it is possible to know what each Subject is thinking of?

Can—That is an interesting Question, which many Portrait-Painters have neglected entirely. I would go so far as to say that it is the most important Aspect of any Portrait. Why is it, do you think, that Portraits are painted?

Laet—To please the Vanity of Patrons. Their Faces will live after them, and be immortal.

Can—True. But what do you have to say of the Vanity of the Painter?

Laet—The Vanity of the Painter is satisfied in the Achievement of a Likeness.

Can—True again. But now, is there not a Conflict of Interests here, a Conflict of Vanities?

Laet—Patrons believe themselves to be better-looking than they are.

Can—Exactly. But there is more. The Conflict may be resolved in Compromise. Each recognises this Vanity in the other, & goes some way towards appeasing it. The Patron is proud to be able to afford a Painter who has so many Commissions that he is not compelled, in the interests of Flattery, to omit Warts,—while the Painter is eager for the Patronage of a Man who is so wealthy that it is understood that not every Wart, after all, should be included. Details must be sunk in the essential and predominant Qualities of Bodies.

Laet—This is not Compromise, Sir, but Bluff. And will not resolve the Question of Warts.

Can—Do you not see? The Warts are quite unimportant. Whether the Painter descends to Warts or not has nothing to do with the true Subject of the Portrait.

Laet—No indeed?

Can—The true Subject of the Portrait is the Bluff. The Subject of a Portrait is that very Negociation with Immortality. It is a Reciprocation, like Love.

I started at this Turn in the Conversation, for Signor Canistrelli's Voice had almost imperceptibly changed in the Introduction of it. I could not but think that I was just then unduly sensitive to the Topic. His Hands all this

Time were moving my Sketches about upon the Table, as if with the Intention of comparing them & indeed answering my original Question. But he had paused beside me, & now looked into my Face.

Laet—I do not think I quite understand.

Can—The Patron looks into the Eyes of the Painter and the Painter looks back into the Eyes of the Patron. This, like Perspective, is the Axis which rules the resulting Portrait. When you look upon a Portrait you are bound to see a Face which, whether arrogant or suspicious, is perceived in the Act of Looking at the Painter who is painting it. That Face, like the Eyes of a Lover, will reflect the Emotions of the Painter. The greatest Portraits, quite apart from the Beauty or Grotesqueness of their Subjects, also reflect certain Emotions, at the very least the Emotion caused by an awareness of that living Axis.

Laet—And Love?

Can—Love is only a Situation where such a Negociation becomes possible. It is nothing by itself but the meerest Fancy.

Laet—Well then, Sir, what of these Sketches?

Can—(a Hand extended) Now I think you are angry.

Laet—I am confused.

Can—It is a Rule in Negociation never to admit to any Thing which may not be turned to your Advantage.

Laet—I think it is you, Sir, who have the Advantage of me.

Can—If I presume upon our own Axis, I am guilty only of bringing it to Light. It is like a May Game. I am only able to tug the Ribband against the Resistance I feel of yourself tugging it. (Long pause, and Confusion.) Well, I must answer your Question. This is the Portrait of a Man whose Knowledge of your Love for him is second Nature

38

to him, and it glows from his Eyes, as he returns it (Grandfather). This is the Portrait of a Woman who would be elsewhere, but has enough Trust in your Affection to reflect it warily back at you. The Nose is wrong, by the way (Dorcas). And this young Puppy is staring you out with an Insolence that tells me that he is completely satisfied by your Interest in him, and entirely expects it (Crowther).

Laet—Now it is you who are angry.

I see that the Account, as I have related it, has failed to communicate the Shock of this Episode, though its true emotional Import & its physical Expression were only momentarily made manifest, removed as suddenly & as directly as they had been introduced, barely disturbing the customary Formality of our Relationship.

But the Moment had occurred, & it was only out of a kind of Delicacy responsive to his own that I thought I put it out of my Mind. In the Arabian Nights, it would turn out that Sig. Canistrelli was the Sultan Haroun al-Raschid in disguise, freely entering the humble Dwellings of his Citizens so that he might be better able to divine their Thoughts, & to rule justly. Smitten with the Orphan's Beauty, he is unable to conceal himself longer. He simultaneously declares himself & his Passion,—and the Orphan, the Light of whose sleeping Eyelids is as of a thousand Suns, consents to be made a Princess.

I would have consented to be made a Painter, & thought I was well on the way to becoming one. But I had been led out of the Garden of my Innocence by my bad Angel, which, like the Wilfullness of any young Miss, leads her on to the most commonplace of Satisfactions. The Child-Woman has only one Gift. She is momentarily ship-wracked between the sunny islets of childish

Imaginacion & the safe Harbour of womanly Experience, & she has nothing during this Time to guide her but the Resources of her Body.

The Person of the Child-Woman, is, in Myth, an Idol for the Devotions of Men,—in Reality it is a Prize they compete for. There is no Help for it but to go along with the Game. When Sir Henry made his Advances, as expected, I could not help it, but smiled in his Face, as at the great Blankness of an Eclipse long-watched-for. When it appeared from what he said to me, so far as I could make out his Stumblings, that his Proposals were intended, not so much to secure my Person for his own Uses, as to save it from those of the dangerous Perry Crowther, I laughed openly. Why, it would seem that Men had Ways not only of going about their own wooing, but of defeating the wooing of Others. It should not have surprised me, for they do it more openly in Business & in Affairs of State. I certainly felt no negotiable Axis drawn between his rather watery Eye & my own, & if I had been able at that Moment to paint his instantaneous Portrait, it would have been a decided Satyr.

Within a Fortnight the Child-Woman began to receive meaningful Attentions from a Dublin Lawyer, Mr. Clifton, who you will readily see is of no Account whatsoever as I have not yet seen fit to mention him. My bad Angel was pleased enough at his Hand-holding & mutterings, but Dame Nature barely stirred from her Cottage Slumbers. I began to take for granted the Likelihood that every Man I encountered of an Age between my own and his Death-Bed, & not prohibited by Consanguinity, would wish to make me his wife.

In these Circumstances, the merry Distance kept by

Perry Crowther intrigued me. Was he insolent? Did he entirely expect me to love him? Should I (the Thought excited me in the Daring of its Assumptions) be <u>kept waiting</u>? Perhaps this was what had happened to my Aunt Kate many years before,—some one had kept her waiting, & she was waiting still, while Dame Nature nodded off, or perhaps had even blown out the Candle and left the Room on tip-toe. Whatever I was supposed to do, I was determined that this should not happen to me.

The haste in the Child-Woman's Desire to change her State is caused by this sudden coming into Possession of her Body & not quite knowing what to do with it. All she is led to believe is that she must do something, or she might die and have never lived. Now that I have survived a great Epoch, & left my bad Angel behind me, I am sometimes not sure what it is I have lived for, but think that I might as well live for ever. I know whose Body it is now,—it is my Body and no Body else's.

In this Realisation I am as content with it as the young Hyacinth is content in his. I, too, watch him standing on the Rocks. He wears only the Air of knowing that Life is an Adventure which the Body instinctively comprehends, as the Blood is but a salt Shaddow of the Depths it greets, as the full Sail on the Horizon feels the Wind but knows nothing of the Cargo. The Sea spouts from his Mouth as from a Neptune in Marble, chasing Sea-Nymphs.

I see him, Percy, as you must see him, and I see him for what he is. He is another Link in the strange Chain that ties us. He is the Agent who reminds us that we are much more than meer Wanderers on the Earth. They were his Fishs, were they not, that you sent me? His Gift, bestowed again? Your Sign to me of the gracious Tenancy we share in this Land of the Salt and the Sun.

The Path from your Villa to the Palazzo is only the dry Dust that is blown about this World, but it is patterned into Wicker Shapes by the Sandals of Giovanni bearing Presents and Invitations, as if out of a courtly Melancholy you yourself kept a polite & knowing Distance. If I had sad Songs I would send them back to you, as Evidence of my own Mourning. The Affairs of Humanity are indeed like a strange Dance, which may not always be conducted at the same Time or in the same Place, and the Dance is a Dance of Incongruities.

The Grasses on my Table still nod slightly in the Breeze. The five Fishs are long eaten, with their many wet Brothers. Since beginning this Story of my Life I have been seized by a fierce Love for all that is passing & for all that has passed, as if the Act of recounting were somehow also the Act of preserving. Do you already know me well enough, Percy, to understand why this struggling Trail of sepia Sentences should nonetheless seem so insubstantial? Here they are on the Paper like the Marks of so many dying Mosquitoes, the Words all Legs and dried Blood, Ghosts of the Insect's niggling Whine that calls it to our Attention when we hope that it is not there. Words are like that, in my Experience,—they insist upon themselves, requiring us to identify and interpret them. They are proud little Galleons in their Purposes, busy at their Enterprise. They suck our Life-Blood, as if to burrow down into our Dreams, & we half believe that they have done so, yet the Dreams as usual fade as they must do, & in the Morning the Mosquitoes are heavier & darker against the Walls.

Mistrusting Words, though I am so deep in them, I have turned again to Paint. The subject is the same—myself. The Portrait is one which I began last Year

& put aside when my Arms grew so tired. Now that it is my Fingers which ake with the holding of the Pen, it is a Relief to use my Arms & to make broader Stroaks, a Motion liker to a Bird than a Mosquito. I instructed Maria & Angelo to move once again from my dressing-Room to the Gallery that great swivelling looking-Glass which stands in its green & gold Frame to reflect the Truth of corporeal Decline & the Follies of Fashion to any who care to stand in front of it. I have seen Maria before it when she did not know she was observd, Knuckles in her Waist, turning from side to side & simpering, as though she were twenty Years younger than she is. Angelo will not look in it at all, even when carrying it, out of a Superstition—what, that he might see a Devil looking over his Shoulder? I do not know. He is a Corsican, and has strange Dreams. Maria tells me that he is a Mazzere, and can foretell Death, but this in the matter-of-fact Tone of Voice in which she will also tell me of his tender Digestion or his opposition to Bonaparte by reason of his family Connexions.

I bless them both for fetching & carrying for me. They are paid for it, but there must be better Service for them elsewhere, with a Mistress whose Legs do not need dressing & with Guests who are better behaved. However, Lady Parker gave Maria a sufficient Sum as well as a Shawl which she found superfluous in this Climate, & the Admiral was entirely more civil to both of them than any Italian would have been. The Glass reflects me at full length, and my Canvas six by four feet is of a size fairly to accommodate the whole Image. I once had made, to assist my Arms, a light Frame which stands before the Canvas. Its transverse Bar, upon which my painting Arm may lie at the appropriate Height, rests upon moveable Pins &

therefore may be placed lower or higher as requird. This I now rely on, for I tire easily.

When they had mounted the Canvas again on its Easel, I was surprised at its State of Advancement. I remembered it as barely begun, a Sketch meerly, designed to distract me after the Death of the Count. I had painted him full-length also, at his Request, in the Accoutrements of his Rank. He was pleased with the Portrait, though displeasd with the Spillage of Oil & Pigment on the fine Parquet Floor of the Gallery, as though a small indoor Rainbow had decomposd there. I would have none of his Complaints, for the Portrait was begun in March and there was no-where in the Palazzo with so much Light unless we were to be out of Doors. He was stubborn, & compelled a decampment to the Terrace, whereupon he caught a chill & died, which was a pity, as the Floor could not be cleaned of the Paint in any case. Well, I was chastened by all this. I would have preferred to paint him as he really was, perhaps sitting on the Bed in his Linnen Drawers, with the mosquito-Curtains caught under one Leg, a look of Surprise on his Face as he slaps his left Shoulder-Blade. But no-one paints Portraits like this unless they are moral Satyrs, & I would have painted mine out of a sort of Love.

My own Portrait I cannot paint out of Love. I look into the Glass curious to know what I shall see there, though I have looked but a half Minute earlier & know that I shall have to look very hard to see beyond that Curiosity. My Body is stained with the green of Veins that travel within & upon the Muscles as if clenched with a kind of Revulsion at having to go anywhere at all in the Conveyance of my Blood. How ungrateful the Body is at the last to do that Service! It shrinks from the Brush as though it were a Usurper of the Soul, & the Painter's Art will find it out. And yet it grasps the Brush boldly to perform the Painter's Will, like a Roman Death. Behind this Paradox, as I conceive it, there may after all be nothing but the original Child-Woman grown old.

My Body has had its Glory, like a Queen now deposd. It has issued its Commands, & they have been observd. I know very well that I should be thankful for this, although it is no matter for an acknowledged History like the wooing of the Sprig Crowther, for it is some Thing that I still must live with, is all indeed I do live with, and Crowther long dead after all. This is the self-same Body that was amorously taken by him in Sir Henry's Coach on a public Road, that consented to have him against my better Judgement & that of my Grandfather, & that concluded the first Act of its dramatic Progress robed in a Crowther & at the pleasant Mercy of a Crowther in a House in Jermyn Street, London.

2

Lux varium, vivumque dabit, nullum Umbra,
Colorem.*

It is in the Nature of Mistakes to be irredeemable. Whole
Religions have been invented which attempt to prove
otherwise, have they not? It is in our Natures to trust to
a Hope in the Impossible,—that is the Corollary. We
dislike the Fact of our Errors, & dream of a World where
they may be removed as easily as a Joint of sacrificed Meat
from a Table that is ready for an aery Pudding. To be
sure, I regretted my Marriage & wondered why, when
Society has arranged Matters so that while it is easy to wed
in Ignorance, it should happen to be so difficult to
become unwed through Enlightenment. My Grandfather
visited us once in Jermyn Street before he died & observd
my Discontent, over Tea.

G—Well, Letty, you would not listen to me, you
know.

Laet—Grandfather, I am glad that you are here, but I
am disclind to hear Lectures.

G—And perhaps that has been your undoing. You
have lived in a World of your own Phantasy & excluded
all Voices of Reason.

---

*The Light produces all kinds of Colours, and the Shadow gives us none', Du Fresnoy,
p. 38.

Laet—How can Reason uncover the Truth of the Heart?

G—It cannot pretend to, but it can perceive the Lineaments of Character & Prospects. It can weigh Virtue with Vice.

Laet—Why then did you not tell me that I should not marry him?

G—Now you are being doubly unreasonable, Letty. Would you have believed it to be in my Nature to forbid it? Am I a Grandfather in a Fable? Would you indeed have obeyed me if I had?

Laet—No.

G—Quite, Letty. You have always been able to make up your own Mind, & the Choice was yours.

Laet—I was carried away, Sir.

G—I do not see why you did not take Signor Canistrelli.

Laet—I did not think Signor Canistrelli had offered himself.

G—I think your Choice of Crowther also involved choosing to forget my Words to you on the Subject. Did you need great urging, my dear? Are you like the Guest who will not eat Cake until twice pressd? Or will take Nothing unless it is handed at your Elbow? Come, I did not think you so coy.

Laet—I do not remember you talking of Signor Canistrelli.

G—Letty, you are now in the Sulks. I do not like to see you like this. You remember perfectly well. I knew that you were conscious of the Delicacy of his Position & his Sense of the Impropriety of his Feelings. I could not press the Matter on his behalf, & he did not know what was in your Heart. It was up to you to give a Sign.

Laet—No Body told me about giving Signs. Why did some Body not teach me this secret Language?

G—You are being obtuse, Letty. Was it then out of some Stubbornness or Defiance that you rushed off with this young Rake?

Laet—(Tears)

G—I blame Katherine in this, who refused every One in the vain Hope of something better, until it was too late. You saw her Mistake, & were determind not to make it yourself. Therefore you made the worse Mistake, & took the first Opportunity that came your Way, without consulting the real Interests of your Heart & Soul.

Laet—I was thoughtless, Sir, & you should have made me think. Why did you not lock me up in my Gazebo until I came to my Senses?

G—There, there, my Dear. Dry your Eyes, & pour me another Cup. You will have to make the best of it.

I had remembered my Grandfather's Approach to me about my drawing-Master perfectly well, & had chosen to ignore it because I was afraid. To imagine Signor Canistrelli in the Role of a Lover was difficult for me because of the Role he already played in my Life as a Teacher & because he seemed old, though he was no older than Sir Henry. Perry Crowther was a Novelty, & behaved like a Lover from the first. It seemed to be his Prerogative. In my Defence I would claim that any young Person of normal Feelings & the usual Inexperience would have been swept away by his Attentions. My Mistake lay not so much in marrying Perry Crowther as in not marrying Luigi Canistrelli. When I looked deeply into my Heart I could see indeed that his Symbol of the May Game & the tugged Ribbands was true. Without knowing it, I had been pulling at my End,—finding the

Ribband not only tightly held but responsive, I had been terrified, & had let it go.

Crowther could sustain no interest in Painting. His early Remarks about my Work were meer amorous Repartee, designd to flatter me & put himself in my Favour. Putting himself in my Favour was the only End for him, it would appear, since once he was in it he lost Interest in me. For my part, I was eager enough to be held in his Arms & did not care if he held my Work in his Esteem. I did not expect him to make love to it, for there is not that kind of Passion in Pigment, & an adventuring Stroak of Indian Ink is never diverted by an Embrace. However, I was much disappointed by my Husband's Attention to my Person. I had expected Ardour, prolonged Adventures & Enlightenment, but what had seemd daring in a Coach was but perfunctory in a Bed. He frequently dined away from Home, & even when he did not, as like as not was in a State of stupefied Drunkenness when he retird.

A drunk Man may the more feel free to indulge in Venery,—yet though he recklessly & speedily approach that Moment of Abandon when (to put it delicately, in Terms I have already establishd) his Errand is in sight & available for its Accomplishment, the Item purchasable & all Negociation abandoned, then he finds he does not after all have the Wherewithal, & his Purse will not come up with the Price. For my part, having satisfied my initial Curiosity about some of the precise Details of the running of Errands, I was content to let him snore. The wedded State was no longer a Novelty to me. I had thought him beautiful, & found him to be but a Man.

On more than one Occasion I brought him to his Bliss with my right Hand while he was completely unconscious. I did it not out of Kindness or Consideration, but out of scientifick Curiosity, to see if by any Motion of his Features his Soul might be said to have ascended to Paradise. Being uninvolved, I could see the whole Process for what it was,—Dame Nature's little Mechanism for propelling the Homunculus into its first nesting-Place. In the absence of the noisy & extravagant Pleasure which usually accompanies the Act, it did not seem to me to amount to very much more than the kind of Shiver we give when some one passes over our Grave, & its product no more than the sad Jelly of an egg-White when we save the Yolk for some Kitchen Confection. The Experiment was, I have to say, an interesting one for a Painter. The Product of this generative Shudder, falling into Loops & milky Shapes upon the Sheet, was very like a Sketch for a Painting, or a series of Blotts that would have delighted dear Alex Cozens* in his search for Inspiration, being in both Design and Substance the Essence of Creation. I remember Samuel Johnson telling me of the Etymology of my Pencill.

Dr. J—It must necessarily be a Thing of no Account, Madam.

Laet—Why is that, Sir?

Dr. J—Why is that, Madam? (His Mouth full of Plums which some One had just set before him.) Why, Madam, because it is the Diminutive of a Diminutive. Your Pencill is the Latin 'penicillum', which is to say a little

---

*Alexander Cozens, (c.1717-86), 'Blotmaster-General to the Town' according to the unsympathetic Edward Dayes (*The Works of the Late Edward Dayes*, ed. E. W. Brayley, 1805), followed Leonardo da Vinci in taking abstract shapes as a basis for his watercolours: 'To form a BLOT . . . possess your mind strongly with a subject . . . and with the swiftest hand make all possible variety of shapes and strokes upon your paper' (*A New Method of Assisting the Invention in Drawing Original Compositions of Landscape*, 1786).

Brush, and the Brush is the Latin 'peniculus', which is to say a little Tail, and the Tail is the Latin 'penis', which I have no doubt you know well enough, Madam, being both a Painter and a Woman, Madam.

He spat out these last Words with much Scorn & two Plum-Stones, while looking me up & down breathlessly as if to defy me into a Response. The only Response I could give him was to offer to paint his Portrait (at which he was mightily pleasd), for which I would naturally need the largest Brushes I could find (less pleasd).

My Grandfather died suddenly one Summer. I received the News unexpectedly, Mrs. Howson bringing the Letter into the Garden, where I was tidying some Bushes of Herbs. Feeling distant from the happy Time of my Childhood, & from the Wisdom that I would no longer benefit from, I rued my Marriage all the more, which was a Romance & no Romance. My Tears fell into the Mint, for my Grandfather, for my Father, for myself, for the very Strangeness of Life itself.

Crowther sailed into his Harbour of Oblivion upon a Tide of Whisky. He regularly received Barrels of it, sent down from the Isle of Islay by a Cousin, to whom he sent Bales of Silk in return. Johnson would say that Claret was the Drink of Boys, Port the Drink of Men & Brandy the Drink of Heros. He did not add that Whisky was the drink of Cowards & Bullies, but if he had known my first Husband he surely would have done so. I frequently had to put Crowther to Bed, & when he was violent I called for the Assistance of Mrs. Howson, who having known him as a rebellious Youth, had ways of dealing with his Whims & Gesticulations which were often more effective than mine. She would, for example, remove the Basin & Ewer to the other Side of the Room or out of the Room altogether. She would hang a Napkin over the looking-Glass, not so much to prevent it being shattered in his Rage as to prevent the Rage in the first place, for Crowther could be so excited by his own sour and puffy Image in the Glass as to wish to assault it & knock it down. He would call it Names, & accuse it of owing him Money.

In truth, no-one owed Crowther Money, for he would lend none. Any Money not in his immediate Possession he was always seeking to acquire himself, or had already lost. He had run through his personal Fortune, & would have ruind his Father's Business into the Bargain if it had not been for the Diligence of his Manager, James Whetton, who remembered well the Prudence of his former Master. Remorse Crowther might well have died a second Time, of Grief, had he known how his Son had neglected his Affairs. His Wealth had been accumulated carefully, as the Poet wrote, like a Cocoon,—now the Cocoon was broke open & become a careless gaudy Butterfly.* It was, as I later came to understand, a mark of this Profligacy that he had been induced by my Grandfather to make a Settlement upon me at the time of my Marriage, my having but a small Portion of my own. This Settlement I had soundly invested on my Grandfather's Advice, & Perry was unable to lay his Hands on it, even when pursued to his very Door by his most insistent Creditors. Most of his Debts were incurred at the gambling-Tables, for the Affairs of the Household were largely neglected, as was his own Person, for being drunk he frequently slept in his Cloaths, & having

---

*Horsepole is probably here referring to Pope, 'Epistle to Lord Bathurst', *Moral Essays* III, lines 169-70: 'Riches, like insects, when concealed they lie, / Wait but for Wings, and in their season fly.'

dismissed his Valet for want of Wages to pay him, was forced to shave himself, which he was neither pleased to do nor much capable of doing.

With or without a Shirt, he lay about so often in a State of Insensibility that I had ample Opportunity to observe his Anatomy, & to draw him from the Flesh, which as you may imagine plentifully made up for my Prohibition, as a Woman & out of Delicacy, from the drawing-Schools. I cannot deny that he was well made, but the Signs of Decline were upon him,—he would have made a doubtful Alexander, & was readier for a Silenus. The Stirring of his Member in Sleep was like the unfolding of Fungus in a wooded Dell, & it shrank from the Finger like an Anemone in a Crevice of Rock. I had to be careful not to wake him, or he would have followed its Motions like a Yokel with an unmanageable Bull, & I should have had much Trouble in keeping him off me.

A decisive Turn in his Fortunes occurred when his Mare Fatima fell in the Steeplechase & had to be shot. He came home in a Temper, & straightway came into my Bedroom, where I was taking a rest against the Pain of my monthly Time. My Maid Jane Penny was ironing some Small-Cloaths in my dressing-Room adjoining, & my little Dog Mustard was asleep at my feet. Upon hearing the News, I expressed my Sorrow in Terms as sympathetick as could be expected. I was sorry for Fatima, whose Portrait I had painted standing against a Group of Oaks, though in truth I was prouder of my Oaks, which were out of my Head, than of the Mare, which had stood long if impatiently before me at the Jockey Club at Newmarket Heath, & of which I had a Sheaf of anatomically contradictory Sketches.

C—I see you are being ironical, Letty. What you mean

to say is that you are sorry that she was made to take Jumps.

Laet—If that is what I meant to say, then I would have said so, Sir. I feel akin to her as a female Animal who has suffered.

C—A female Animal, hey? You intend to say that you suffer, lying here upon your Bed all Day?

Laet—You well know what all Women suffer, Sir. Taking Jumps, too, if it come to that.

It was my Misfortune to have learned how easy it was to be witty at his Expense, since Whisky had made him stupid. It had become my sole domestick Pleasure, which I wearily indulged when I was not in my Attic at my Easels. Pleasantries of that kind shamd him, & therefore angered him further, for he had put me through fewer Jumps than Fatima, to be sure. I counselled him to be quieter in his Rage so that Jane would not hear every Word he uttered, but soon my Voice was raised, too. He accused me of being barren and a blue-Stocking, while I told him that his Breath stank of a Peat-Bog. When I retreated into my dressing-Room, he followd, and, taking up the smoothing-Iron which Jane had just put by to cool, he hurled it at me & broke my left Shin. Mustard then bit his Ancle, & he stamped on her.

I knew of the Frailty of the human Shape, & of human Hopes, & was touched by Death in my early Life, losing as I did both Parents while yet a Child. But those Events were still to me an emotional Idea, a kind of Myth assisting in the Delineation of my Life, which Life in any case was at the Centre of the entire Universe. To be affected by Loss is not the same Thing as to realise that one may be lost oneself. Every One, I do believe, has some Moment in his Life when this Realisation arrives, like a Shaddow cast upon daily Objects that transforms them for ever. From that Moment I knew that I was breakable, like a Tea-Pot.

But I did not have to be shot, like Fatima. Mrs. Howson called the Surgeon, who did what he could for me. My Stubbornness in trying to ignore my Condition (more out of Disbelief than Consideration for the Feelings of the Perpetrator) contributed to a Fever that put me in the most Danger, but the Leg did not heal well either & ever after I have walked with a Dip in my Gait like a Camel. I was relieved of the difficult Business of responding to an Apology or of negociating a Reconciliation, since within Weeks Crowther was found drifting in the Thames near the Isle of Dogs. I do not think that it was his Shame that pursued him there, but his Creditors. It would have made a grand Finale to a set of moral Tableaux, the Spendthrift Heir, with the River Scavengers & their grappling-Hooks coming to him like Devils from a Judgement.

It was indeed Judgement he felt, if the dissenting Practice of his Family had had any effect on his upbringing. I suppose I have never known a less pious Man so intimately, but some of the Assumptions of his Father in respect of Divine Grace had contributed to his doomed & graceless State, & I had the Impression that his shameless Exterior concealed a fatal & gnawing Guilt within. He had no Will to resist the Conviction that he was predestined to waste all that his Father had amassed.

I have often wondered at these cyclic Changes in human Nature, where the Ant is succeeded by the Grasshopper. If I had borne him a Son, would the Son have turned out an Ant again? His Hopes of an Heir, so vocally frustrated, may have been intended in this Way to bring the Family back into Virtue & Fortune. I cannot believe human Nature to be so preordained, & I doubt that Perry truly believed it. His Beliefs lay rather in the Beneficence of Luck, in which he blindly trusted.

Now I hear you object, Percy, that Grace & Luck are equally unknowable, imponderable and illusory, & that a Scoundrel might as well believe or disbelieve in either. But if so, what is there for a Saint, or Poet for the matter of that, to believe in? We know our Conditions, but wish also to know if they be just. And if after all there is such Justice in our Lives, how shall we act? We look forward and see no Path, but we look back & see clearly the Path we have followed. How can this be? Was the Path not always there? I wish you had not returned to Pisa, for I would dearly like you to visit me to talk it over, you & your whole Tribe of Otaheite Philosophers.* For of the Paths we think we create for ourselves, Marriage is the strangest. Those who speak & write against it cannot understand the Paradox of the willing Yoak even as they mock any Idea of a Legislation for Love. It is like Peachum's Remark to the wretched Polly—'Do you imagine that your Mother & I would have remained happy so long together if ever we had been married?'† These Ideals of a free Society never sufficiently acknowledge the Desire in our original Ancestors to be so bonded.

However, being left a Widow wealthy in Silks, I had little now to prevent me from pursuing another Path that lay open to me, that of my Painting. I have in my Time been accused by Criticks of an Indulgence in my Art for

---

*i.e. believers in free love (Otaheite = Tahiti). The phrase was Claire Clairmont's and was picked up by Byron, from whom Horsepole must have heard it.
†John Gay, *The Beggar's Opera*, I, viii, misquoted.

want of Offspring, but these Criticks are prejudiced against my Sex in general, & their hollow Jibes conceal a Fear that Women may invade their private Haunts & reservd Occupations & find them out. The Theory itself is ridiculous, as if I were to be seen wiping the Nose of an Ink-Wash or fondly tracing the Progress of a Mezzotint in a Go-Cart. I shall have no more to say on this Matter.

The Path was unknown, its Difficultys not therefore to be feared. In Retrospection I was amazed to discover that I had not been lost on the Way. The Traces of Endeavour, as of Suffering, are often invisible to their Owner, as all my old Bruises were to me when uncovered by the Surgeon who attended my broken Leg. But at the time we put up with Adversities one after the other as they arrive, & think not of them in the Mass.

Without Signor Canistrelli's generous Letter of Introduction to Francis Hayman* I should have early strayed. As it was, caught in the Toils of my marriage, I had little opportunity for the social Intercourse that in a Man constitutes no little Proportion of the Effort he expends in his Vocation. I was encouraged to attend at St. Martin's Lane, and sometimes during the long Hours in which Crowther was engaged at his Tables I made my way there to draw from Greek Plaster (though not from the Nude) and to despise the petty Antics of the Followers of Gravelot which, as a Woman, I was expected to admire,—all Texture & Decoration in my View, meer Toys of Art. I preferred the Humour of Hayman's Work, and liked the Man. In the five Years after the Drowning of my Husband, I came to know him well & was the

---

*Francis Hayman (1708–76) was one of the principal members of the St Martin's Lane Academy, and President of the Society of Artists from 1766 to 1768. He became Librarian of the Royal Academy in 1770.

Confidante of Mrs Hayman & their Children. The Children treated me like an Aunt, a Role I was happy to play, bringing them Tops and Windmills & other Gewgaws on my Visits,—and Mrs Hayman treated me like a Daughter, serving me with Tea & encouraging me in my Aspirations, while scarcely understanding any of them. She was the least jealous Creature I have met in my Life, for any Wife might expect her Husband's Association with a young Widow to conceal a Liaison, despite the common professional Concerns which might excuse it. She, however, seemed really to have my Interests at Heart, & pleaded my Cause at every Opportunity.

Mr. H—You will be pleased to hear, my dear, and you too, Letty, that I have indeed received the Commission to decorate the new Music-Room with some of the glorious Transactions of the late War.*

Mrs. H—Oh, I am so pleased to hear it. Are you not pleased to hear it, Letty?

Laet—It is an Honour that could not fall to a worthier Hand.

Mrs. H—It is a Work that will need the Assistance of many Hands, will it not, Husband?

Mr. H—I expect my Studio to sound like a Summer Hive. I have in mind a Series in which Britannia bestows upon her Heros the usual Accolades.

Laet—The Generals are to be crowned with Oak, Sir?

Mr. H—And to appear in noble Stances upon the

---

*Hayman decorated the Vauxhall Gardens Music Room in 1760. His subjects were the surrender of Montreal to Lord Amherst, Hawke's victory at Quiberon Bay, Lord Clive receiving the homage of the Nabob after Plassy, and Britannia distributing laurels to a group of leading generals headed by the Marquess of Granby. It is extraordinary that Horsepole was assisting in this project shortly before her thirtieth birthday.

Vistas of their Conquests. Ah, I see. You are being satirical, Letty.

Laet—Never, Sir, as I am a true Patriot.

Mrs. H—And a true Painter, my dear, though one of our Sex. Husband, you will give Letty work in the Studio, will you not?

Mr. H—Of course, of course. What shall I give you now, Letty? You would like a Bird, would you not? Perhaps the Feathers in a Huron Head-Dress when the vanquished Savages come to pay Tribute to the Flag?

Laet—We are a civilised Nation, Sir, & should take no extravagant Pleasure in Humiliation.

Mr. H—That is spoken like a Woman.

Laet—It is felt like a Christian (not altogether what I meant).

Mrs. H—Oh yes, my dear, how true.

Mr. H—But is it not our Christian Duty to civilise the Globe? The modern Artist has become a Witness of this Process of Civilisation. He is a privileged Historian of the Empire.

Laet—He may be, Sir, but is he not also—and is *she* not also—a natural Philosopher of the Appearances of Things? I should be interested in your Huron Cap of Feathers for what it might tell the Onlooker about its Wearer's Desire for Immortality, since the borrow'd Plumes doubtless signify the Hope of Flight into the Unknown. And for the matter of that, I should be perfectly content with a Cloud. Or a passing Gnat, that is ignorant of all History, even its own.

And all this was true enough. Painting in those Days had exalted Ambitions, or it had none at all. On the one hand you had Painters whose whole Purpose was to provide a visible Setting for the national Destiny,—on the other were those who cut out Silhouettes with a Pair of Scissars. I excepted those who, from a satirical Purpose or out of a Genius for comic Observation, could represent Life as it is lived. Hayman himself had studied the Dutch Painters with profit. Joseph Highmore will be remembered, and William Hogarth, for Satyr upon the Manners of the Day. I do not intend a Lecture upon Art,—there were Painters I liked better, who will not be—have not been!—remembered. But the whole Drift of that Century was to invest Scenes from everyday Life with the Dignity hitherto reservd for Subjects from Holy Writ and from Antiquity. I find that I have required quite the Opposite of such heroick Transformations, & look to Painting to capture in physical Form, however fleeting, the hitherto unknown. It is like giving Body to the Soul.

We marvel at Painters who show us the Unseen in Nature. Lightning was never still enough to be painted, nor the Wave tumbling on the Shore. From the Mountain Summit the Surface of the Clouds beneath has become an Ocean. From the Eyes looks out, as from suddenly drawn Curtains, the hitherto confind Spirit. These are Things not seen, & there are many other Things seen but not looked at. The Painter looks closely at the World, & brings it to book.

My Life in Jermyn Street was now my own. I ordered my Husband's Manager to close three of the Warehouses, & to dismiss the greater Part of the Employees. The Business could never be the same again, but it was possible to pay all Debts by doing what Crowther had never contemplated—abandoning to Fate the sole Source of his Wealth, & making publick the Extent of his fatal Claims upon it. In particular, he had feared the Disapprobation of Whetton, whose own father had served

Remorse Crowther throughout the rapid Growth of the Business with a Skill and unstinting Application that seemed to give him a Family Right in its Affairs equal to any material Share. I had no such Fear, but consulted Whetton fully about Retrenchment. I was, of course, rewarded with practical Advice, & thought it prudent at last to make him a Partner. With careful Management I had no material Cares.

I resolved to be active in all Aspects of my Art, & to busy myself with Projects of every Kind. I perswaded my Aunt Katherine to gather her Courage & her Skirts, & to make the great Journey to London, bringing with her the Fruit of my Father's Work on Fevers. When I was younger I was powerless to prevent her innocent Appropriation of it. For her it had been an Object of superstitious Reverence, like a Saint's Knee-Cap in a Monstrance. We were Rivals in our Worship at that Saint's Shrine indeed, but whereas my aunt had nothing but her Relics, I had my Life before me. But now I was secure in my Prospects, & in a Position to bring this Work before the World. Aunt Kate could not pretend that the Relic had greater Efficacy shrouded in secret & sisterly Feeling in Dublin than it would have in the Hands of a London Printer, & appeared in Jermyn Street in a Flurry of Excitement & Usefulness. My one Fear was that she would be full of Reproaches—or of prurient Curiosity—about Perry Crowther, & for some Reason that I did not fully understand she was the one Person to whom I could not represent his Failings in their true Light. I sensed that in some Respects my Situation compared badly with her own, as though I had erred & she was inviolate. But I told myself firmly that to make a wrong Choice is better than to make no Choice at all, &

that Age & Spinsterhood alone gave her no moral Authority over me.

However, she did not take it upon herself to assume it, but entirely put herself at my Disposal for the Space of her Visit, & it was together that we began the difficult Business of piecing together Joseph Connell's Papers. Despite my resolve, I soon discovered that I could not have begun this Project without her Assistance and Encouragement. She was my Kin, & closest to my Interest. The Project, as the World knows, was brought to a successful Conclusion.* It was from the Publisher of my Father's Book that I consequently received Commissions for Engravings similar to those that I provided as Decorations, Versions in suitable Disguise of the Bird-Fevers I had sketched as a Child, Phantasies deliverd over into rococo Friezes. Though they were unsuitable for an Encyclopaedia of medical Discovery, the Publisher was pleased enough to have them, & they pleased me,—they lay at the Head of their cold Pages like new Flowers on a forgotten Tomb.

They came not from a cold Heart, for that was full of rememberd Love, but from a cold Spirit. I lay in my Bed of Nights as though it were itself a Tomb, & dreamed of God reaching down with a Sigh to draw a Veil over my Existence. I would sometimes wake & light a Candle, or if the Moon was full & casting its blue Light into my room I would lie in its welcoming Mystery, hearing nothing but the retreating Creek of a Cart in Piccadilly &

---

*Pharmakopion Okeanikon: An Account of the Fevers, Dropsies, Calentures, and Illnesses peculiar to Sea-Voyages, with their effectual Treatment, now first published from the Papers of Capt. Joseph Connell, MD, by his Daughter. Printed for S. Bladon, in Paternoster Row, MDCCLXII. Handsomely printed in one volume, octavo. Price Six Shillings, bound and lettered.

the Pulse of my body that was Flesh after all, & not Stone. I had been reminded at the Printing of my Father's Book that I was now older than he was when he was taken by Fever. I had been married and damaged, like some Article that cannot be returned to the Shop. I wanted to travel. I wanted to learn Greek. I wanted to find out what another Man would be like. Yet at that still tender Age I half thought my Life to be over. My Aunt seemd to be curious about nothing, & had already lost some of her Teeth. I took her as a Model of my likely Self twenty Years in the Future, shuddered & took her as a Model of her own Self instead.

It was at that Time perhaps the best Portrait I had painted, & I thought it might not have disgraced the Studio of any of the Flemish Masters. I placed her at her Sewing, her Face looking up questioningly & half amused, as if pleased to be distracted from a domestick Task patiently undertaken but not quite as interesting as Gossip. To keep her patient during the Sitting, & to preserve the Expression, I told her as much about my Life with Perry Crowther as might be proper for two Women to converse of, with Jane Penny likely to bring in the Tea. There was much at which she was incredulous, & not a little at which she was shocked. I like to think that the Success of the Portrait was due as much to my Skill in Conversation & Judgement of Character as in Painting, & often as we sat together I remembered the Words of Sig. Canistrelli, that the Subject of a Portrait is a Reciprocation. It was not enough to convey to the Onlooker that here was an unmarried Woman of Fifty, brought up in Rectitude & blessed with Humour, inclind to wear such-and-such a sort of grey Dress & to wear her Hair so, & to wrinkle her Brow, & to catch the exact

Length of her Nose or Depth of her Chin. I had to paint her Relationship with me, her Feelings about me & her Sense of being the Object of an unusual Scrutiny by Someone of whom she was still fond but after some Years perhaps a little uncertain. To sit for a Portrait is a kind of Judgement. That Truth which is the resulting Verdict is beyond the Painter's Control,—it is a Survival of the human Spirit which the Mystery of Art guarantees. It is in the Face, & of the Face, but is not only the Face. It is in its Essence invisible.

I thought then that all Painting attained its glory in despite of the Mass of the World in its Colours, which weighed it down. The purest Canvas would be of an impossible single Quality of Light, which was the single Divine Truth, before Creation, & before our imperfect Understanding of it. Every poor Representacion of the Forms of this World was striving to understand the Essence of these Forms, & to paint that if it could,—not this Niobe or that Juliet, but Grief or Love itself. Even as I worked for Hayman, thrilled that any small Part of my Work would thereby come before the Publick, I was conscious not of the particularly grand Personages beneath whose planted Boots I touched in little trampled Flowers of the New World, nor of the Occasions commemorated, but of the Feelings of the Vauxhall Assemblies as their Hearts were stirr'd by Symphonys & Thoughts of the great Machinery of Property and Empire.

My Portrait of Katherine Connell was shown at the second Exhibition of the Society of Artists, & was received favourably. From that time Commissions came my way as they do to any working Artist, & I soon acquired a sufficient Reputation to be continually busy. It might be thought that to be launched in this way with an admired Portrait of a Woman, & being a Woman myself, that the Commissions would come from vain Actresses or idle Noblemen wishing to immortalise their Wives. This was scarcely the Case, for I soon found myself in demand by the Navy, whose gallant Officers seemd to like nothing better than being stared at intently by an independent young Woman with coloured Stains on her Smock, sitting quite still in their powderd Hair & bright Uniforms with the licence to flirt all the long Afternoon.

At that Time there could be no more secure a way to re-enter that Society I was in Danger of never having in truth entered in the first Place. Crowther had kept no Table but the one in green Baize he had constantly sought for the Manifestations of his Goddess Fortune. For myself, even in my Freedom I dined almost nowhere but with the Haymans, & preferred for Company the few Remnants of my own Household, my Aunt Kate, who showed no inclination to return to Dublin, Mrs. Howson and her odd Brother Elkanah, an Enthusiast of the old Kind, who would bring me Roots from his Garden & entertain me with Philosophy. I soon, however, saw that I was in Danger of becoming a Recluse, the Hermit of Jermyn Street, a Woman so tall that when she limped off a Pavement, dipping from one Hip & ballanced by a Basket of Ochre on the other, with a forgotten painting Brush still stuck through her Hair above one Ear, she seemed like a stooping Eagle to frighten the very crossing-Sweeper into forgetting to beg for his Penny.

I was informd as much by the first and most genial of my naval Subjects, James Horsepole, as I stared him down into a harmonious Posture between a Curtain & a Globe of the New World, upon which I instructed his Fingers to play as if performing a sprightly Victory-March upon a Keyboard.

H—Indeed, Mrs. Crowther, I feel that you have me now. You have the unblinking Eye of a Bird, & I am your Prey.

Laet—The Eye of the Artist, Sir, is a passive, not an active one. It receives, but does not seize.

H—Quite so, but the subject may nonetheless have all the Appearances of a Victim, quite transfixd & helpless.

Laet—I consider my Eye, Sir, to be an open Door through which my Subject is invited to step into my Mind.

H—I am at the Threshold, & may not turn back!

Remarks of this sort were perfectly familiar to me, & I considered a Man of valiant Deeds & Decisions the less a Man of his Kind for being backward in witty Civiltys to a Lady. But there was a considerd Gravity in his Manner, & a magnetick Glow in his own Eye, that produced an Effect quite different from the Pleasantries of his fellow Officers. My Instinct was to assume that he would no more take Advantage of me than he would insult a Duchess, & I was right.

He admired the Progress of his Portrait, & wished me to paint his Son Robert. This was most conveniently to be accomplishd at his own House at Greenwich, & I soon became intimate with his small Family. There were but two Children, Robert, who was six Years old, & Daisy his Sister, little more than two. Their Mother had died in giving Birth to her, & James lived with his unmarried Sister Frances as Housekeeper.

Robert was a solemn Child, a Miniature of his Father but with the Stiffness of a Being as yet incompletely formed. He missed his Mother, & was frightened of me until I let him mix my Paints & take Pieces of Charcoal for his own Scribbles. He had no Talent for drawing, but liked to make Boxes, which he filled very slowly as much with heavy Breathing as with any Accuracy. These boxes were his Fleet of Ships, & he drew lines from them into the empty Spaces of the Paper which he said were gun-Fire. Thus was his Picture a Plan of his Empire & nothing more. He was perfectly satisfied with it, put it away & straightway forgot all about it.

My Portrait of Robert was designed as a Companion to my Portrait of his Father, although I knew they would never hang together. Where James's Fingers rested upon their model Hemisphere with the Delicacy & Ease of political Assurance, his Son's Fingers rested upon a Hoop. I did not need to point this out to James, who laughed aloud when he saw it.

H—Thus it is, you think, Letty, that we make Toys of our Conquests?

Laet—I dare think no such thing. Rather, we learn of the World through our childish Models of it.

It was at this moment, seeing him laugh, & finding myself giving him an Account of my little Garden-Academy in my Grandfather's House in Dublin, something that it would never have occurred to me to offer to Crowther, that I realised I had an Affection for James Horsepole that would not be satisfied by anything but the closest Ties possible between a Woman and a Man. I had a good enough Understanding of his own Interest in me to conclude that there was little to prevent such a Relationship from rapidly coming to pass. His Overtures to me were of the most tender Character, & so without Lewdness as almost to disappoint a Woman of eager Blood, as I was soon reminded I was.

Our Understanding was well-watered & soon shot up to an Engagement,—before the Spring had quite warmd the Earth anew, it had blossomed into Nuptials. His Part in wooing me was soon done, but mine was in some degree to woo his whole Household. I had no fear of his Children, for I had befriended them already. With Robert, our Treaty was ratified with a Box of Lead Soldiers. Little Daisy needed no more than the latest & warmest of a long Series of Huggs. But what of Sister Fanny, whose severe Demeanour (so like her Brother's, though more forbidding in a young Woman) promised Disapproval, & Resentment at being displaced? I feared Enmity in that Quarter, for my Overtures of Friendship had never been visibly reciprocated.

My Fear was groundless. Within a Month of our Marriage Fanny was off & wed herself, to an obscure Norfolk Cousin with whom she had long had a secret Understanding. At least, James confessd himself utterly surprised. Later I was to wonder if her Departure had not been long threatend, putting him in need of a Replacement. I never thought that he did not love me in his quiet Way, & I was never in Danger of finding my self to be a meer Convenience, but sometimes our Path in Life is conditiond by the Circumstances in which we find ourselves. The prompt Appearance of the Cousin, & the ease of Fanny's Arrangements for Departure, suggested that James had been threatened with Mutiny & Abandonment or was aware of its Possibility, & had bethought himself of the appropriate Adage, any Port in a Storm.

As for the Œconomy of my own Voyage, I was now enabled to disburden myself of some unnegociable Cargo & therefore to sit lighter in the Water, for seeing another Man on the Horizon, my Aunt Kate proposd to return to

Dublin at last. I did not think that I would feel so sorry at this Decision, for I did not know when I might see her again. I proposed that she convey her Portrait instead of herself, & see if her few Friends would notice the Difference, but she saw no Humour in the Proposal, & packed her Trunks all the more speedily.

James Horsepole was in most respects the precise opposite of Peregrine Crowther, cautious in his Dealings, constructive in his Humour, respectful of my Person, modest in his Pleasures, & sober in his Habits. He had begun to give up Wiggs, & would wear his own Hair. This seemed to be a Sign of plain-Dealing in all the Spheres of his Life, for he did not dress to impose himself on others, nor cast off Formality at Home the more credibly to act the Brute (as did that Rascal Perry), but bore himself as a Man at all Times. He welcomed me not only as his Wife, but as Mistress of the Household, & when I sold the Jermyn Street House insisted that I need not dismiss my Servants also, for Fanny would wish to take her Cook with her, & Mrs. Howson could well fill that Role. There was a small Cottage at his Disposal in which her brother Elkanah might live in return for working at the Livery Stable. There was also a Room for Jane Penny, who could continue as my personal Maid. His Servants welcomed mine with the same good Grace as I was myself accommodated in the Greenwich Household. All was arranged as though our Places had long awaited us, as though James had lookd back at me from his vantage-Point in our Future & had calld out to me to make haste to catch up with him.

And what did Nature make of this pretty Picture?

Nature—In haste again, Letty? Have you not learnt your Lesson?

Laet—It seems that I would like to learn it again.

Nature—And you believe that I have commanded you to this pleasant Docility? You know that my School teaches the Fashioning of Posterity, not the Indulgence of Pleasure.

Laet—But if I am barren, may I still not have the Pleasure, & without the Pain, too, with which our first Mother was judgd and burdend? My Posterity is my Art.

Nature—Then should you rather paint what your Art requires you to paint, & put an end to these ten Guinea Adventures into the Heads of Men, whereby a three-quarter Window on to their Likeness requires them to stare back through it at you without Aversion.* It is no Wonder that you have so easily found another Husband.

But this I did not truly believe. I had a lofty Brow, & dark eyes, & an Abundance of dark Hair, & knew well enough that I could command the Attentions of Men without the Excuse of rendering them immobile. To me as a Wife, my new Husband rendered all the Hommage I might expect from his Courtship of me as a Widow,— and because we were neither Novices, nor in the Bloom of Youth, we dispensd both with all the Niceties sometimes attendant upon such Engagements, & with the Clumsiness as well.

The delicate Reader would not wish to ask if I were at all disappointed in the natural Outcome of this Relationship, but (Percy) I can see you in my Mind's eye silently & quizzically posing such a Question. Let us say that my natural Errand was successfully run. Where Crowther in the very occasional Extravagance of Passion

---

*Horsepole was doing well enough to receive ten guineas for a three-quarter length portrait in the mid-1760s. Reynolds was getting twelve guineas in 1755, although by 1780 he could command fifty.

that he could be prevaild upon to muster would arrive at his Joy at any Time or in any Place, regardless of my Wishes in the Matter, & to pay as little heed of it as slipping from his Saddle when taking a Fence, Horsepole came conscientiously & reliably to his Purpose in a steady Manner about which it would seem surprising of me to complain. I did not at that time complain, of course, although my later Experience put the Business in Perspective, & even then I was surprisd to find myself reflecting that there were some Things that I would do with the odious Crowther that somehow I might not dare to do with my beloved Horsepole. But all in all, I felt the Errand complete.

My husband did not forbid me to continue to portray the handsomely-inhabited Uniforms of the Profession he served, but I sensed that he expected, now that I was again married, that I would consider this particular Episode over, or now to be brought to a Conclusion. For quite different Reasons from his, I was almost ready to concur. In a short Space of Time I had painted what seemed like a whole Sett of Naval Characters, almost like a Suit of Cards, enough to grace several publick Rooms of the Admiralty. It seemd like a portion which I brought not only to my Husband in Marriage, but to my Husband in his publick Office,—it seemd like a completed Tribute.

But this was not the only Reason for wishing to be finishd with such Trumps. For a time I was diverted to the floating Timbers of the Vessels which housed my former subjects, safely impersonal Images which Horsepole was authorisd to procure, & which he saw no reason not to procure from me. Three Days in the driving Rain at the Chatham Yards, however, convinced me that no new Man o'War was worth my catching my Death of Cold. And if a Ship has a Soul, as Mariners say it has, then I had not yet discovered the Truth of the Claim, nor would ever do so on a quay-Side with a folding-Stool & oild Umbrella, nor yet from a windy Mole on the Hampshire Coast for all the unfurling Beauty of Sails, & the scurrying up Rigging, Activity as distant & tiny as it might be that of Insects among blossoming Flowers.

At that Stage of my Life there was not much visible that I could not paint, & had not in some Form painted. But I knew that I could never be appointed Serjeant-Painter, and Painter to the Navy, nor did I wish to fulfil such momentous Commissions as to cover the great Hall at Greenwich Hospital by the square Yard.★ Francis Hayman offered me Work continually, tempting me with the Passages in Shakespeare which stimulated my true Love of the Mysterious & the Unknown—

Ye Elves of Hills, Brooks, standing-Lakes, and Groves,
And ye that on the Sands with printless Foot
Do chase the ebbing Neptune, and do fly him
When he comes back—

The Fashion had not yet come in, as it was to do, for the romantick Aspect of Shakespeare's Genius, & if I had proposd to paint an invisible Spirit the Publick would have clamourd instead for their favourite Actress in a Breeches Role. In this Respect the Publick ever believes in a stubborn Patriotism of standing no Nonsense, & to Glendower's 'I can call Spirits from the vasty Deep'

★It was Sir James Thornhill who painted the great hall at Greenwich Hospital, at 25s the square yard. Thornhill procured his son to be appointed serjeant-painter, and painter to the Navy.

would play the veritable Hotspur.* To the Million, a Sign-Painting is wonder enough, if veild.†

You, Percy, have talkd to me of veild Mysteries so much & so fiercely that you remind me of myself in those Years, & I reflect that I was then not much older than you must be now. It is an Age when the restless Appetite of Youth for the Novelties of this World has not yet been succeeded by the resignd Wisdom of Age, & when something of both Restlessness & Wisdom run together, like the Pulse of a Mountain-Stream as it spreads across the flooded Sands to join the eternal Ocean.

Whence does Mankind derive his News of Eternity? It was never hung up for casual Perusal in the Coffee-Houses of the Spirit. No secret _Gazette_ was ever passd into eager Hands that listed Appointments in the New Jerusalem to Office everlasting, without Envy or financial Encouragement. That Path to Preferment was the worldly Interest of my Husband, who had the daily Expectation of being sent out across the Seas to govern the Heathens. I had no views on such a Future, being inclind to deprecate the Flogging of Men, whether they be the enlisted Christians of Spithead or the enslavd Indians of Madras, or some such Place. It was Mrs. Howson who first pointed out to me that there might be some Justice in my new Husband serving the Interests of the old, for the Trade of the House of Crowther would be protected by the iron Administration of a Horsepole.

---

*Hotspur replied: 'Why, so can I, or so can any man; / But will they come when you do call for them?' (_I Henry IV,_ III, i, 53). Hayman's scenes from Shakespeare were painted for Vauxhall Gardens. Tyers, the proprietor, valued them so much that he took the originals for himself and had copies made.

†Horsepole is alluding to an exhibition of sign-painters in 1762, held at the upper end of Bow Street, Covent Garden, and organised by Bonnell Thornton. Some of the paintings were concealed behind curtains, as though indecent.

Laet—You are right, Mrs. Howson. If there is an Uncertainty in Silks and Ribbands it is as likely due to the Energy of Pyrates as to the Vagaries of the Tides.

Mrs. H—It could not be more appropriate if you had planned it from the Beginning, Madam.

Laet—If my Life had been so completely planned, it is inevitable that a third Husband be requird to enter the Calculation. Do not look so shocked, Mrs. Howson. If I have a Husband who is to keep the Peace of the Seas across which another Husband has transported his lucrative Bales of Cloth, why should I not have a third Husband whose Business lies in the Manufactory of that Cloth? Thus Marriage might at last become a useful Institution, a veritable Pillar of the Œconomy of the Globe.

Mrs. H—Ah, Madam, how you do always gladden my Heart with your Quips & Quibbles!

Laet—A Joke is a more serious Event than you may imagine, Mrs. Howson. It is like a Child, which is conceivd in a light Moment of thoughtless Pleasure & yet lives to confront its Originators with Intentions of its own.

Indeed, I spoke truer than I knew, Percy, as you shall discover hereafter. For such Jokes are the only Children I have had. Yet this One, though promising in Conception, turnd out still-born.

The continual Requirement of my Husband in the Duties of his Office threw me much in the Company of Mrs. Howson, who became of inestimable Value to me both in the Regulation of the Household & the Needs of my Painting. The House stood at the Head of Croom's Hill, with a fine View overlooking London. Despite its odd gothick Turrets it provd adaptable to my Purposes. I had large Panes of Glass let into an upper Storey, which gave on to a westward Prospect across the Park. Two Rooms on this Storey I had broken into one, & this servd me perfectly as a Studio. Mrs. Howson became my Assistant, & when she was not basting Fowls & stirring Puddings she was priming Canvasses & grinding Pigments.

My Husband's Children were old enough to be in the Care of a Governess, & I was allowd to have as little to do with them as I wishd. Since I had no Responsibility for their Education, nor Jurisdiction in their small domestick Quarrells & Difficultys, I was able to indulge them or neglect them equally. I have discovered that this is without Question the most effective Way to befriend Children, & therefore ultimately to controul them. The Procedure is enshrind in the Practice of sending male Children away to School, which institutionalises this Neglect, & allows Holidays to attain an Unholiness bordering on Riot. It was not long before Robert was sent to Christ's Hospital.

For some Years I sought a new Subject as my Husband sought political Advancement—it seemd imminent, but ever postponed, like the Dawn at five o'Clock in the Morning when Sleep will not come again & it feels too cold to rise. The Contentment in my recent Work lay entirely in Details accidental to the central Purpose—in my naval Portraits I discoverd, if I could, the private Stirrings in the publick Countenance, the small Distractions of his physical Existence that my Subject believed he had put aside in the donning of his Uniform, but which lingered to betray his Humanity. In my nautical Subjects I took an Interest in Clouds, & in the changing Moods of Light by which Nature appears to show an Interest in our self-important Affairs which by Rights she should not have.

There seemed to me at the Time to be no Contradiction in these Interests, for they represented the same Mistrust which I had of the sanctioned Purpose of painted Images, which was to confirm, & if possible to elevate, the Significance of material things. A Painting of a Ship is no better than a Model of a Ship, & a Model of a Ship is no better than a Toy. Men might well move such Toys over a Table in a darkened Room, & believe that they rule the Seven Seas, just as they can look on a certain Shape in a Map & know it to be England although it were never seen like that in the Reality. Maps are indeed the Toys of the world. They are like Pictures with blank Spaces in them to be filld in by Children, or fired into at random by their charcoal Fleets.

But Light itself, without which the World were a Blank to us, what does Light represent? The Paintings of a blind Woman would, I declare, be to me the most mysterious of Objects. When I said as much one Day to Mrs. Howson, she told me of a blind Artist known to her Brother, of whom he had often spoken. He lived in the City, she said, & fed & maintaind himself without Help from any Body. He worked by Day in a printing-House & made Pictures of his lightless World by Night.

Then he will have little Need of Candles, said I, & resolvd at that very Moment to pay him a visit.

I was taken there the following Sunday, very solemnly, by both Mrs. Howson & her brother Elkanah. They prepard for the Outing as if it were a Pilgrimage to a Saint of benign Repute. Elkanah brought Leeks & Lovage from his Garden the Night before, & his Sister made a Pie which she decorated under his Instructions with three raised Devices on each of the four Edges of the Crust.

It was a fair Day, so we walked to the Ferry with our Basket of Food, which was not, however, for ourselves but for Smagg the blind Printer. I expressd the Hope that he would not be offended by our bringing him Provisions, as if in Presumption that he were in Need of Charity. Elkanah assured me that the Pie was no Charity, & less a Pie than a Sacrament. It was brought to Smagg as from one Worshipper to another, on a Holy Day, as a Sign of Community. This Community was no less than a Church in his opinion, & in the Intentions of their Elder, who had had a Vision of the New Jerusalem in the year 1743 & preachd it ever since.

Laet—So, Elkanah, here I am seated in the Ferry with a Church on my Knee?

Elk—I know that you are a rare Woman, Mrs. Horsepole, that has an Ear for the Truth, & would rather have a Church at your Knee than a Weanling.

Laet—Well, I am certainly not a Ewe, Elkanah.

Elk—You are very much yourself, & your own Woman, as ever, Mrs. Horsepole.

Laet—So what is the Significance of this Decoration? It leaves the Pie well fortified, against the Devil, I suppose.

Mrs. H—Why, Madam, these are the twelve Gates of the New Jerusalem, which signifies the Church which is to be hereafter establishd.

Elk—A new Heaven & a new Earth, sayeth the twenty-first Chapter of the Book of Revelation, & in Verses twelve to fourteen—'A Wall great and high, & had twelve Gates, & at the Gate twelve Angels, & Names written thereon, which are the Names of the twelve Tribes of the Children of Israel—on the East three Gates, on the North three Gates, on the South three Gates, & on

77

the West three Gates—and the Wall of the City had twelve Foundations, & in them the names of the twelve Apostles of the Lamb.'

Elkanah had stood erect in the Ferry to declaim these Portents of Scripture. I thought the other Passengers had been like to throw him out of it as a Madman, & for myself I was embarrassed to be the bearer of such potent Symbols. The twelve Apostles of the Lamb! Why, you would think the Pie had made a greater Effect as a Mutton-Pie than as a Pie made of Leeks & Lovage, fit only for a cold-blooded Devotee of a Tailor. But I bow to your Views in this Matter, Percy, for the Vegetable-Diet suits your Philosophy.

I wonder, however, what is your opinion of the Philosophy of Mr. Swedenborg (for the Elder of this Church-to-be was none other than he) & what you think of all those of his Kind who are privileged to hold intimate Conversations with Angels? I had looked long in my Greenwich Sunsets for something like an Angel, & had been likelier to have seen a Camel. The Printer Smagg, as it turned out, was a Great Conjuror of Angels. We found him in an upper Room in Blowbladder Street near Cheapside in the Company of an Engraving Press & a Chamber-Pot, both of which made a mighty Impression. It is no Wonder, is it not, that labouring Humanity, which stinks manifestly when it takes little Care of its corporeal Presence, should be enamoured of Creatures that have nothing to do but roll Stars about the Sky like Nine-Pins & were never known to pass Water in their Lives?

For Smagg's Engravings were all of Angels in the most friendly Postures—Angels on Garden-Stools, Angels under Apple-Trees, Angels holding Conversations,

Angels taking Tea. It lifted the Heart to think of this Man, alone in his Blindness, so befriended by Spirits that he never saw. They were his Society. They were his Audience. They appeard to listen with infinite Sympathy. The Heavens were neglected while they sought his company. I wondered if they were waiting for us to leave, so that they could return & eat up the remains of the Leek and Lovage Pie.

Smagg himself had nothing to tell me about the Angels he saw, or how he could see them, being blind. My Mystery remaind. Or was redoubled, rather. For a Man never to have seen a still-Life of Chrystal, Oysters & Lemmons, with Highlights upon them as upon Jewels, & yet draw such a Thing, was wonder enough—but for a Man never to have seen Creatures that no Man ever saw at all, & to draw them as if he were surrounded by them all Day long, beggared Belief.

We talked at some Length about the relative Merits of Sight & Touch in the Conceptions of the Imaginacion. I was at Pains to flatter his Productions & spoke of the sightless Great, such as Homer & Milton, but I could think of no blind Painter. The Principle of Representation, followed in Darkness, could lead to no sure Outcome, I was convinced, but Smagg explaind that he was familiar with all Forms by the feeling of them. He pressed into my Hands a small Stone, & told me that from it he could as perfectly deduce the Idea of the spherical as could any sighted Man. But what it might be at a Distance, I responded, he could never know. The Senses so frequently deceive us that the Source of our Vision itself, the blessed Sun, could look at Times no larger than a Guinea-Piece, nor more spherical. How could he hope, without the Benefit of Light falling upon its Surface, to represent the Sphericality of his Stone? Smagg meerly smiled & moved his Fingers over his Engravings, as if he should say, Here are solid Objects enough. In my Frustration at the Circularity of this Argument I asked him how he might even know that it was one Stone and not two? The answer was again a Demonstration. But I seized his Hand & made him cross two adjacent Fingers & to feel the Stone between their crossed Tips. It is an old Trick, taught to me by dear Canistrelli. The Stone is, despite all Evidence to the Contrary, obstinately judged to be double. Even the Howsons were deceived.

I was in due Course to attend a Lecture of Mr. Swedenborg's, & though affected by the Sincerity of the Man, did not believe that these Angels with whom he claimed to be in Fellowship could be anything more than the Phantasms of an intense Imaginacion. He claimd to have seen them 'as Jacob did on the typical Ladder' & to have been 'long in Holy Shudders'. I had observd the effect of Quantities of Whisky upon a Man, & well knew what the Shudders looked like.

A year or two later, when his Book was printed that gave an Account of Heaven and its Wonders 'from actual Information & Observation', my Sympathy was severely put to the Test. I looked for Mapps, which our Informant (having in his earliest Employment been a Mining Engineer) might surely have been expected to provide, that we might the better find our Way about the Place when we get there, instead of asking for divine Directions to Eternal bliss like some Country-Cousin lost in a Thoroughfare.

I concluded that the ingenious Smagg had used Plates like Mapps, to explore Lines cut by others & thereby to find his Way about the visual World with sensitive

Fingers—as must any blind Man do in any Case. His Employment in the printing-House gave him Access to a vast Range of Images through Touch alone, & therefore the World that was closed to him at a Distance opened up to his ingenious Hand, through Imitation.

The Sighted do no better, perhaps. What we have not seen, or cannot see, we paint by Reference to the Representations of those who have, as by Recourse to funerary Vases for the Dress & Deportment of the Ancients, or to Vistas of Citys we have never visited. And the Faces of the Dead, like the Faces of Angels, often have to be borrowed—'tis from a hand-Maid we must take a Helen, as the Poet said. Yet Poets cannot be so particular in their Likenesses as Painters must be. If I were to paint an Angel now, I would have Giovanni's Son, our water-loving Hyacinth, to sit for me. Or rather, he would stand, tip-toe upon a Rock—and I should picture him as if he had just alighted there.

But Smagg's Angels were out of illustrated Editions of Milton, and wore Nightgowns. And they carried no Colour. It was sufficient for Mrs. Howson, whose God no doubt wore a similar Nightgown, but it was of no use to me. I have seen angels accoutred like mediaeval Knights & I have seen angels with Roman Breast-Plates, & all were appropriate in their Place. I have seen the Spirits of Shakespeare (as have we all) represented of Necessity by human Actors who had little to bring to their Parts but the Voice. But I am a Painter, & a Painter has no Voice. Why should I be compelled to give the Publick a Titania dressd in best Drury Lane muslin? It would be meer unthinking Habit, as it surely was when the afore-mentioned elder of the Nova Hierosolyma described in his *Arcana*, with great Self-Satisfaction, being call'd 'to a

Holy Office by the Lord Himself, who most graciously manifested Himself in person to me His Servant'. Gracious, indeed! Goodness is gracious, & absolute Goodness may be absolutely gracious—and graceful, for the matter of that, but not like a provincial bishop in an unoccupied Hour before his Dinner.

This is not the pure Radiance of the Eternal, but like the colloquial Angels of Smagg, the meer black-and-white of our poor dualistick World, meer Ink-and-Paper, meer Bread-and-Cheese.

I pretended to the Howsons that I was delighted, but I was to become no Devotee of the Church of the New Jerusalem. I had done better at this stage of my Life to take care of my Fame. I had double Reason to have no need of Fees from my Painting. My domestick Situation was comfortable, & I received the greater part of the Crowther Profits securely in my own Name. Whetton had been adventurous in introducing Noveltys, though he was forever warning me of Competition from cheap Cotton from the new Mills in Lancashire.

But to make Money from Paintings is not the same thing as making a Name. It were an easy Matter to be recommended in Society & to be for ever filling Chimney-Compartments with Satyrs & Fruits, or supplying Landscapes on half-length Canvass for forty or fifty Shillings. It had been meer Fashion indeed that brought me to face so many aquiline Noses & amused Glances, so much gold Braid, & so many inflated & decorated Breasts, & I had become heartily sorry for the Haste in which my Portraits had been executed. But the Canvasses had to be coverd. I had no Assistants to fill in the tedious Areas while I applied myself (as I truly wished) to the Soul of the Sitter. Would I had been a Kneller, who would paint Heads and Hands only.

My best Portraits I exhibited where I could, with the Society of Artists, with the Society of Incorporated Artists, or with the Society of Disinherited Artists if it come to that. I took no Part in the internecine Warfare among Painters in those Years, & save that I would no sooner trust any Committee than I would allow a Cat to churn Butter, I did not doubt that the best Painters would find their Patrons—and that Patrons would get the Canvasses they deservd.

God is the only Patron who is never pleased enough.

God—Who is next?

St. Peter—Benjamin West.

God—And what, pray, has Mr. West performed?

West—If it please you, Divinity, I had Favour of the King in 1768, & was commanded to paint 'The Departure of Regulus from Rome'.

God—Show it me. Is that all it is? This Thing?

West—It was the best I could do, Divinity.

God—I had been better pleasd with the Departure of Benjamin West from London, which is a Place where Money is more regularly sought than Truth.

West—I cannot say that I ever made more Money than I deservd. When I showed my 'Pylades & Orestes', my Servants made 30*l.* from the Showing of it, but no-one asked its Price or commissioned another.

God—Friendship such as that between Pylades & Orestes hath no Price.

West—How would you have had me live?

God—By selling all thou hadst & distributing it amongst the Poor.

You will see, Percy, that you are not the first to perceive that Christian Precepts have never been a Part of the Morality or Œconomy of this Country. Poor West died this very Year, as did the mad Monarch he was so proud of pleasing. The Academy is with us yet, but is as capable of being blind to the Truth as ever. You will not know that in the Beginnings it was a grand Society for the Encouragement of Arts, Manufacture, & Commerce, and had benevolent Aims. But I now do not think that Painting can ever be, nor should be, confused with material Objectives. It would be enough for one Spectator who had never set eyes on her in Life to see my 'Katherine Connell' & observe her Attention divided between busy Needle & the being painted to know a Truth about the human Mind, & to know it through the Being of my Aunt Kate.

Painting enables us to recover the Sensation of Life. As God breathd into the dust & raisd our first Father, so we Painters reach into the Earth to create our Forms. These Forms can be nothing but the Illusion of Things as they are or as they might be. To adapt Samuel Johnson's Apology for his Adventures in Lexicography in his Preface to his <u>Dictionary</u>, I also never forget that <u>Pigments</u> are the veritable Daughters of Earth, & that Things are the Sons of Heaven. But to create Light out of Earth, & that Light not only the Sunlight of Reason & the Moonlight of Imaginacion, but the very Light of the human Soul & the Harmony of stellar Light which Vision imparts to the Whole, is one of the most Sublime of human Facultys, & was now securely my fiercest Ambition.

3

Supremum in Tabulis Lumen captare Diei,
Insanus Labor Artificum*

When I wrote of the five Acts of my drama, Percy, I did not elaborate upon my Model as I might have done. But consider the Pattern as it commonly appears—quiet Development—Conflict—Crisis—quiet Development—Resolution. The Pattern is varied in every Form it takes, but the common Shape establishes as the very Centre some vital Passage where the Outcome is in doubt. In Shakespeare, we find it is the Habit of the Poet to remove his hero in the third Act to a place of Ordeal. Thus it is that Lear arrives at his tempestuous Heath, or Caesar appears before the Senate, or Othello is transported to the Heat & Passions of Cyprus. The third Act of my own Life finds me in a Place I never expected to be, in Shipwreck upon the Coast of Madagascar, at the Mercy of a Storm raisd neither by my own Folly nor by my own Ambition, yet as well consequent upon a little of Both.

Less foolish, less curious, less discontent with Society, I might have stayed at Home with Margaret—Robert being now at School—and continued to paint Faces. I

---

*'Tis Labour in vain to paint a High-noon, or Mid-day Light in your Picture [because we have no colours which can sufficiently express it]', Du Fresnoy, p.50.

might have painted the Lords of the Admiralty at that time if I had wished, & put my Signature upon their Future. As it was, they put their Signatures upon my own Future, for their Names, E. Hawkes, C. Spencer, C. J. Fox, were attached to the Commission which sent my Husband to India. This inky Authority was ignorant of the Part I was to play, as ignorant as was Shakespeare's own Ink of the Career of Mrs. Barry.*

It was ignorant, indeed, of the Circumstances of the Shipwreck, & I dare say as little caring of our Fates and Fortunes. It was Horsepole's desire & Duty both, to put himself thus at the Service of Empire—I had no need to follow. But at that Time of my Life I had no Wish any more to paint the known World. I was as weary of my Subjects as a Tyrant is, who will let them starve out of meer Boredom. Whereas, I conceived the Possibility of a new Interest in those Parts of the Globe less familiar, & without any particular Claim on our Sentiments or Institutions. My Model would therefore come from the East, & be rather that humane Monarch Haroun al-Raschid, whose Curiosity about his Subjects sent him out, disguised, into their midst. My Resolution, when this Opportunity offered itself, was to set out in Disguise, like Haroun. My Subjects were still unknown, but by adventuring forth, more like a Pyrate than a Painter, I would surely find them out.

I need not tell you that Horsepole was opposed to my accompanying him, for he had supposed my Place to be at Greenwich, to maintain the Household. I argued that he could hardly deny, as Head of the Household, that the Household must exist only where he himself was to be

---

*Elizabeth Barry (1658–1713), the Restoration actress.

found. It was only through such self-denying Arguments, & by no means through the Earnest of my Spirit & my Profession, that I could prevail, & be permitted to follow my Master into his Exile, like a Jacobite indeed. And if I were to accompany him, so must little Margaret. Robert might continue at Christ's Hospital, & come out to us if he wishd, when we were establishd in Bombay.

It was not to be, for we never saw the good Bay of Bombay.* We had many Weeks of the Voyage, & I am sure that they would have been described by any of the hardy Mariners who tenanted our creaking wooden Estate as uneventful, though they were not so to us who were Novices. There were Creatures of the Deep that showed us their glistening Backs as they kept up with the Ship, & my Pencill itself could scarce keep up with them. At Madeira and at St. Iago I had opportunity to see how the Populations that lived more directly beneath the Rays of the Sun absorbed more of its continual Light. Their Bodies were as Prisms, richly hued with the Refraction of all Colours. I had seen a Negro before, as for example Sir Gregory Page's Page, whom it was his quaint Pleasure to call Gregory, at Blackheath House when we were invited to view his Coriolanus by Imperiali & there was more Attention paid to a broken Tea-Cup than to the Painting. Little Gregory in his powderd Wigg seemed but a white-eyed Poppet compared with the Negroes who approachd the Ship in their Canooes, half-naked, with the Muscles of their bodies working like Ropes to steady their Craft in the Waves & to haul at their Baskets of Roots which they offered us. This Black of their Skin containd many

---

*The old derivation of Bombay from the Portuguese 'Bombahia' or 'Good Bay' is false. The name derives from Mumba Devi, or Mumba Bai, a goddess originally worshipped there.

Ochres & an iridescent Blue as of hung Flesh, & if I had painted their eyes, as of Gregory's, plaintive & terrified at the Tea-Cup, I had need of Yellow Lake & fine Points of Cinnabar.

But the Motion of the Waves did not allow of Painting, beyond the quickest Sketches on Paper in Sepia, which I made sure to have by me. My Canvasses & Pigments were secured in a Chest in the Hold of the Ship, in Preparation for my Indian Paintings. What these should be, I knew not, save that in this new World I was as prepared for Revelation as St. John upon Patmos. In my Heart I had a Suspicion that I would be put to the Faces of Nabobs or Vistas of the great Bazaars, but I was as determind in my Search for the Light as is the Turnsole, or trusting Heliotrope.

My Husband, wishing to be my only Sun, & to draw my Orbit about him, had been long perplexed to find his Influence so frequently in Eclipse. Like most Men, who freely admit the Mysteries of the Moon, he allowed to a Woman her Obligations to that Sphere, & was perhaps unduly ignorant & even afraid of them. In all human Intercourse that was not clearly regulated by the Formalities of his Profession or the reservd Understanding of the masculine Character, he was inclind to hesitate his Opinion & obscure his Will, as if before a Relationship imperfectly understood. I knew, for example, that he did not care for little Margaret's freedoms on board, as unbecoming the Daughter of a Personage of his Station, but as the least arrogant of Men he could barely say so.

Laet—What is it, Sir, that you object to? Should she keep to the Cabin and learn plain-Work, which she might do in London where there are no shoals of Dolfinns to see?

H—Of course, she must see the Dolfinns.

Laet—And all the Excitements of the Voyage? To see the Sailors clusterd on the Mast like Wasps on a Bottle left in the Garden, & the Sails unfold like a Summer Flower?

H—You mistake me. She is too familiar with the Sailors.

Laet—A Child of Six has no notion of Dignity. She will sit on an old Sailor's Knee to hear Sweet William's Farewell to Black-Eyed Susan as readily as she will sit on your own Father's Knee to hear Tales of the Constellations. I am sure you do not think that any of them will do her harm?

H—She runs bare-footed on the Deck & brings Streaks of Tar into her bed-Linnen.

Laet—Would you have her wear Shoes & Stockings in this Heat? Or be seated like an Infanta beneath a silk Ombrifuge, canopied from the glorious Light?

H—Never.

Laet—Well, then. And for the matter of that, look at my own Feet. Are they not spotted as black as a Pudding made with Raisins of the Sun? Come to me, old Bear, and kiss me.

Indeed, little Daisy loved her Wooden World &, like the aëry Spirit, 'flamed Amazement'*. To please her Father we drew together a Mapp of her Kingdom & its allowd Places, where, since they were cunningly written & designd, with our private Names for them, she was content to be confind. During the Storms of the Cape we all kept to the Cabins, & for a time thought it ill-namd as we had little Hope of ever being ourselves again.

Yet soon after, we set steady Sail once more, & I looked

---

*Ariel in *The Tempest*, I, ii, 198 'now on the beak, / Now in the waist, the deck, in every cabin, / I flamed amazement.'

out again for the flying Fishs. There is more of Life in a dorsal Finn than in a powderd Wigg—more of Life, too, in bare Toes however sun-burned & grimy than in a buckled Shoe. I would rather Daisy had grown up free in the benign Influence of marine Nature, than have married the Duke of Rutland. Better, indeed, that she live the life of the poorest naked Fisherman's Wife picking over Netts on the sandy Shores that we passed than to be the Duchess of Rutland, who was so vain that when she came to sit for Reynolds tried on eleven different Dresses before she was content to be still & pose before his inquisitive Eye.

My favourite Station on the Ship was in the Fo'c'sle, where I might best observe the Ocean at that Moment just before we entered it, which I felt to be a lively Conceit for my Experience of Life, limited & yet impetuous as it seemed to be. Sometimes, as I sat in my solitary Contemplation, the Captain would take the opportunity to approach me. Captain Fell was a little stout Man who existed in a manifest State of Unease, perpetually grinding of his Teeth, so that the reddish Hairs of his Cheeks danced in alternate Motions together like scouring-Brushes. With the Excuse of a Tour of the whole Ship, in which his Idleness was more apparent than his Duty, he persisted in his Overtures, whose whole Purpose, as I discoverd, was to find out my Husband's Opinion of him. I told him as clearly as I could that I was ignorant of the Matter, & that it was none of my Business, but that if he were to convey us to Bombay without Mishap, he would not (I dared to say) stand in ill-Repute with us.

Little did I think then of my Words having particular Meaning, but as I now think, the Man was abashed at the Conveying of a Naval Officer of such Distinction, who might easily see through his habitual Short-Comings, & make a critical Report of him. In particular, it would appear that the Ship had sprung Leaks at the Cape which had been better attended to immediately than left, as he had left them, to some future Repair. With the Chain-Pumps already at work, we met with a hard Gale some hundred Leagues south of Madagascar, & were obliged to lay under a Foresail for the space of ten Hours, which occasiond the Vessel to make more Water than she could free with both Pumps. We set out again, & with the Captain's Intention to put in at St. Augustine's Bay. He was loath to lighten the Ship of any of its Cargo, which would have lent us Speed & allowd us to lie more comfortably in the Water. Before long, the Water overflowd the lower deck. The Captain, who was without Certainty in the Matter, but observing a Sand which ran along for two Leagues & we within three quarters of a Mile of shore, he let go an Anchor & then cut down our Masts & Rigging & at last threw our Guns & heaviest Goods overboard. His Hope that we might return & save the Vessel seemd a thin Hope to me, who felt its Torment beneath me like that of a wounded Creature tethered to a Stake that it might soon uproot in its Pain.

We could scarce get into the Yawl, being thirteen in number, and Horsepole was hit on the head with an Oar as we made our Way. We took one Keg of Water, & a small Supply of Biscuit, & of cheese, & two Bottles of Wine. I had little thought of the Danger, but was all the while in Amazement at the Suddenness of our Misfortune, & was concernd, by telling over some robust & familiar Stories of comick Mishap, to divert Daisy from her real Apprehension of our frail Situation.

The Weeks of the Voyage, like the Years of our Life, had seemd by their regular Motions likely to perpetuate our enclosd World without Impediment, as Time itself seems to draw on the Hands of a Clock. Our very Existence, under the burning sun, was as under Glass, the Ship wound to its steady Motion through the Waves, & the Masts creeking like the Tick of clock-Work. And then, overnight, all was changd. We were wrecked & in Peril, the Prospect of Bombay deferrd, perhaps for ever, & our Fortunes depending upon an unknown Shore & the Uncertainty of Salvage.

But here I am in another Danger altogether, of descending to the Particulars of Incident & of Adventure, which as a Woman I am vowed not to do. I leave that to the Drurys* of the World, who may live for ever by their Lives of Violence. This is not to be a Maritime Narrative, which are two a Penny in these Days of the travelled Globe. This is the Story, Percy, not of my wandering Person but of my Soul & my Vision. In pursuing this to the Source of Light across Oceans I set myself up by Accident as a Venturer, but Accident it certainly was, for I fell by chance into my Eden, & thankfully not into my death. Take care you learn to swim, Percy, for if you find yourself on board for however so slight a Journey, there is no certain guard against Wreck. Take your Practice now, in the Shallows, for the Mistral comes in the September of our Days, & we must exercise against Storm. Let the agreeable Hyacinth teach you, holding his firm Arms about your pale Body.

---

*Robert Drury published his *Pleasant and Surprizing Adventures*, perhaps ghosted by Defoe, in 1729. He ended his days as a common porter at India House, telling his story of shipwreck on Madagascar at Old Tom's Coffee House in Birchin Lane. He died some time between 1743 and 1750.

Though at first we feared a Crusoe-Existence, eating Wilks & Conks,* & brackish Water from the rocks, for our Biscuit was wormy, we were eventually found by some Fishermen of those Parts, who, though respectful of our staind Splendour, seemd not unused to the Sight of Europeans, & even offered some Words in our own Tongue. We were taken some Miles to the North, to St. Augustine's Bay, where we found a Fortification long abandoned by the British, who had been lured there in Hope of Gold & Pearls & had been cruelly murdered. The French, it seems, had greater Success in colonising, and several other Islands were theirs, such as Ile Bourbon and Ile de France,† but in general the warring Princedoms of Madagascar itself forbade successful Settlement. We were lucky to have been found by Fishermen & not by a War-Party of young Bucks who might have considered us fit Targets for their Sagayes.‡ We had small Possessions about us that servd as handsome Gifts, so that we were fed, & honoured, & grinnd at, as much as any terrified and salt-water-bedraggled Party might wish for. They gave us boild guinea-Corn & Milk, & Carravances, which is a Kind of Pease-Pudding, & their Drink Toake, a kind of Mead fermented of Honey & Water. There are few Calamities which may not be blessedly appeasd by the rudest of Banquets. We gave them the rest of our Wine, & chearfully taught them the customary Toasts, which we then freely exchangd.

We made known by Signs & by some Words which they seemd to know, the Situation of our Vessel. The Promise of Salvage in exchange for Protection &

---

*Whelks and mussels.
†Now La Réunion and Mauritius.
‡Assegais.

Assistance seemd to be understood, & we were taken to the Lohavohit, or Village-Elder, who then took us to the Lord of the District, the Voadzir. The simple Lives & Manners of these People made them trusting & curious. If we had been Pyrates or Traders in Slaves (from whom without Doubt their slight Knowledge of our Tongue was originally derivd) Matters might have stood otherwise, but we were after all a pitiful Party, with Women & a Child, & had clearly not disembarked from a Man-of-War.

Within the Week we had taken what we could from the Vessel, which we had little Hope of putting afloat. The principal Cargo was too heavy & useless, but we took off what we thought proper for Trade, viz. Cloths, Brandy, Knives & Razors, together with Chests of Physick, & such Baubles as all Ships carry to please Natives, as Pewter Utensils, Silver Toys, & Glass Beads. Nor, despite the Friendliness of our Hosts, did we fail to secure to ourselves a Supply of Powder, Gun-Flints & Musquets, &c, as a necessary Protection. Some of the Cargo we had thrown overboard earlier had lodged on a Sand-Bank, & that, too, we conveyed with the Assistance of Canooes & Porters.

You will ask, what were our Hopes at this Time? What did we expect to occur? It is a commonly observd Truth that the larger Expectations in Life are perpetually adjusted & postponed, according to the Circumstances in which we find ourselves,—but that our immediate Needs & Gratifications can tolerate no such Alteration. Our Thoughts were of Food, of Shelter & of medical Needs, & then perhaps of Communication & Rescue. These were Instincts of the Body. The Ship's Surgeon dressd Horsepole's Head, which needed to be stitchd, & there were other Maladies & Contusions requiring Attention.

Captain Fell's immediate Plan was to take two Men & some Weeks' Provision with him in the Yawl, & make for Mozambique, where he might find a Ship that would at least take us to the Cape. Horsepole was of a contrary Opinion, that it might yet be possible with Assistance to float the Ship, & that it would besides put us at a Disadvantage to separate the Party. But his Arguments did not prevail. The Injury to his Head brought on a Fever, & he was too distracted to use his Authority. I believed that Captain Fell, with his Experience of Fevers & fearing them cravenly, thought only for his Comfort, & by Pretence of a heroick Journey to fetch help was in fact saving his Skin, for indeed, no sooner had he left than within Days the greater Part of the Remnant came down with Fever.

When, in extremity, the Body has survivd threats from without, viz. a swinging Boom that might have crushd an Arm, a Wave steep as a Roof that might have capsized the Yawl, the armed Native who is pleasd with a Bauble & does not think to gain more by Force but becomes a Friend, and what not else, such as Animals that do not fear the Night-Fire,—when it is thus assured of Survival, as if charmd, it is a worse Calamity to find the Body assaild from within, by those invisible Squadrons that feed and rage upon our Weakness.

After the Salvage we acquired Fame beyond the Locality, & were visited by the second Son of the King, who made a Journey of three Days to inspect us. A sorry Sight he found us, in the Huts which the Voadzir had put at our Disposal. At the very Moment of his Arrival I was, with some Women of the Village who had offerd to help, disposing of some Calabashes of Slops. At their prostrating themselves, I felt constraind to give the young Man a Bow of Sorts, which was little more than a Nod in the Circumstances. The Nod was returnd, with an inquisitive Smile.

I liked the King's Son from the first Sight of him in the ceremonial Lamba which he wore in our Honour. The Lamba is a Cloth commonly worn around the Waist & reaching to the Knees. Ramboasalama's Lamba was of white Cotton reaching as far as the Ancles. It had a deep Border of Silk marked with black & red Stripes & trimmd with silk Lace of the same Colours. He also wore a silk Cloak. Being of the Merina Nation he did not have the negro Features of the Fishermen of the Coast, but (like most of the Inhabitants of the Island I saw) lookd more like the Huron of America, with a noble Profile & a Hue of Copper. He carried a Stick tipped with Iron, & ornamented with a Tuft of Cow's Hair.

Although Ramboasalama carried himself with regal Dignity at all Times, he was by no means distant or fastidious, but showed himself to be humanely concernd with the pitiful Inhabitants of our Village-Hospital. He spoke to the Ill severely, as if addressing not them, but their Fevers. This alarmed me at first, but he reassured me by his Smiles. He muttered Imprecations, & thumped the earthen Floor with his Stick. There was something about this innocent & useless Way of dealing with a Fever which appeald to me, for if it could not be driven out with British Physick except (with good Luck) in but one Case out of three, why indeed should it not be argued with, and bullied into Submission?

It was as if the Almighty had condescended to argue with the Rebell Angels before he drew up Battle Lines, which might well have exhausted their forensic

Resources so boastfully displayd in Pandæmonium & brought them early into the peaceful Fold of Right Reason. Yet the Phansie of reasoning with Disease, while it might give Heart to the Healthy, was built on a hollow Joke to those in its deadly Grip. Such was the View of the Ship's Surgeon, who having ministerd to the first three of the Crew to fall ill & seen two of them reach their fatal Crisis, had now himself sufferd the first Violence of an Attack.

He had no Need to remind me of the Course of the Treatment that he himself now requird, for I carried my Father's Book of Fevers everywhere with me, & it was the third Thing which I made sure of when we abandoned Ship. At the Onset, a Dose of Tartar is given as an Emetic, the next Day Ipecacuanha then Quinquina & Ptisan until the fifth Crisis. After this, the Patient is blisterd, but only Prayers might attend the lethargic Drowsiness & continual Delirium with Hope of Cure, for there is nothing more that Physick might do, & the probable End consists of the most terrifying & abject Ravings & Convulsions, as if the Soul were being drawn to its eternal Torment.

Can this Weakness of the Body be the Consequence of our fatal Human Error, as was in my Youth so widely believd? For from Sin (so the Divine Fable runs) was begotten Death, who was from that moment of Rebellion licensd to hound all created Things, like a Mastiff releasd into a Summer Park of passive brooding Fowl. But we draw these Analogies only from their own Examples & Consequences, for that Dog itself will die. Nay, even the tiniest Creature that carries the terrible Wrath of God in its Body of air must itself die. My Father knew, though it was not then generally known, that this Fever which we sufferd was carried by the Agency of the Musquito. But to know this, is not to possess a safe Passport through their whining Kingdom.

Laet—Signor, you have had your Fill of me, & of my Family & Servants, & your Body is now a meer Sack of Blood, which you bear with Difficulty through the Night.

M—I took but one Drop, which as a Lady and a Christian you can well spare.

Laet—One Drop! which would overwhelm your freighted Body were it not foully & bloatedly contained there as in a greasy distended Bubble. You must think nothing but Blood or it would spill you, & blott, like the Point of a Sentence that will never end.

M—It is my rightful Booty, for I am the Prince of Darkness, though shrunk to the Point of Punctuation, & my Point is the Point of Interrogation, & my Punctuation is of the guilty Body whose Sentence is indeed endless.

Laet—You are too small. Let me see your Face.

M—I fly in the Zone of Damnation, furthest from the Holy Light. I am the Dark Angel. If you were ever to see my Face, you might see your own.

Laet—Because you have drunk my Blood does not allow you Rights over my Existence or Appearance.

M—I will leave you for dead, & speed the Globe of Earth in its hastening Shaddow of Night to do my Mischief, my Rapier & Buckler before me, singing of my own Deeds in a Humm of Triumph.

Laet—Your Interrogation shall have an Answer, if you will stay for it.

M—On, on, on!

Laet—The Grave hath no Victory!

M—But yet there is Death in a Sting! On, on, and on! The Motions of the Dark Angel had become my own

Motions, as I had become his Creature. I was carried in a gigantique Leaf which seemed to me a sort of Cradle, which though it cradled my Body yet gave it no relief, for the Pain in my Head pressed it against the cool Ribs and Veins of that Leaf, which now seemed not cool at all, but hotter than my Head, which knew not what it did. Inside, the Brain and conscious part of my Head wished to rise up in the Air, and indeed seemed to do so, in my Dizzyness, while the Skull itself rolled heavily in its Sling, like a Hogshead lowered from a Brewer's Cart. I did not know how I got there, no more than a summer Caterpillar that finds itself crawling with first-unfolded Wings from the Leaf that once it meerly ate for mindless Sustenance.

Was this my own Transformation? Was the Fever but the enveloping Pupa of a new Existence, from which I might rise, in new Colours? How much of the old Body may be taken up to make the new? To see a Man dead of the Fever, racked in his Sweat and Stink, is to have little Hope. To see him lain in a shallow Grave, more a Trench than a Grave, more a Furrow than a Trench, little more than the tearful scraping of a hard Hour to lay bare the red Earth of a strange Island & to close it again upon him, is to have no Hope at all of that Body. What can the Soul be, that is of so firm a Conception while we are alive? If, as must be true, it is itself the Agent of that Conception, and slips away in utter Sleep, where then is it? If the Soul recognises itself in our Being, that Being is but the Wakefulness of the Soul, of which the best Image is the unprepard Glance in the looking-Glass, that accidental Self-Portrait in reflected Light which surprises & sometimes terrifies us with its indescribable Truths. On, said the Leaf, on, on & on!

This rowling Darkness may be a Ceremony, whether of

Death or of Life I do not know. There is a Sweetness at my Nostrils, as of an aromatique Gumm, & something hung about my neck like Feathers. Shall I be encouraged to fly, like Icarus, to escape this Labyrinth of Death? Is this a Journey with a Destination, or is it but the poor Shadow of the original Fall, the Crumple of Wings, a Descent into Darkness? On, on, & on!

I was in a Delirium, & did not know myself. Of Place, and Time, I had no secure Idea, save for the Phansie of being led by my Fever into some new State which awaited me. The Mind, cut adrift from its safe Harbour & given free Passage, makes many wild Journeys. I spoke in Tongues with my Grandfather, who turned to me & showed me a Stone. He gave me to understand that he entrusted me with this Stone, as being his best, & his only Gift to me, & held it out towards me with a grave Smile, though weeping, as if for Joy. The Property of the Stone was to defy the Distinctions of Reason & Language, as a kind of Key to the important Work to be done in unlocking the Mind from its Shackles. I was to take this Key, & keep it securely about my Person. He held it out towards me, & I saw that it was neither red nor green but all One in the Colour of the Stone, not in Iridescence only, as the Reflection from a Silk, but a new Colour that was both Ruby and Emerald together. Though there is not such a Thing in Nature, it was given to me to see it, & later when I reflected upon this Vision I knew that by it my Grandfather meant to tell me that One might be both dead & alive at once, as he was, & that our Distinction between such States of Being was false. The Colour that I saw was therefore a Transcendance, yet I was easy with it, for it was plain before me, & it was indeed a Colour, & not a Savour, or a Shape, or a Sound,

& therefore like enough unto the Ruby or Emerald which it resembled, or (shall I say) reassembled, for it was a Stone & I was like the astonished but confident Miner who had discoverd it.*

Then in my Fever I saw my Husband lying dead, and a Voice saying—It is all Worms. How much of this was true & how much imagind, I do not know, but later when I was told of his Death I would not let them spare me the Details, but learned that in the Height of his Convulsions, when they removd the Dressing from his broken Head, they discoverd it to be alive with Maggots who had made it their Habitation, too deep to be washd all away. Of other Voices, & strange sounds too, I heard many in the Mazes of my Fever, and I did not know which of them might be real & which imaginary.

When I did wake from my Fever, I soon learnd that of the entire Ship's Party I was the only Survivor. Why this was I do not know, & you may imagine that at the time it brought me little Comfort. The greater bodily Fortitude of Women is not a Fact that you will hear much proposd among Men, who have need to make claims upon its Counterpart for themselves, but it is true. I learnd that Jane Penny & Daisy had been the last to die, & Daisy only because in the heat of her Phansie she had wandered off into the Trees & had been found bitten of a Snake which was Taboo to kill.

My Informant was Prince Ramboasalama himself, who was seated in the Lamplight of my Hut with Women-

---

*Horsepole's speculations about her vision have an interesting scientific basis. Ruby and emerald are paradigmatic of red and green, yet their crystal structure and chemical composition are quite similar. Both stones owe their colour to the same impurity, chromium. The difference in colour is due only to a weakening of the crystal field strength in emerald as compared with ruby.

Servants busy about him when I woke. His Manner was compounded of the watchful Concern of a Host & the formal Manner of an Ambassador. His Authority over the Women, which must in truth have been absolute, was laid over with a Reserve & Deference which suggested that they had been made over to my Use, & that there were Matters which as a Man he would not interfere with, though a Prince. His Position as Ambassador was threefold: to me as a Woman, as a Briton, & not least as a Survivor, for having been sick nearly unto Death, I had been of that other Kingdom which of all Kingdoms is worthiest of deep Respect.

The Merina have a saying—*izay marary andriana*, the Ill are noble; which is the Ground of their Beliefs about Death & the Continuity of human Life. In Europe this is not so, for we despise the Sick out of our Fear of them, & we fear them because we fear Death itself. On the Island it is understood that the Dead have simply passd over into another Form of Life. They are not only rememberd but consulted as Presences, & their Remains are frequently exhumed to be cared for, & to be reparcelled in their Cloths and Unguents. If the Merina perform this Service for their Dead, how much more will they care for their noble Ill. The Prince had brought us away from our feverd Village to his own People. We had been carried in Palanquins of Baobob Leaves on the Shoulders of his young Men, & treated with the Herbs & Roots of his own Tradition, which (as I was to learn) though very different to our own, was not inferior.

Since the Men of our Party had by Necessity worked together in their Attempts to save the Vessel, & in their Salvage of it, Distinctions of Uniform & of Rank had been lost. I by my Dress, & some poor Remnants of its

Quality, was taken to be the Queen of the Party, & treated accordingly. The Merina have a Respect for Women no less than our own, & in some Ways greater. The Inheritance will often pass not to the King's Son, but to the King's Sister's Son, & a Queen may rule, as I am told is the case to-day.

The Feathers I had thought to be my Wings of Death were but a Part of a Charm which, due to my Distinction & deemed an Honour, had been placed about my Neck. This Oli, as they call it, is a sort of Teraphim which represents the Guardian Angels of a Merina Family. I found it still around my Neck when I awoke, heavy enough & rather a Stock than a Necklace, a wooden Demilune set with Alligator's Teeth, Bones and Scarabs, with Tufts of Hair & some Scraps of Bark letterd in a kind of Arabick. It seemed a hideous Fetish, but to Ramboasalama smiling at me in the Light of the Lamp it had saved my Life. To him I was grateful for all his Care, & there was no other course but to become his Friend. He removed the Oli with some Ceremony from my Neck, taking it with his own Hands. In my weakened State I could not forbear Tears, & I took his Hand & kissed it. His Nod was an Acknowledgement of all these Dealings between us, & our Understanding was complete, though with little Language.

I was thus delivered from Death, but, Percy, this was not itself the Crisis that I wrote of. If I had indeed been a Heroine of Shakespeare's Stage, my Husband & his little Daughter might have been magically restored to me. Robert would have set sail to find us, still clad in the Habit of his School,* and his own merry Adventures made an instructive Part of the Story. I could hope for

---

*i.e. the blue coat and yellow stockings of Christ's Hospital.

none of this. Thus the Crisis surmounted of my Struggle with the Dark Angel could play no Part in the Crisis of what might be done with the rest of my Life, which was yet to be engaged.

And as I soon reflected, for I now had Time for infinite Reflection, there was no need of my being in Madagascar to decide this Question. In our mid-Life, Percy, as you will soon enough discover, we all of us find ourselves in our own Madagascars, where our particular Path has been so narrowed as to set up a fearsome Challenge to our sense of Purpose. You yourself are already in the perplexing Involvements of your own Second Act, your Progeny sown, your Mistakes alive before you like Guests that you once freely invited but who now will not go, your Art still in the fiery Crucible of its Conception, &c. You will, I dare say, find your own Madagascar in good Time.

Bring me wine, Maria! for I am at the Heart of my Story. The Air is cooler at this early Hour as the Year draws in, but the Morning Sun is sparkling on the Rocks & the Day will be warm. There is a Bird flying over the sea that believes in its Direction, though straightway it is lost to all view, & no-one will ever tell where it went. The Air stirs a loose Curtain by the Window, but the Noise it makes is no louder than the Sea. At such Moments I feel the Peace of knowing where I am & of being precisely here, so that I have used up long since all the grief at what I have lost, like a Cloth that has drawn into it what has been spilled, & has been wrung out in Tears, & long hung up to dry.

I had Freedom to mourn then, for I thought I had lost the whole World, & I had all the time in the World to mourn. But what is this World? It is only what we make it to be. To your Philosopher, the World is nothing but what has been put in your Head, & while there may be much that is sensible there, of which our Senses are reliable, there may be a good many Chimaeras as well. But I believe that our Minds are our private Theatres, & though we must learn our Parts, we do not write them—& the more we act our Parts, the more we shall learn what they are about. And there you may find a wondrous Revelation of Truth, I dare to say, a fifth Act of still Music and moving Statues.

In my Palanquin of Baobob, as I wrote, I thought myself to be metamorphosed into a new State, though it was only my Fever spoke of Wings. Perhaps it is a Presumption to expect full Knowledge, for why should the Grape on the Vine, asleep & sticky beneath the busy Feet of the Wasp, think of becoming a pink Wine that fits cool in the Mouth as this does, speaking silently of the dozing Shade of Summer? Who is able to write the Regrets of the Caterpillar? Perhaps I had not lost the whole World, but meerly gaind it, & the first World were but an Ouverture, or Dream. The Merina have a name for their Island, which is *izao tontola izao*—that is to say, the whole World. Their Conception brooks of nothing else. But this is no different from our Understanding, where the compassing of our own World takes ourself as its central Point. The Philosopher surveys the Horizon of his Kingdom. He is its Jerusalem.

In such Beauty as I found there I was soon enough ready to be born again, for it was a Place of Creation. Another name which they give the Island is *ny anivon 'ny riaka*, or, in the Midst of the Waters, which you may think a meer Description of Geography, but which to my Ears spoke of God brooding upon the vasty Deep. I felt his Finger on the trailing Vines of the great Forests, his Voice in the rustle of their Leaves. I felt indeed that this ancient Place may well have been that first created by Him, & therefore was the Earthly Paradise lost by our first Parents. In the Shafts of Light that occasionally penetrated their arborial Glooms, strange Creatures were to be seen, Animals indeed, but with the Hands & Feet of Men, & their Howls were Howls of Joy most like—although at that time the Instrument was unknown—the falling Shriek of an untutored Clarionet.

Later I made friends with these Creatures, of which there are many kinds, whom they call the Maki.* They are piebald black and white, with large intelligent Eyes of lemon and black. Some hop upon their hinder Feet like Men, & converse in Affection & Concern. One I kept, as an Orphan that needed Protection, & he grew to love me & would pick over my Hair to keep it free of Insects that collected there. I calld him Zoma, for I found him on that Day, which is the Merina word for Friday. Although they found the Practice of keeping a Pet a strange one, I had no fear that they would do it any Harm, for they called the Creature *babokoto*, which is Cousin to Man, & there was a strict Taboo against killing it, for they say that they are People who never came down from the Trees.

Many of the Fruits and Creatures on the Island were of such a great Size as to seem to be the very Originals of Nature, which had sufferd no Degeneration. I saw Bats with a Wing-Span of four Feet, a Rat the Size of a Rabbit which roard like a Lion, a Hedgehog the size of a Cat, & a Yam the size of a Man. There were no Lions or Tygers,

---

*'Maki' is the Malagasy word for lemurs. The kind that go upon their hind legs are the *sifaki*; the kind that Horsepole kept as a pet seems to have been an *indri*.

& no Creature preyed upon any other, but all was peaceful, as in the First Innocence. Multitudes of Chamæleons walkd like Dragons among the Orchids, & the Fruits of Nature offerd themselves to the Hand for the taking and eating. Of the Uncertainties of Agriculture and the Anxiety of the Seasons there was little. Ploughing was unknown. Of Crops, only Rice was grown, & that so easily and plentifully that it was not only the common Food, seasond with white Pepper, but the Measure of all Things, a Currency & even a Clock, for it was common to refer to the Preparation of Rice as a Period of Time from which all Activities might be computed. The Merina Religion has no Knowledge of our Eden, but their sense of it is well expressd by their Saying—*Ny tany vadíbea 'I Zanahary*—that is, The Earth is the First Wife of God. This Zanahary is sometimes called Andriamanitra, which means 'the scented Lord', a Phrase which always put me in mind of Christ in Matthew when his Feet are anointed of the quiet Sister who adored him. And soon enough it put me in mind of Ramboasalama, who himself walkd in a fine Perfume, like burnt Honey.

I acquird the Rudiments of their Language more speedily than you might think, or I could ever have hoped, for some English was known at their Court, & Ramboasalama was my ready Interpreter. Indeed, when I was first taken into the Presence of his Father the King, or Ampansacabe, I found him seated on a grass Mat with the Lamba around his Stomach, or as much around his Middle as it might decently go, since he was very fat, & on his Head a Dutch Grenadier's Cap a Foot and a Half high, with the Insignia of the Dutch East India Company cut in Brass upon it. The King had European Words of all kinds at his Command, which he producd indiscriminately, & in Quantity, as though they might, without much Intention on his Part, sufficiently cohere together to convey to me some Meaning or other. I confess that the Performance brought a great Smile to my Face, as much of Wonder & Admiration, as of Amusement at the Eccentricity of it. My Feelings were of great Curiosity & Sympathy, while at the same time my mind was greatly put upon its mettle. This Combination was like nothing so much as finding oneself in the Presence of Johnson. The King resembled Johnson, & he spoke in the assertive Periods of Johnson, albeit it was a nonsensical Macaronic to my Ears. Ramboasalama was patient with him, but—as I thought—concernd that his Father should make an Impression on me, & I on him. My smiling put every One at his Ease, & soon the King was shouting with Laughter & calling me to him to have my Stays felt, as if he could not quite believe in the Shape of my Waist. This he did with little Delicacy, but without Lewdness, & he touchd my Cheek with his fat Finger as if to put me at my Ease like a Child. What I found to say I hardly remember, but the King burst out laughing all over again, until Ramboasalama came forward to lead me away.—Today Brandy speak, he said.—Tomorrow King speak.

I did not know if this was a Promise or an Apology, but it was the longest sentence in English that I had yet heard the Prince speak.

Language is a strange Faculty. The little we need of it to make our Wants known is but a false Assurance of our Control over Circumstance, for we learn to need only what we can recognise. I soon found Ways, with Ramboasalama's Help, & with the Help of his Women with whom I livd, to name the Objects I saw and the

Food I was given. To the Prince, who had a Thirst for Knowledge, I was able to supply in many Cases some sort of English Equivalent, but for the Things his People lackd, the Words had no Significance to him. To say that the Merina had Musick, or Writing, or Paper, or Firearms, or a political Assembly, were to give as false an Impression of their Society as to pretend that they had none of these Things. Their Musick seemd to me at first as monotonous as a drunken Irish Crowder playing on one String, although in Time I learnd to enjoy & understand the Intricacies of their Performances on the Valihou, which is a kind of Lyre or Guitarre made from a hollow Bamboo Tube, & their comick Songs of Courtship. Encouraged to provide some Example of our own Songs, I stood before the Assembly & lustily gave what I could of a Chorus from the Messiah of Handel. My Head was full, as I did so, of remembered Harmonies & the grand Timbre of Violins & Trumpets, but my Voice is a poor crackd thing, & I saw the Company looking at each other in Bewilderment. Their Paper or Writing is a Mystery guarded by their Ombiasy, or Wise Men, who possess Charms & Histories in a kind of Arabick Writing on Bark-Cloth. I could not interpret such Legends, & neither, I suspect, could the Prince, though he had them shown to me with Veneration, as they were holy Relicts. As for Firearms, the King's Armory was furnishd with two Guns with broken Locks & one Pistol, whose touch-Hole was near half as large as its Bore. Their Assembly, calld a Kabary, was something like a Quakers' Meeting, full of bold Claims & meandering Sententiousness, where little seemd to be decided but much Brandy was taken, & the King at last made his Will known. Thus all these Words, which might have suggested Something perfectly familiar to you, refer to Versions of themselves which you would not have visualised. The Painter, who presents all to the Eye, has no Problem like this—save for those words which are unpaintable that the Philosophers use.

I livd among the Women of the Court—a Word as far from the Idea of silk Breeches at a Levée as is a red Herring from a Sturgeon, though both be Fish—and for Months could hardly discover if they were Wives or Slaves. Ramboasalama's elder Brother, who by another unexpected European Acquisition like the Grenadier's Cap was calld 'The-Prince-of-Wales', came sometimes among them to take them away for his Pleasure, but he was the Warrior of his Family & was so frequently abroad terrorising the neighbouring Kingdoms that I did not have much to do with him. His Enemies were the Menabe & the Boina, who had been powerful in the Island, & he went into their former Lands with such Ferocity that Reprisals were little feard. The Merina laid claim to the Whole of Madagascar, & spoke in such terms at great Length in their Kabaries, though the Reality were in Truth greatly different.* Our own Nation has seen its Kings of Mercia & Wessex & the like, nay & its Irish Rebellions & Scotch Wars too, & peaceful Union in a Country may be long delayd.

Ramboasalama was very different from his Brother, & by Nature more concernd with the civic than the martial Arts. Nor did I observe him take much Interest in the 'Wives' of the Court, though there were Children who calld him Father. It was he who took Pleasure not in the Quantity, but the Quality of the Kingdom, & showed me

---

*It was not until 1817, perhaps, that Radama I of the Merina could realistically claim sovereignty over the whole island.

the many Improvements made in Agriculture & Manufactory.

I was most interested in their Process of making Paper, for little of my Materials had survivd, save what I had kept about me. For many Weeks, in my Weakness & uncertain Thoughts of Rescue, I had no Opportunity or Inclination to draw or to paint. But the little Captain who had been so eager to set off in the Yawl was not so eager to return, or perhaps in his Incompetence had capsized again, or had been captured by Menabe Warriors, or had been overtaken by the flying Fever he had hastened to elude, or any of a Dozen other possible Fates. I was forced to conclude that no-one would come for me, that no-one knew where I might be, & that there was no-one to tell Robert Horsepole what had happened to his unfortunate Family. When my Tears were exhausted, as you may imagine, I was ready to draw, to paint if I might, the Paradise about me.

The Paper of the Island, the same as that of the magick Books I have mentiond, which they call Taratasy, was made from the Bark of a real Papyrus, which they call Sanga-sanga. I was shown how it was made. They take the inner Rind, & divide it into very thin Pieces, which when sprinkld with Water are layed together variously, crosswise, & pressd down hard. This then is boild in a strong Lye made of Wood Ashes until it is completely soft & supple, then reducd into a Paste in a wooden Mortar, then washd yet again. Then it is pourd on Mats of exquisitely fine Reeds or Rushes, twisted & joind together very close, on which it dries & becomes Paper. They size the Paper with a Decoction of Rice. It is somewhat yellowish, but if well-sized will not blott. The Prince freely procured me much of this Paper, in return,

as he hoped, for my teaching him the English Language.
I enterd gladly into the Bargain, & said that if he would
give me Ink as well, I might teach him how to swear. He
did not understand me, but I got my Ink. They make it
from the reducd Sap of the Arandrante Tree, with a little
Verdigris added. It is not so black as British Ink, but more
glossy.

Immediately I set about my Drawing, covering the
Paper with Representations of all that was unfamiliar to
me, & it was like a return to the Drawing of my
Childhood. For years I had been accustomed to reading
Faces, like a Gypsy at a Fair, here modifying a Sneer, there
dignifying a Simper. The Formality of a Face designd for
a Wall may be acquired with a few Tricks common to
every Physiognomy that in Nature is animated & less conveniently in a self-satisfied Repose. There is Time for an
Outline of the Head in flake-white, lake & black. There
will be a second Sitting, at which Naples-yellow is
introduced. And so through the familiar Process, with
Conversations, & Mrs. Howson serving Tea. But on
Madagascar Nature did not willingly sit to me. Nature
went about her Business with a thousand Faces of
unselfconscious Grimace, a thousand Faces of profligate
Beauty.

I was minded of the Flowers here at the Palazzo, which
is a Reason I am glad to end my Days here. But the
Storms of September have jealously ruind them. The
Blooms of the Bushes are thrown & crumpled by the
Wind, like coloured Handkerchiefs discarded. The late
Roses look singed. The last of the orange Lilies has fallen,
leaving its brown Spikes to point at the racing Clouds.
The Leaves stir, & the Wind & Sea together make a
continuous Roar that seems to hang inside my Head like

a Prelude to some greater Sound that never comes. At a Distance the Sea is scratched with white on the blue, like Creatures moving in it. Nearer it is all moving Marble, & when the larger Waves break, they are scrolld like the ribbed Green of Bottle-Glass. The Season gives my spirit a Sense of Expectation, as do all the larger Manifestations of Release. I see Giovanni sweeping the Terrace of the empty Villa, & chasing a Leaf that will not keep still. I move between the Terrace, where I compose these Memoirs, & the Gallery, where I stare at my other Portrait. Which of these, Percy, will be the more faithful to the Truth? How can we trust with such extravagant Hope that simple Marks of one kind or another on a flat Surface will preserve something of ourselves, and that continuous Roar in our Heads, for the future World to think on? One thing I know, & that is that I doubtless will appear a more rational Creature of the Terrace than of the Gallery.

It was my Frenzie & Delight to record over 300 Orchids on my yellow Paper,* and to observe from Comparison how each kind in its Involvement of Parts represented a kind of Struggle of the Vegetable Life for articulated Movement. The Disposition of a Petal, varied in its characteristick Angle to the Stem, or to the rude Stamen choked with Seed, was in each different Specimen like a single Picture of an animated Process whereby the Flower might attain the Power of Flight, though forever locked to the Earth it grew from. I had some idea of a Conclusion to be drawn from this, that an

---

*There have been more than 900 orchids recorded on Madagascar. The first naturalist to visit Madagascar was Commerson, accompanying Bougainville in 1769. It would appear that Horsepole's work, though in scientific terms that of an amateur, predates Commerson's. Neither Commerson's nor Horsepole's drawings have survived.

Insect was but a Flower in a more advanced State of Development, & I thought it a telling Evidence of such a Notion that Insects were drawn to these Orchids in great Numbers, & Birds too, some of which were no bigger than Insects moving in sudden fluttering Lurches, a Blurr to the Sight save when they approach the crimson Bell of their Desire, hung open like a wet Lip, whereat they hovered & became more exactly visible, like the end of my Thumb with a Needle for a Beak, sipping at the rich Nectar that gave them their accelerated Energy. I wondered how a Bird might be so small, or a Flower so large & so seductively designd.

I drew the Chamæleons & the Maki, which also varied greatly in Size, some being as large as Monkeys & some others as small as Mice, though I made many Portraits of Zoma, who knowing me would keep still enough—when he was satisfied that my Brush was not delicious to eat, or he was tired of hanging about my Neck. It was this varying Scale of Being, as much as the Strangeness of Form, that impressed me in the natural Life of the Island. We are well used to Creatures as just the Size they are, no more and no less. But if a Bird may look like a Moth, or a Maki like a Man, who knows but that the One may be a kind of the Other. If my Zoma was one of the People who had never come down from the Trees, what might that Idea conclude of People who did not live in Trees? I did not think that such a Line of Argument was far from the bitter Pleasantry of Voltaire & such Philosophers as would dress an Ape as a Macaroni & challenge us to expose the Imposture.

The Children of the Palace would crowd to see me draw, & wonder at the Illusion, for the Merina have no comparable Skills. I write 'Palace' as is my Instinct to do, though it were but a Gathering of Wooden Buildings like Barns within a Palisade, none much larger than 15 feet, & roofed with Palm. But all Words have their Uses & their Parallels in all human Life, though on the Island there was Hunting without Dogs, Warfare without Maps, or Dining without Tables or Glasses. There were, too, marriages without Wives, though there were perhaps many Wives, & there was Death & Generation without Fear or Shame, for the Dead were always among the Living, & Boys and Girls were allowed to Copulation very early, as young as twelve & ten years old. And I thought, at the Chatter of Voices about me & the young Fingers tracing the Ink Lines of my Flowers & Animals, that although I had not been on the Island for more than a few Seasons, if Daisy had survivd with me, she might by now have lost her Innocence, living in Freedom & in the Customs of my Hosts. All of us act the Roles which Society gives us to play, & a Child may be a Woman before her Time, as a Fop may be but a belated Baboon.

Wanting Colours, and therefore Pigments, I at last with the Prince's Assistance found ways of procuring them, as by pickling Gunshot in Vinegar for White Lead, & from the Clays, Insects & Plants of the Island contriving Ochres & Dyes. Freed from the little brown and yellow leaves of my Flowers & Animals I made haste to procure Boards on which I might perform a larger work, for the Bark Paper did not take my Pigments well. I wanted a Subject, which though but one of the many possible, should represent the Island as it seemed to my Eyes. If there were something like Divinity in that Place, it was not of the Order of Smagg's Intuition, for I considered it not latent but manifest. It was not to be expressed by any Domestications of its Spirit, or conforming to the civilised World, but should meerly be itself, in its Fullness of Being. What need had I of a New Jerusalem, when I had found the Old Eden?

But first, out of Politeness, out of Gratitude certainly, & also out of Friendship & Affection, I offered to paint the Portrait of Ramboasalama's Father. It was not a hard task for me (though the old Man could not keep still) & perhaps something of Timidity in me put off the Decision of what I was to paint if I was to paint the Portrait of Madagascar. If I could not yet paint its Angel, I could paint its King.

The Painting was brought to him at a Time of Heat, I remember, when it was the Practice to sprinkle the Floors of our Chambers with Water, to create a kind of Fresco in them & to employ the younger Servants of the Household in fanning us with Murchals made of Peacocks' Feathers, four or five Foot long, in the Time of our Entertainment, which this was, for we had much Dancing & Flute-playing & Songs of young Men teasing the young Girls who go to the Well to fetch Water. The more that I learned of their Tongue, the less strange I found their Notions, for these lewd songs could have found a place in D'Urfey without alteration.* After the Music, the Portrait was brought in, veild with a Cloth like one of their Dancers. When the Cloth was removd, small Sighs of Wonder filled the Room. I did not know what the King might think of his Image, but I might well have expected him to laugh at it, for this seemed to be his Custom. He was, however, attentive & silent, & perhaps a little afraid. He turned to his Wives for approval,

---

*Thomas D'Urfey's *Wit and Mirth, or Pills to Purge Melancholy* (1719) was a popular collection of sometimes risqué songs and ballads.

uncertain whether even their Verdict might be believed, & with his great fat Finger—the finger which investigated everything, particularly his Food, & which silenced Speakers at the Kabary—reached out to touch the illusory Surface of Paint. It was my Suspicion that not only was Representation of this Kind naturally unknown to the Merina, but that neither had the King ever seen himself before, there being no looking-Glasses with them, or none that I had come across. He looked at me closely, with a low Sound of understanding, nodding his Head. Truly I was an English Ombiasy & not meerly a sometimes comick Visitor. From that Moment, not only Ramboasalama—who was my Confidant, & who understood me—but the whole Court accorded me a real Respect due to my Profession, which to them was little short of magickal.

At that time, while I was causing to be prepared a larger wooden Surface for my Painting of the Spirit of Madagascar, which was not easy, needing as it did four Planks of Wood securely fastened side by side, & smoothly connected, a Disaster occurred among the Merina.

Ramboasalama's elder Brother, 'The-Prince-of-Wales', the warlike Prince who was continually leading his raiding-Parties into the Territory of their neighbouring Nations, was trodden upon by a Buffalo & brought back crushd, whereupon he died within a Day. I had witnessed the hunting of the Buffalo, & could hardly think of it as other than a kind of harmless Game, particularly so as the little Boys all played a Game based on it, wherein one enacted the Buffalo with a Frame of Withies & Hide, & was suppos'd to escape, as the Buffalo mostly did. To hunt

Buffalo, you must get them to the windward & creep slowly towards them, pulling at the Tops of the Grasses to let them believe you are not young Men with Sagayes, but only Cows, munching. How could the Warrior Prince-of-Wales, who had survived countless bloody Encounters with Boina anxious to deal him a Death-Blow, be killed on a peaceful Day by a harmless Buffalo? There was Suspicion at the Kabary which followed, but no-one to dispute the many Witnesses. The-Prince-of-Wales, who had already thrust at the Buffalo & lost his Weapon, had leaped upon its back with a great Cry & drawn his Dagger. But he slipped, & was trodden on as the Beast made its Escape. All the hunters swore that this was true, on the Graves of their Ancestors. Before he died The-Prince-of-Wales had no Breath to claim otherwise, though his Eyes rolled in his Head, fearful with unspoken Accusations.

The Burial was the greatest Ceremony I had witnessed in all the time I had been among the Merina. Everyone joind in the Procession, the Women in silk Shawls & decorated square Caps or Hoods, the Men with Cloaks & Staves. The Voadziri from many Miles about were in attendance. There was Music made of a great Consort of Flutes which followed to the burial Place, which was approached with a slow Movement more like Dancing than Walking, although the old King was carried as too fat to walk much. The Tombs were like a whole Village of the Dead, brightly decorated with painted Turrets & Emblems, & coloured Palisades, more like a Fair than a Graveyard, & there with much Singing & Talking & Laughing. The-Prince-of-Wales was laid to rest in 80 silk Lambas, inside a Canooe made of solid Silver.

Ramboasalama had warned me that the Ceremony

would include their Famadihana, or Turning of the Dead, whereby the deceased Relatives are given a new Shroud every few Years. I knew and did not know, as is the Case when some Thing is feard & not easily to be faced, whereupon the Mind denies it, that this might also be done for the Members of our own English Party. I did not forbid it, since to forbid it would be to acknowledge that it was going to occur. I have ever held something like the Stoick Philosophy in the Dealings of my Life, whereby the Circumstances likely to obtain were not to be strenuously diverted from their Course—nor yet proudly welcomed as a sign of Fate's particular Attention to one's Self—but simply accepted, & made the best of, as likely thereby to bring the greatest Happiness, or at least, Peace of Mind. To live thus without Anxiety or Resentment has made no little Contribution to my great Accumulation of Years. I have seen many die whose bodily Weakness was aggravated by an ill-containd Defiance of what they conceived to be Misfortune. I believe with Seneca, that it is our Duty to make our Life acceptable to Society, & our Death acceptable to our Self. Taken in the true Spirit, I dare to hope that Death will be an Event hardly to be noticed.

And yet, no Philosopher can ignore the Momentous-ness of that unique Event, & we all live now, do we not, Percy, in an Age of Philosophy? Momentousness is of the Moment, as the *Dictionary* will assert, and yet to be convinced throughout Life of the Momentousness of the Moment of Death is foolish, We cannot call a Moment of Time such a Thing until it be over & done with, since until it is over & done with it might easily by Extension prove too long to be a moment, & be something else, as a Dream, an Eternity, or perhaps no Event at all. We

119

judge an Event by what it is when it has happened, yet when we are dead we are in no Position to judge what it is that has happened to us. In such a Case, it might as well not have happened to us at all, for all we know. There is my Philosophy, Percy, make of it what you will. You may add Grandma Seneca to your little Band of Freethinkers, if you like.

So when at last they descended into the Tombs, in a Place like a Badger's Sett beneath the painted Monuments, & handed out the Bodies in their Shrouds like so many Carpets rolled up for removal, I showed myself calm enough, though my Heart made itself known to me in my Chest like a Drum & beat its own fearful Musick with the chearful Catechisms & Responsions of the Crowd. For their Time of Lamentation had turned into a publick Holiday, where Families are reunited, & Merriment is the Rule of the Day. The Lambas were untied & rolled back, & the Contents given a hearty Spring-cleaning. Limbs were turned, indescribable pieces lifted & sorted like Vegetables at a Market, Bones dusted. I found myself of necessity caught up in the Process, & as in a Dream, once more caressed the mortal Shapes of those I had known so well in Life—silent Jane Penny with the Mole on her nether Lip—fleet Daisy forever disappearing round Corners & leaving but a Shout upon the Air—dear Horsepole stout in sentiment & a little stout in person, whose Shoulders I had claspd in those Moments of Intimacy which make our greatest Claims upon the Future. These & the others, though now no more than Charnel-Relicts that you, Percy, might shriek & faint to look upon, were at that Moment impressd upon my Soul so forcibly that Tears of Grief & Joy stood silently but suspended in my Eyes. My Heart was full as I refolded the funeral Cloths. I blessed the Dead, & felt that they were with me, as I now felt at one with the Merina. The Song passed among them, Men to Women, Women to Men, Family to Family, & I was comforted in sharing it with them. Thus went the Famadihana, which gave me an understanding of their Possession of the Island which they called *izao tontola izao*, the whole World.

On the Evening of that same Day I walked with Ramboasalama, up from the Houses along a Track into the Forest, & from there to a great Stone from which it was possible to see a long Way. We sat on the Stone, & each had our own Thoughts of the Past & of the Future. When we talked, our Exchanges were as full of difficult Silences & tender Misunderstandings as always, but my Mood of Meditation & his of slow Resolve brought us to a new Intensity of Feeling.

Laet—Now that your Brother is dead, you must be The-Prince-of-Wales.

R—Yes. And must be King, too.

Laet—Shall you like to be King, Ramboasalama?

R—Today now Prince-of-Wales. Yesterday Ramboasalama. Tomorrow King. Tomorrow Ramboasalama, too. Not like-to-be King, but must like-to-be King.

Laet—We must all like to be what we are, but it is harder sometimes if you are able to choose.

R—Choose? What is this Word?

Laet—Between one Thing or another Thing. Between one Path or another. As I choose to be a Painter. But you cannot choose not to be King. God chooses between the Sheep and the Goats, Ondri & Osi, the good and the bad. We must choose the good Life, not the bad Life.

R—Osi cannot be Ondri. Osi born Osi.

Laet—It is like a Story, Ramboasalama, a Story of the English Ombiasy. A Story about the Spirit.

R—So, in Spirit, Osi can be Ondri?

Laet—Osi bad, Ondri good. We must choose.

R—Choose is very good English Word. Better Word than must. Ramboasalama choose like-to-be-Ondri. Not King.

Laet—But you will be a good King. I think you will be a wiser King than your Brother.

R—Hard Thing. Ramboasalama must now be King, and must too now choose-to-be-King. Other ways not happy. Prince-of-Wales all ways say—*Ny riaka no valamparihiko*, Sea is the Limit of my Paddy-Field. Now Ramboasalama must say this Thing. This is what King must say.★

Laet—But what do you want to say yourself? It will be you who will be King, not your Brother.

R—Yes. I am not my Brother.

Laet—Ramboasalama, you must choose what kind of King you will be, Osi-King or Ondri-King. No-one will tell you.

R—You will tell me.

Laet—No, I can not tell you. You must choose for yourself.

R—Yes, yes, I choose, I choose Ondri-King. King must not drink Brandy & make War. King must make Merina happy People. You help me make happy People.

He placed his Hand on my Shoulder, & looked at me closely & directly. And I, who all this while had been thinking to myself of how little I was able now to choose

---

*Ramboasalama was proclaimed king of the Merina nation in 1787, whereupon he took the regal name of 'Andrianampoinimerinandriantsimitoviaminandriampanjaka'. He is indeed known to have announced 'Ny riaka no valamparihiko.'

my own Destiny, suddenly saw in his Eyes the Light of a Soul searching like me for some Thing it had lost, or perhaps never found. I took hold of his Hand, & quite suddenly, as Rain will finally break through the long tormenting Closeness of an after-Noon, I wept away the Tears that had pressd upon me at the Famadihana, & I seemd to weep away all my Life, for there seemd at last to be nothing in the World left but the Shoulder I wept on.

When we came down from the Stone, the Crickets seemed to sing even more loudly their dry Song in praise of the Moon. Whatever Song the Moon sings, the Imperfections of our Ears are closed to, but I could feel its Light as a strangely conscious Acknowledgement of all that occurred beneath it, though looking still askance as it always does, like some One surprised or distracted.

Below us the Houses seemd all on fire, & I pointed this out to Ramboasalama in alarm. But he said that these were only the Herecheroche, the Fireflies of the Night that come out in such Numbers when they are mating. Each Fly glows in Passion, & hopes to attract another, rising and falling in the Darkness as does a glowing Smutt in a Chimney. As we came closer through the Trees, I could see that this was so, & that the general Conflagration or Clamour of Embers, was each a little Life making those Choices which it must make, doing the Errands that Nature sends it on, & not thinking too much about it. That Night I considered myself to have found a Husband for the third Time, & though it was not & never could be calld a Christian Marriage, on the Occasion itself I thought the dancing Herecheroche Ceremony enough.

We were in a paradoxical Fashion linked together by the Languages that we imperfectly understood, & our

Languages expressed Differences between us that were both the Difference of Civilisation & the Difference of Gender. I had once asked him if he liked the English Language, & he smiled at me & clasped his Ears & rolled his Eyes, & said—'English is Language of Head.' Then he put one Hand to his Chest, & said —'Merina is Language of Heart.' He had then pondered profoundly for a while, with raised Finger cautioning me to be silent, until he said—'English strong Head, Ramboasalama strong Heart.' By this he referred to me as well as to himself, for he did not presume to address me then by any Version of my Name, but identified me in the third Person as 'English' as though I was—as in all practical Terms on the Island I was indeed—the sole Representative of my Nation. Then triumphantly, as at a Proof in Logic,—'English Man-Woman, Ramboasalama Woman-Man.' And he afterwards blushd & laughd, & looked away from me. I had perhaps then thought him to be talking Nonsense, but after the Famadihana I began to understand the Insight that he was struggling to express. Just as our Kinship originally resulted from our Exchange of Language, so our marital Relationship, if such it was, seemed to draw upon an exchange of the Male and the Female Qualities in subtle Ways that I had never experienced with Crowther or Horsepole. To them, it was clear, a Man had a Role to play that might have been consulted in the Law Books & followed to the Letter. When the Letter was broken, there the Man had faild to be a Man. Ramboasalama acted in all Things as a Human Being, as I had come to believe I did myself, without Distinction of Gender, & just as there were many of my Countrymen who may have thought it absurd for me to pursue my Profession, I dare say there were many Merina who would not credit

Ramboasalama's Reluctance to be King. Cleaving to his Body, I could think of him as indeed nothing other than Andriamanitra, the scented Lord, whose Gentleness & Self-Knowledge completely transcended the carnal Appetite as I had come to know it in Men. What we performd together in our Tenderness of Difference, rising & falling like Fireflies, seemed to have no Distinction of Subject and Object, nor of Age & Youth, for Nothing needed to be spoken of.

Afterwards, he liked to play upon his Sody, which is a little Flute of six Stops, on which he made a continuous Melody that without Resolution seemed neither joyful nor melancholy, but in its tranquil Persistence to express every Thing whatever that is in human Experience, and to make it all one.

The King seemed to accept me without Demur as now some kind of Member of his Family. It seemed a happy Resolution of my Position as a permanent Visitor, & a happy Way of somehow controlling my dangerous Magick of trapping the Spirits of Men & Beasts on wooden Boards, wherein they became imprisond & could only be releasd by the Subject staring on them until they flew back into their Body again. Ramboasalama told me that this was how the King felt, but I observd that it in no way discouraged him from frequently approaching his own Portrait in a kind of Glee & Awe, & of squinting at it a few Inches from the Surface in an attempt to understand how it was done.

This I was able to witness because I was now more freely privileged in my Movements than before. Ramboasalama took me into the Apartments where many of the Treasures & Objects of State were to be found, & the elaborate Olis of his Family that warded off evil

Spirits. He showd me the King's Throne, which I had seen at a Distance at the Kabirys, but not before examind. Its Legs appeared to be constructed of great Thigh Bones or Shins of Oxen, & its Arms & Back naild with innumerable Objects that were not only of Merina Manufacture, but had been salvaged or collected from Visitors or Wrecks about the Island, viz.—gold Moidores, Venetian Sequins, votary Limbs of stamped Tin, Rows of Beaks, & Cowries, & Alligators' Teeth, Belt Buckles, a ceramick Bambino, Indian Cornelian Beads, Brass Nails, Feathers, & what-not-else. Here, if I had known it at the time, was the first Sign to me of what I should make the Subject of my Painting of the Angel of Madagascar.

It seems that I had accepted that Part of my Life which had little to do with my Vocation without much Difficulty of Decision. What was it indeed, in Ramboasalama's Phrase, to choose-to-be? I thought that my Choices of Life had seemed like Choices only after they had been made, & even then were like Paths taken only through Whim, in meer Ignorance, or Things offered & accepted without Resistance. I thought of my not having accepted the hand of Sig. Canistrelli out of Blindness, & out of a Prejudice of our respective Ages. That Relationship was but an Inversion of Ramboasalama's Relationship with me, where the Substance surmounted any Disparity of Years as easily as the Seed of the antient Tree finds the Soil of the Forest Floor & grows again. But could I be said to have chosen not to marry him, any more than I had actually chosen to marry Crowther, rather than being swept by that Rakehell, as by a Tide of fleshly Curiosity, into the bleak Bay of my Disaster? And in the Case of my veritable as well as my figurative Shipwreck, I had surely been as much wrought upon as acting freely, & I could not confess to Dame Nature, nor to God—if I had thought on Him much—that in gaining Ramboasalama I was happy to have lost Horsepole.

We view the Past as a mapped Country because we have moved through it, & sometimes regret that we may not retrace our Journey. But why do we not also view the Future as a mapped Country? That we are not yet in it is not very different from our not now being in the Past. The Past we know may not be changed—the Future when it has happened may not be changed—but what sort of a Thing is the Future until it has happened? When we conceive of the Future it is never as a Blank but as a Set of Events that shall have happened, & that is perfectly reasonable, just as we cannot think of any Thing at all but as the Thing it is intended to be. For example, if I had said 'the next King of the Merina', I had intended to mean my dear Ramboasalama. Yet, a month before, the Words had indicated his Brother. Now, it may have been, by some Mischance that I could have no Knowledge of, that the next King of the Merina should have been some other Person, as if my dear Ramboasalama should have stepped on a deadly Snake. Yet whoever it was to be, would be that King, and the Fact as certain as that the present King was the fat King, Ramboasalama's Father. These certain Facts are hid from us by the iron Door of Time shut in our Face, which we may open but a Crack each Day to let in the Light of our Lives.

I talked much of these Things with my Prince, which made him smile & hold his Head in his Hands. The Merina do not think of the Future with Anxiety, nor even with the persistent curiosity of our Philosophers, but simply feel & accept the Continuity of Life. To die like the Moon is a necessary Phase before a Rebirth. To die like the Tree is only to know that the Seed has begun to grow again. To the Merina, one dies like the Moon or the Tree. I lived through too many Cycles of the Famadihana not to understand the Strength which such Beliefs brought them, but as for me, accepting that my Life was not blessed with Children & with a Brain made too much suspicious by Astronomy, I could no more see my Immortality in a Tree or the Moon than I could in the Nova Hierosolyma. If I had been carried off by the Fever, I had by now become no more than a Parcell of handled Bones, & why should my Soul's Life be linked to the Lunar Shadow? And yet I dare say, like all of us poor sublunar Creatures, Percy, I could not answer the Mystery of how our Souls exist within these perambulating Parcells, or where they may be found when our bodily Facultys are lost to us.

No wise Man counts the Months of his Happiness. I was aware of the Seasons only as the Merina were aware of them. In the New Year, after the first new Moon of March when the Cyclones have passd, I helped with the sowing of the Rice. My day did not seem long enough for all that I undertook to do, for I helped the Women with the washing, hanging the Cloaths in the Sun to bleach them, as a fit sign of my Belonging, & I talked with Ramboasalama about the Methods of producing Cloth that his People might be more largely put to for the purpose of Trade. He sadly pointed out that the Men of the Merina Nation would rather make War than Cloth, & that if all the Women made Cloth then there might be no Rice. I told him of the new Machines they had in England for the Manufacture of Cloth, & I told him of my Interest in the House of Crowther. It seemed like a natural Proof in Logic to conclude that between us we might make Madagascar into a great trading Enterprise for Silks, Cotton & Cloth of the Raphia or the Cocoanut, or Cloth of all Kinds indeed. Ramboasalama looked at me & nodded gravely, but it was plain to see that such a Prospect was beyond his Comprehension. How would we sail to England to procure such Machines? How would we begin to make enough Cloth to justify the Expense of further Journeys? How could his People be taught to operate the English Machines? They are Children, he said. And he told me of the people on one of the smaller Islands who were used to eat the Chrysalis Silkworm & to throw away the Silk.

One Morning, an old Man & a Boy of the Antanosy came before the King.* Their Purpose in coming such a Distance was, I think, to seek his Support in protecting them from the Encroachments of the Antandroy, but the King was suspicious of them, since the old Man claimed to be the Father of Prince Crindo, & said that the Boy was Crindo's Son. The King wanted to know why Crindo had not come in Person.

A Kabary was held that Day to discuss the Power of the Antandroy, & what was needful to be done. I had not much Interest in such Deliberations, as usually concluding in Bloodshed, but I was indeed interested in one of the Presents which the Father of Prince Crindo had brought for the King. This was, when the oiled green Cloth was carefully unfolded which contained it, a gigantic Egg.

With this Egg, when I saw it, I had an immediate Sense of Præcognition, as when something for which one

---

*The Antanosy were a tribe living in the South West of Madagascar.

yearns, though one knows not what it is, is suddenly presented to the Senses & though quite unexpected, even outlandish, is familiar. Its Shape & Size struck my Vision like the Answer to an antient Riddle, which I had long pondered. It was like the Continuation of a Story broken off long ago, yet hinting at a Conclusion which I may have often dreamed.

Ramboasalama then told me of the Vorombe, or giant Bird of the Island, called the Elephant Bird, which was supposed to have existed from the Survival of its antient Parts, but which was not now seen, though he thought that someone had claimed to have seen one at a Time shortly before he was born. Eggs & Fragments of Eggs were sometimes found in Stream Beds after the Rains, but mostly in the South in the Country of the Mahafaly & the Antanosy. It appeared that those Bones that formed the Legs of his Father's Throne which I had thought to be Ox or Buffalo Bones were belonging to this prodigious Bird, which when I looked again at them were longer than my Arm. The Egg itself was almost as long as my fore-Arm.

My Imaginacion thrilled at the News of this great Bird. To see with my own Eyes the veritable Egg, which might contain the Embrio of its vast Shape now lost to Fable, was a Privilege which excited me as a Woman & as a Painter both, for this ivory Shape, which the Antanosy Boy could scarce carry in both Arms without staggering, seemed like the Cradle of a great God, who though he may have disappeared from the Earth, could be brought to Life again by some Miracle. The Meaning of this chance Epiphany flashed upon my inward Eye in an Instant—I could bring the Bird back to Life if I could but see it, even in a Vision. The Egg was half a Fossil, & contained no vital Spirit. It was but as the Relicts of the

Virtuosos of my Youth, who made Theories of what they found in the Rocks with their little Hammers that accorded with that partial Loss of Creation in the Great Flood. It now seems ridiculous to suppose an actual Ark, & Species lost to us by their not being taken on Board. The finding of Bones in the Rocks & sedimentary Layers of our World may have far other Explanation, as I have since heard discussed, & as the Survival of these sterile Eggs presupposes, given that the Bird is itself remembered by those who have spoke of it to the Living.

And there was good Reason to think it not forgotten of Noah, for surely it was the same Bird that carried off the Sailor Sindbad, the giant Roc of the Arabian Nights that so delighted & terrified me as a Child? Sindbad voyages southwards from Arabia, & makes his Fortune by Trade & Luck. That Island on which he ties himself to the great Bird's Foot, & is carried off—as I conceived my Father to have been carried off by his Fever—could be none other than my Madagascar. Indeed, I later discovered this to be true, for it is spoken of by Marco Polo in the Thirteenth Century, who calls it a Rukh.

I wished to see this Bird because it represented to me the Strangeness of the natural World of Madagascar, but it represented much more than this alone. I have written of some of the many unique Creatures that I saw on the Island, & there are others that I never saw, like the Aye-Aye, the raw-faced Man-Beast that is a Harbinger of Death, but none of these Prodigies impressed me, seen or unseen, as did the Idea of the Roc on the Day that the Antanosy brought their Egg as a Gift to the King. It was both beautiful & a Challenge to me, as to say,—I stole your Father from you many Years ago & flew away with him & you never discoverd the Place. Here is a Hostage indeed, make of it what you will, but you can not bring it to birth. You have no Children, & you have no Father. I belong to that World of featherd Shapes which removes Men from the World they know, to a World that they can never speak of. I am Angel. I am Fever. Pursue me at your Peril.

In an Instant I conceived that it was my Mission to do what I could to pursue the Roc indeed, at whatever Danger to myself. It was not Revenge, but a sense of Wonder. From the Egg & Bones, I computed that the Creature would stand taller than the King's Palace. I could not be a Foster-Mother to that Brobdingnagian Egg, but if I could find the Roc itself, I could by painting it bring it to Birth in the Womb of my own reflecting Eyes.*

Where was the Creature to be found, if it could be found at all, being quite dead? I set for myself the Task of acquiring all possible Information about the Bird, & for Months visited the oldest of the Merina for Accounts of its Legend & the Memories of their Fathers' Child-hoods. I collected what Remainders & Fossils of the Roc I could find, to assemble the Fragments on Bark Paper into something of an Anatomy, whereby its true Size and Proportions might be established.

It was ever likely that my Quest for a Sight of this Rukh or Roc would take me into the Territory of the Antanosy, an Expedition to which Ramboasalama was firmly opposed, as being certain to put me into the Danger of the Wars still being fought between the Antanosy & the Antandroy. For, however I was to proceed, I could by no means travel alone, & so accompanied by a Party of

---

*Horsepole's fancy here suggests that Shelley may indeed have read her memoirs. See Appendix B.

Merina could scarcely fail to be mistaken for the Leader of a Warring Excursion. Either the Antanosy would believe me hastening to the aid of the Antandroy, or the Antandroy would believe me of the Antanosys' Persuasion. It was useless to protest that I was no Amazon, nor looked like one. Nor that Prince Crindo would surely give me Protection, having sought the same from the Merina. Ramboasalama believed the Prince's ouvertures to be a Design upon his Nation's Trust, & to be therefore suspected. If I were found among the Antanosy I would surely be taken Hostage, he proclaimed sadly. I thought it all a Nonsense, for we had not kidnapped Crindo's Father & Son when they had appeared with the Embassy of the Egg, so why should he think of kidnapping me?

At the last, after many Months of imagining the Roc & distracted by domestick & economick Events of a Magnitude to require my Care & Concern, I made Plans to travel with no-one but a Woman who served me, whose Name was Saka, & her young Brother, who would be the Bearer of our Provisions. I did not, in my Innocence, believe that we could be mistaken for Warriors, though I took the Precaution of a Pistol. We were, after all, a sketching-Party, practically a Pick-nick, & did not intend a journey of above a Week.

Such Errors are always the Result of some fatal Enthusiasm. Having first fallen into the Sea, I found that I had fallen into an Eden. It is Perversity of Human Nature to be discontented with a happy State, & to be ever in search of some newer Thing. I was happy with Ramboasalama, & did not conceive how easily I might lose him.

After some Days making our Way towards the Mountains where by my best Calculation there might be a Chance of finding a surviving Roc, eating our small Cakes of compacted Rice & drinking Rain-Water from the fleshy Centre of the Raphia Palm, a Bounty that lent to it the common Name of the 'Travellers' Tree', I had a Dream of the Prince. He appeared to me in the Cloaths of a great Man of my own Country, now almost forgotten but here reminding me sharply of the Delicacy & Pomp of State Occasion, as of national Mourning, where there is personal Grief as well as publick Ceremony to be endurd by the principal Actors in it. Ramboasalama looked down upon me as an Admiral might look upon the chart of his Voyage that had led him past Rock & Shipwreck. He spoke to me, & Fire came out of his Mouth, saying gently—It was your Wisdom I needed, not your Body.

When I was again awake, I had an Intuition that his Father had died, & that he had already been calld to the Kingship of his People. I considerd at this Moment that I would immediately return to him, but soon put off the Idea as born of an unreasonable Superstition. Rather than return, I made a contrary Plan of proceeding even further than better Reason told me was practicable, for Saka had related to me, as we sat at our evening Fire, many Tales of the Fishermen of the West, in whose Religion the Vorombe was venerated. In the unusual intimacy of our Expedition, she became voluble & confiding, who was usually quiet & uncommunicative, & described the Lives of the Vezo, as these Fishermen were calld, with the Familiarity of one whose Cousin had married into that Tribe. Their Boats were decorated with the Symbols of the Birds, as a Sign that they might fly across the Waters, & their Houses are so decorated as a Sign that Life itself may not be restricted by human Flightlessness. And—as at last she told me, when the Boy her Brother was asleep—these Vezo believd that carnal Intercourse with the Vorombe would bring them the greater Wisdom of understanding the painful Passage from Life into Death, & therefore described upon their Tombs uncommon Performances of Acts of Pleasure between Men & Birds to signal these serious Hopes of Survival. In my Mind there was a wonderful confusion of Purpose, in which the Revival & Ascendancy of Desire which I had experienced in my Years with the Merina became the Instrument of my larger Vision, as if I should reply to Ramboasalama in that Dream World where my Spirit encountered his, 'not Wisdom alone, but the Body also'.

All this Time, Percy, you will have been casting your Mind about to calculate by what Method I ever came to depart from my Eden, for here I am, writing this Memorial of the Red Island of Madagascar from the twilit Terrace of my old Age, looking out upon the Sea of Italy & of Youth, where your Hyacinth is at this Moment attempting to sit as still as he can in his little green Boat so that he will not affright the Fishs he purposes to catch & eat. As I write, it is hard to believe that I am not there still, as once I believed that I might be for ever & ever, & perhaps the first white Queen of the Merina. It is painful for me to remember now the means of my involuntary Removal, & I will say little about it.

We were encamped upon a Height from which we could see a good Way into a remote Valley, led there by the positioning of some antient Vezo Tombs which we had found, which appeard to be station'd as Stages of Approach. Some Vezo Tribesmen whom we had encounterd in the Bush had been not unfriendly to us when addressd in their Tongue, which Saka could speak a little, & perhaps were induced by the Sight of my Pistol as much as by our Questions, to reveal some thing of the Significance & Direction of the Burial-Grounds. I had gone ahead upon waking to look down more closely into this Valley, which, though wooded at first, extended beyond into a grassy Plain. I left the Pistol with Saka, as better Protection of our Encampment, whose Embers might give us away. I was there for several Hours, picking my Way among the Rocks for a better Vantage-Point, for I thought at the first that I had seen some Thing in the Distance. When Saka's Brother shouted up to me, I made a Motion with my Arm for him to be quiet, for at that Instant I had seen again the same Movement that I had first seen. If it were the Creature I most wishd it to have been, it had been a Miracle indeed, you will claim, & rightly. Yet Miracles will occur, & the long Looking for some Thing is as likely to find it as to preserve it lost to Sight, as the strange Revelation of the Needle in the Pie which I told you of, which my Father produced from between his Teeth like a biblical Sign. This Creature, whatever it was, was long-necked like a Needle, & might have been grazing, when the Sound of a Pistol Shot startled it, though at a Distance of perhaps a thousand Yards. In a Moment it fled down the Valley, tiny indeed to my Eyes, yet considering the Distance as by every Means at my Disposal I urgently attempted to do, with all conceivable Accuracy, I estimated its Size as larger than a House. If I had been close to it, as by stalking it I should have dearly liked, there had been no earthly means of keeping up with it. Percy, you must some Time or other have seen a Partridge run—this Creature moved like a Partridge, & I beside it had been a meer Mouse.

Often in Reverie I have revisited the Place, & felt again

that Excitement & Sense of Loss at its prompt scampering Trot, its Neck thrust out in an Urgency more comickal than a Panique, the utter Silence of its Motion at that Distance from which I observd it. At the Time, I had no Opportunity to reflect on its Escape, nor to plan a lengthier Pursuit, for now the Reason for Saka's Brother's shouting, and for the firing of the Pistol, was reveald to me. Our little Party had itself been pursued the while, & not to be wonderd at nor painted neither, but to be taken into Captivity. Saka had fired the Pistol in the Direction of our Captors, but to no Effect beyond the wounding of a harmless Tree, & very soon we were all in the Hands of a Trader in Slaves.

4

Foeda, cruenta, cruces, obscæna, ingrata, chimeras,
Sordidaque & misera.*

At the Distance of Years, the Tediousness of Discomfort
is levelled with the Alarms of Pain & the Thrills of
Pleasure—the Wonder is rather at all we have endured, &
as much forgotten as secure in our Memory. I did not
intend this Account of my Life, Percy, to be made up
exclusively of nautical & tropical Adventures, which were
meerly the Accidents, as now it appears to me, of my
Dream of the great Bird. I need say as little of the
unlooked-for Captivity that removd me from the Red
Island as of the Wrack that landed me there, for once
again afloat, although in such alterd Circumstances, it
seemed little more than a Dream, though a Dream that
had occupied Years of my Life.

I had thought the Days of the great Pyrates, viz.
Caracciolo, Thomas Tew, La Buse, Thomas White,
William Kidd & the rest, to be long passed, & indeed they
had been suppressed by Commodore Matthews above
sixty Years previously. All Ages of Man have deemd
themselves more civilised than their Predecessors, & now

---

*'[Shun] also all things which are obscene, impudent, filthy, unseemly, cruel,
fantastical, poor and wretched', Du Fresnoy, p.56.

we reckon that no longer would a Privateer terrorise the Trade Routes nor a Nation—though as rude as the Dutch—plunder Mauritius for its Ebony & eat up the Dodo to Extinction. That is as may be, but it is to reckon without the Traffic in Slaves, for what a Man may be shamed into giving up because it is lawless, he will persist in if it seem but the sole Means of the Achievement of a great Enterprise, and the Law will follow tamely.

This I learnd from Don Pedro, our Captor, who claimd to keep the civilised World supplied with the prized Luxuries of its Table, as Sugar, Rum, Coffee & the like, which the New World could produce only with the Labour of the African Slaves he sold there. These slaves he took as freely as a Man might take fish, though he claimd fairly to pay for them.

So they are betrayed for Baubles (I replied) by those of their Countrymen who should most be their Protectors.

But privately I thought the Majority of the Wretches whom Don Pedro herded into his Ship had been taken in War by the Antandroy.

He was surprised to find me not a Native of that Island & ordered his Fellow to untie my Arms from the wooden Barr across my Shoulders, which was the Posture in which his human booty were controlld until they could be more securely shackled by leg-Irons in the Slave Hulk that awaited them at the Mainland.

Nay (I told him) I am not a Milkmaid, neither, to be so yoakd, but a British Gentlewoman, & known to Admirals.

I did not expect either to be believed nor better treated for such Information, for the Man was nothing but a Blackguard, but it was my Duty and my Need to secure my Safety as I best might, & for Saka and her Brother too.

In my Lamba & Pagna* & my Hair long & undressd, as of Necessity it was during my Years on the Island, I could not have appeard less like the Person I was, or at least had once been & now pretended to be. Don Pedro stared at me, as if he had found him a Dolphin in a Net of Tunny, & when I recited to him the Words of the Requiem Mass in incomplete but ringing Latin, my Conquest was complete. If there were Dangers in seizing a baptised Native, there were added Hazards in crossing a crazed Prophetess. He would consult the Captain of his Vessel, which awaited him at Ibo, but he had no Intention of releasing me.

In the Vicissitudes of Tales & the convenient Logic of the Stage, this Captain would inevitably turn out to be the very same Captain who had abandoned us to our Fever after wrecking us on the Madagascar Coast, though pretending to seek Assistance. And so it was in Reality, though you might scarcely believe it, for when Don Pedro brought me to the Captain's Cabin, like a Riddle to be solvd or an Irritant to be appeasd, as by a Test of Nationality or by returning the Offence to its Source, it was little Captain Fell who faced me there, his Jaws still naturally working in Perplexity & his Side-Whiskers dancing, as if Life had had no Thing but Trouble to offer him in all the Years since we had last set Eyes on each Other. In this Moment in which I knew my whole Future hung in Ballance, I made without Hesitation, but not without moral Revulsion, the most politick Decision of my Life. I pretended to Captain Fell an immediate Confidence & Friendship, as of old Trust & Exploits, with no shaddow whatsoever of my natural Disgust of him,

---

*The pagna was a kind of cotton shawl.

both for his former Betrayal & for his present mercenary Profession. On his part, I reckond a like Dissimulation, for between Guilt & Ingratiation he steerd a self-protective Course, claiming—as might for all I knew have been true enough—to be finishd with his present Traffic after the Passage to Jamaica, & to be returning to Bristol & his Family with a Cargo from the Plantations. I took it upon myself to presume that he would take me safely with him so long as I did not interrogate him upon his Failure to have effected a Rescue, & thus we chatted away merrily upon such a Basis of mutual Fear & Scorn, suppressed by Expediency. The Freedom of Saka and her Brother I secured by swearing that they were my indentured Servants, but this was the most I could do. The Fate of Hundreds of Africans chaind in that stinking Hulk, including the Cluster of Vezo & Antanosy of which I had nearly been a fatal Part, I was powerless to avert. They were sold at Kingston three months later, or rather those who survivd the Journey were sold, for not a Day went by when the Dead or Sick were not thrown overboard to avoid Contamination of the rest of the Cargo. This was done without Compassion or Ceremony, but as a Measure of economick Efficiency only. I kept my Silence to secure my Passage. I had no Thing to bargain with but my Rank & Contacts, & knew that at any Time the Reputation of the odious Captain might be as easily securd by my Disappearance as by my Preservation.

At Kingston, human Dignity was exchangd for a Cargo of Rum, & I was allowd to acquire more suitable dress for myself & my Servants. It was not until I stood once more in Petticoats that I fully understood in what Danger I had been, for it is by Dress that our Nature & our Rank is known. Put the meanest Wretch of that Slave Cargo into gold Braid & there is not a free Man of Portsmouth who would not have saluted him. As it was, they were put to their involuntary Labour thousands of Miles from their Homes without raising any Suspicion of Injustice among those who purchased them like so much Cattle.

But for myself, as you may imagine, that Sense of Injustice remained. I was able to save Saka & her Brother, but at the same Time felt that I had betrayd their whole Race. Saka was more resignd, for as she said, the warring Nations of her Island had no Hesitation in taking each other into Slavery. It was the natural Condition of the Defeated.

I thought of Ramboasalama not wanting to choose to be King, but choosing to be like the Ondri. He understood, as he had had ample Opportunity of understanding, that perhaps it was not after all possible to choose Both, that Power could not be exercised without the Frustration of some human Interests, or the Denial of some human Rights. It was evident that my Portuguese Bone-Merchant never for one Instant considerd his Cargo to be human at all, & something of that Attitude underlay the Refusal of Parliament to listen to the Wishes of the People in the many Petitions presented to it concerning the Slave Trade, for the Number of sitting Members with Property in the West Indies forbade it. After I had set about my Work of stirring publick Opinion on the Matter by speaking at Meetings organised by my Quaker Friends★ I was accustomd to reflect on the relative Impotence of my Role despite my direct Experience of this Evil. Had I remaind among the Merina, & playd the

_____
★The Quaker Anti-slave Trade Committee was set up in 1783.

Part expected of me by my Ramboasalama, my general Ignorance of European Politicks had been no great Matter. To him I was a 'Man-Woman' of uncommon Wisdom & Magic, & I might surely have been a Grey Eminence of the Madagascan Union.

In England I had no Wish to become a Drury, seeking Fame for a Past Adventure, & yet it was not so easy to become again myself. I had much to do to convince Captain Fell that it was in his Interest to advance me Money in addition to seeing me safely into Harbour, for even he had not so much Self-Importance as to believe that I could—even an I would—bring him into Credit at the Admiralty by my Report of his Actions. I offered to paint his Portrait, & privately thought that with enough Time & an Inclination to the old Myths, which had never much pleasd me, I could make of him a credible Charon, ferrying lost Souls across the dark River. But I was content with the Pittance which he paid me for a Kit-Cat,* since it provided me with a Lodging from which I could find my Bearings. I had brought no Thing out of Madagascar but these Skills, & for a time feared that I would have to prove who I was, or not be believed. But my Story was printed in the Bristol Newspaper, for which I was also paid. I had Money for Letters, for Travel, & for my entry once more into that World where One is defind & appraisd by those Customs which have made One what One is, rather than being thrown upon One's Wits.

And yet this World, through having proceeded upon its way without Pause while I was absent from it, becoming ever more like itself in its Discovery of its true Aims &

---

*The Kit-Cat size (from Kneller's portraits of the members of the Kit-Cat Club) was 36″ x 28″.

Corrections of old Errors, was not quite the same as it was. In polite Society the Ladies' Heads were higher, & the Gentlemen's Heads their own. Waists were higher, too, and Dinner later. It was as though every Thing had been screwed up a little tighter by that attentive Watch-Maker who keeps us all in perpetual Motion. Every Drawing Room contained a new Fortepiano & a pert Miss to sit & play at it, every Garden a Frame of Cucumbers.

My Aunt Katherine was, I discoverd, still alive & hale enough. I resolvd to visit her when it would be practicable, to share again the Memory of a Brother & a Father, & to re-acquaint myself—as it was my Phansie to think her—with a kind of Image of myself fifteen Years hence. I had no other Relations that I knew of, beyond some Bristol Cousins on my Mother's Side, who I had thought knew & cared nothing for me. But they, reading of my Experiences in the Newspaper, made Ouvertures to me to renew such Family Ties as might be thought to exist between us after so many years, which to be sure for my Part I considerd negligible. They, however, whose Afternoons & Husbands were as unrewarding as Limbo, were pleasd to open their Houses to me, which was, in truth, an Assistance to me in my Re-establishment as a Citizen & a Speaker of the English Tongue.

Whetton, though believing me dead, had not yet appropriated my Ownership of the Crowther Business, though this was not for Excess of Sentiment or Delicacy, meerly out of Deference to the Procedure of the Law. He stared at me as if at some tragick Ghost returnd in sulphurous Light from the Underworld, & when I informd him of the mutual Advantage to be gaind by taking our Business into Madagascar, all but told me to my Face that I should return to Cloud-Cuckoo-Land forthwith, where such Dreams belonged. He was relievd to hear that my Dreams were not of material Profit, & readily consented to my taking a comfortable Annuity out of Crowther & leaving him in effective Charge of the Rest.

Mrs. Howson was as well as ever, & living in her Cottage, though her Brother Elkanah was now mad & confind in Bethlehem Hospital. The House in Greenwich had been let, & Robert made Ward to his Aunt Fanny in Norfolk. He, however, had taken his Degree at Cambridge, & done so well that he showed no inclination to leave, but lived there still in Fellowship with those who liked to ponder on First Causes. To him I was also a half-forgotten Wraith, the hobbling Step-Mother of Fable, who had taken his Father away from him & ended his Boyhood. All this was so much in the Past for him that he could pretend an Interest in the News of my Adventures, once satisfied in the Manner of his Father's Death, & the sufficient Honour of it. He was becoming a Replica of his Father, though strangely stouter, & far from the Image of the pale running Boy of my Memory. He asked kindly, yet formally, after my Means—the Horsepole Estate having passed to him—& I was able to put him at his Ease by saying that I would make no claim upon him.

Laet—And yet, Robert dear, there is a Favour that you can easily grant me.

R—Gladly, I am sure.

Laet—The House on Croom's Hill, you remember, where you used to come up to my Studio at Noon to see the golden Sphere on the Observatory descend? And the Cannon?

R—Of course I remember. I was frightend of you, &

frightend of the Ball, & thought it magick, though I had to see it.

Laet—The House is lett to a Captain who will have a Command within a Twelvemonth, & no Family to dispose of. He must rattle emptily in those Rooms, like a Crab in a beached Schooner.

R—Captain Bligh.

Laet—Exactly. Well, Robert, I should like the Tenancy of that House, & I should pay you for it. Or can it be that you are minded to live there yourself?

R—Unless I were to take a Living in some Country Parish, I shall always be content to reside in College.

Laet—Good, it is settled, then. I designed the Studio there, & it will suit me still. Besides, Mrs. Howson kept many of my Paintings out of a Fondness for my Memory, & they are crowding her out of her Cottage. She sits by the Fire with half-a-dozen naval Officers at her Shoulder, & takes her Tea off an Oilcloth of a Fleet Visit. I should like to relieve her of them, & give her some Space for Thought in her declining Years.

R—This is a happy Outcome. You shall live there gratis, & perhaps I may sometimes visit you there, to see if the Astronomers celebrate the End of the Morning in quite such a theatrical Fashion. And as for our Relationship, I am happy to celebrate in you the End of Mourning, & a particular Happiness of my Father.

It was a gracious, if clumsy Speech, & gave promise of the Sententiousness of Village Sermons. I could have wished them to have quite given up Theology at Cambridge in favour of the Mathematicks, but it was not to be. I left Robert gownd not in the Advancement of Thought or the Liberalisation of Opinion, as was the noble Endeavour of his more celebrated Contemporaries, but in the Solemnity & pious Devotions of his Guardian and Aunt Fanny. His one Claim to Distinction, I fear, is to have been for a time Tutor to the Poet Wordsworth, whose Sensibility cannot have been much sharpened by the Contact. I had Wordsworth's Poem *The Excursion* sent out to me a few Years ago, & found it dull beyond Belief. It is no better than the sentimental Moralities of the previous Age & gives me nothing of the Terror or Frisson that I require from true Poetry. I am told, on the best Authority, that all his poetic Notions derived from his Sister Dorothy, who made them over to him as a Surrogate for the carnal Complaisance that even their Revolutionary Society would not tolerate. I find no Delicacy in such a Substitution, having seen Incest for the natural & generative Performance that it is—when not proscribed by Holy Writ—in the Villages of Madagascar. Mr. Wordsworth would have found his beloved Nature, Nutrix & Godhead in one, a more perplexing Force if he had been reared among the Merina & not among the dutiful Peasantry of Cumberland.

It was inevitable that our Mr. Wordsworth would fall out with his former Friend Mr. Coleridge, whose Mind is as the Summer Lightning to the former's November Fogs. His poetic Instincts lay ever towards the Grandeur of History, the Origin of Human Institutions, & the Workings of the Mind—but these profound Subjects were colourd with such wayward Knowledge of savage Customs & Superstitions, Færy Lore, scientific Scraps & gothique Fables, that his Wisdom came at you obliquely & surprisingly from his Verses, like a Demon King in the Pantomime.

I indeed first met him in his Youth, when quite unknown, some years later, at the House of one of my

Cousins who did Business with the Family of his young Wife. I was there on Business of my own, a Commission to paint their Husbands, who were Moguls in Bristol Trade. It was a Period of my Life when I was less eager to take publick Commissions, & yet a Fee almost on my own Doorstep was not to be lightly turnd aside. What Mrs. Coleridge was doing there I could not imagine, except perhaps to escape for a Time into the bosom of her material Family from the Rigours of an immaterial Marriage. Mr. Coleridge walked over twenty Miles to retrieve her, & burst into the drawing-Room sweated like a Cart-Horse & apparently in mid-Sentence. My Cousin & Mrs. Fricker pretended not to be outraged, & Mrs. Coleridge was perhaps truly imperturbed, & all of them continued frostily to eat Cake, while Mr. Coleridge soon found some Benefit in directing his talking at me rather than at my Cousin, or at his Wife or Mother-in-law. He asked me about Madagascar, & became excited when I told him about the Elephant Bird.

Col—What Place does such a Creature have in the Pantheon of their Beliefs? Do they fear it as a Raptor?

Laet—Indeed not. It is in their private Dreams an Instrument of Love between the bodily Life & the World of the Spirit (& I told him of the Images of bestial Engendering on the Vezo Tombs).

Col—So then these peaceable Fishermen are all happy to imagine themselves willing Ganymedes, & their strange Eagle a Bearer of divine Wisdom? A pretty Annunciation!

Laet—It seemd when I saw it a more gentle & clumsy Bird than an Eagle. There was even Comedy in its Manner of Perambulation.

Col—Nevertheless, you might paint a Vezo

148

Annunciation—if you could find a Vezo Church which would pay you for one.

Laet—I painted freely among the Merina, but they were content to see Nature in Paint. Their own Faces were as much Truth as they could bear in Art, & with that I too am content, though the Truth is not so often found upon Men's Faces as it should be.

Col—Indeed, but the Truth can be a Figure, too, and the figure of a Bird for that, & of the Truth of any human Failing as of human Ambition.

Mrs. Col—I wish you would stop talking, Sam, and take some Tea.

I had indeed begun to think that the Self-Satisfaction of that Class of Aggrandisers who come fully into their Content when hanging on their own Walls rather than the publick Scaffold was not very different from the Bravado of those who amassed their Wealth outside the Law & were found out. My work towards the Abolition of the Trade of Slaves brought me into Contact with many who were no better, & who were guilty of the Robbery not of individual Property but of the whole of Mankind from the proper Happiness & Relationship with the World we inhabit. Yet here I was, agreeing to flatter the material Pride of such Men by creating for them the Images of their Self-Worship. From my Marriage to Horsepole I continued to benefit from his naval Connexions, & was aware that in some Circles I had become known as 'the Admiralty Widow', though whether with a desirable Notoriety I was not so sure. In any case, I was a Pluralist in Widowhood, & felt most strongly my most recent Parting, albeit not one over which Death had yet presided. To paint naval Officers was by no means to paint innocent Men, even less, contrite ones, & the Act of painting restord nothing to them of their sense of Sin. I thought of my Peace Offering & financial Passport, the Likeness of the odious Captain Fell, & compard it with Mr. Coleridge's portrait of <u>his</u> sailor in his Ballad, I complicit in the Man's Esteem, he brought fully into the Relation of his Guilt—and with a Bird, at that!

I knew that I had to find a new Way of painting not the flatterd Individual but the arraigned Representative of general human Failing, & not by the old Allegories, either.

But I am stepping ahead in my Story, like a weary Pilgrim who sees interesting Vistas ahead & visits them in Imaginacion before the Track which is to lead to them has been laboriously traversd. In truth, those Years when I met Mr. Thelwall & Mr. Coleridge were more settled for me. I had been one of the first who had worked for the Abolition of the Trade in African Slaves & had learnt through the Frustration of Committees & official Contumely all the Limitations of that worthy Work. It was, however, a renewed Encouragement to myself & to the great Cause to bring Inspiration to the Young, who always have the Readiness to right the Wrongs of this World but are too frequently ignorant of the Ways it may be done, like Gunners in the Heat of Battle, in the Din & the Smoke, free with their Powder, but careless of Aim. Their Sentiments are fiery, but likely to be sufficiently exhausted in the Manufacture of a Greek Ode to Freedom, or distracted by amorous Adventures. In the Soirées of the Merchant Families of Bristol there were Opportunities for the latter in Abundance, even for those young Men whose social Accomplishments did not extend much beyond the former. I doubted that Miss Fricker had been charmed by Greek into turning herself into Mrs. Coleridge, just as I am sure that her Husband must have forgotten his radical Principles when he allowed himself to be accepted into her dull Family.

It was at a Soirée of similar Compromise, not long after I had returnd from Madagascar, that my Life was again changed in a Moment. We are, I have discoverd, unable to predict such Changes, which is perhaps to be expected—but we are also unable to learn anything at all from this Failing. It is one thing to be ready for a likely Disaster, as we might with good Reason have been on that leaky Vessel sailing from the Cape, but Life does not offer us always the precise Warnings of wet Decks or seeping Cabins, nor the happier Omens of our particular good Fortune. We must read the Signs as we can, & we cannot read them soon enough.

You will now discover why I have come to believe in second Chances—those illusory Gifts which the gods promise us if we acknowledge their Power to bestow them, a cruel Trick to keep a Sceptick unhappy, if I ever heard of one—when I tell you that I stepped into a London drawing-Room on a June Evening, expecting as usual to be bored as the Price of an Introduction to a profitable Face, & at once met with my former drawing-Master, Luigi Canistrelli.

All my Indecision of the Past, or rather my wrong Decisions, were upon me in an Instant, like a Blush, since although at first I could hardly believe it was he, & was sure from my Experience of Time's Passage that thirty Years or more must change a Person utterly, he was in despite of Theory the very same, & after ten Minutes of eager Conversing seemed no older than he had at my Grandfather's House in Dublin. A Gentleman in his later Sixties with his own Hair may look very well to a Widow approaching her half-Century, where the very same Man to a Hoyden of fifteen will appear a grave Methuselah, though he be no more than thirty-five. These calculations will be beyond the mental Capacity of Youth, which has a Conception neither of the Persistence of Emotion nor the Brevity of Life. To the Young, all who are not young are as a different Race of Beings, who may once have read of Love in Books, but can have scarcely experienced it.

Now that I was old myself I was readier to understand the Desires of others, to tolerate them, even to share them. And further, to share in even a Lack of true Desire. I remembered the Dream I had of Ramboasalama saying to me, not as a Confession, but as a plain Fact & without Regret, a Description of a State of Affairs belonging to the Category of the Unique, & beyond Defiance or Argument—Truly it is your Wisdom I want, & therefore I take your Body. In the civilised World how many eager Wooers will say such a Thing to their Mistress, pretending to make her a Goddess of Divine Wisdom? And all the same seeing her as no more than the yielding Shape of their Gratification? But for Ramboasalama it was a strange Truth that my Person was for him, in the Oddness of its Lineaments, in its Colour & Boniness, not a customary Object of Desire like the familiar rounded & dusky Matrons of the Merina Court, but the Vessel of my Spirit, so foreign to him &—though I say it—inspiring to his Nature.

From being a Plaything to the miserable Crowther, indeed a Doll to be broke by him at his Pleasure, I had been a respected Object of Curiosity to Horsepole, but at the last something more directly like myself to Ramboasalama, who after all had no means when he found me on his Island of expecting me to be any Thing but what I was, since he had never known One like me. To be allowed to be what One is in this way with a Man is the true married Freedom, & I have feard no Man since.

And yet for the space of an Evening I feard Canistrelli. I feard him for his Knowledge of my native Abilities & for his known Criticism of them; I feard him for his early Authority over me—more than I feard it at the time, for I doubt that I feard it at all then—; I feard him for having refusd him when I was a Child-Woman without his quite knowing that I had refusd him; I feard him for whatever my Grandfather may have said about me to him; I feard him for his Dimple, which was still there in his Cheek when he smiled, as he did often that Evening, like a Man who has found a lost Guinea in an unlikely Place, such as the Buckle of a worn-out Shoe, where it has been all the time & preservd its Value unspent; & I feard him because I did not know if I should ever see him again & did not know how I might make it perfectly plain that I should very much like to do so.

We know that Fear is a necessary Emotion, to preserve us from Danger. How could I have imagind any Danger in Canistrelli? The Danger lay in the Possibility of losing some Thing that I had already through my own Carelessness mislaid for so long.

At Lady Brock's that evening we talkd of Portraits— what else?—out of Deference, perhaps, to my small Fame. Canistrelli, who had now become an Architect, a Designer, a Tutor, a general Master of Works or what-not in the Household of his Countryman the Count Chiavari—and was later invited to oversee the Creation of his new Palazzo—proclaimd that he was tired of

England, where Art was now the Toy of Commerce & in servitude to base mechanical Reproduction.

Can—Why, have you not seen them? They came in while you were enduring your Adventures. Mr. Boulton has ensured that the Painter need go no-where, nor observe any Thing. Give him a printed Canvas, & he may apply his Colours by rote, like a Gardener pricking out a Bed.★

Laet—I have seen them, Sir. They are but a logical Extension of the Furniture Print & stipple Engraving. If your modern Families will have Paintings, they must have paintings they may recognise.

Lady B—Is it not a great debasement of polite Taste?

Revd Slythe—Your Ladyship is correct, of course, but consider—the Volumes in your Ladyship's Library are but Reproductions of an Original, which, were Printing not allowd, we would have to seek out in some gloomy Cloister—

Miss B—Heaven forbid!

Rev^d S—where the Author's Words would be found rapidly fading on wormy Vellum.

Miss B—And why is Printing to be forbidden?

Can—It is the Government's Intention to protect young Ladies from a Tide of Corruption emanating from Novels.

Laet—With the Addition of Stamp Duty on Fans & Powder Puffs—

Can—And of course the publick Execution of the Fortepiano.

Miss B—I see that you are in the Habit of teasing, Sir,

★Matthew Boulton's 'mechanical paintings' were briefly popular in the late 1770s. An aquatint plate was printed on to coated paper which was then applied to the canvas. After the application of vitreous colours by hand, the result was varnished and framed.

& would be obliged to be handed that Dish of Comfits at your Elbow.

Rev^d S—It is all very well, but as a Protestant Nation, Sir, we believe that the Word should be in the Hands of the People, & if the Word, why not the Image also?

Can—I bow to your Religion, & to your Sentiments.

Lord B—All Paintings look the same to me, except those that are different.

Lady B—Edward!

Lord B—I mean, there are different kinds, are there not? Like Dogs?

Laet—Your Lordship speaks a great deal of Truth. Your modern Studio is but a form of Manufactory. I believe that Reynolds presented his Subjects with a Collection of Prints from which they might select a Pose. The curled Poodle? The supplicating Terrier?

Can—But this is in order to concentrate the more properly upon the Face.

Laet—I grant that the Soul is in the Face, but the Character is in the whole Body. Did you not yourself teach me this, Sir? It is but a short Step from the Practices of a Reynolds to the Conveniences of a Boulton.

Can—You are right. The proper Occupation of the Painter is the higher Truth made visible in the Uniqueness of Form. I sometimes think that even Colour diverts the publick Eye from higher Beauties. In our Lifetime, Art has been degraded to a meer sensual Pleasure, an Implement of Luxury, a beautiful but trifling Bauble, of a splendid Fault.

Laet—Rinaldo & Armida upon a Wardrobe!

Can—In sepia Medallions!

Laet—Paradise in a Watch-Case!

Can—And the Inferno upon a Pole-Screen!

Rev^d S—I could wish you to bow to my Religion with more evident Sincerity, Sir.

Miss B—And I could wish you to try one of these delicious Comfits.

The Honourable Miss Brock was to be commended for her Instincts in bringing this Conversation to a Close, since the only Participants in it who knew Anything at all about the subject had not only discovered that they were in complete Agreement but also—as was later confirmed —that they were heartily enamoured of each other.

For a Pair of our Species to have survived in Health & Vigour to our respective Ages at that Time was perhaps a kind of Wonder, Eden in a Watch-Case indeed, where Time itself was suspended, or even wound back upon itself. And it was nothing like January & May, bitter Conflict indeed, but rather November & September, which frequently share an equable & temperate Climate. And from the need of a timid January to tug at the Ribbons of an elusive May-Pole, we had moved to a more confident encircling Dance, where Hands may be directly claspd.

We first embracd in my studio at Greenwich, upon a drapd Sofa, like Actors in a Melodrama, & in my thrilld Expectancy I did not know whether I was embracing a Dimple, or the founding Deity of my Vocation. It was, however, a Surprise to both of us to find ourselves in the attitude of Maid & Swain, & though our Minds were attuned like Instruments in a drawing-Room ready for an Evening of Sonatas, our Bodies creakd a little at the Exercise. Canistrelli had been married, to a daughter of a Cousin of the Earl of Macclesfield, but she had died in Child-Bed twenty Years before, leaving a sickly Child which itself expired soon after. The Marriage was a melancholy Affair, though it repaird Canistrelli's Fortunes & renewd his Determination to develop his architectural Ideas. He had for some Years been associated with his Patron Chiavari—who pursued political Interests in this Country of an inscrutable Complexity—and, as he told me, did not think that he should ever marry again.

I told him that I did not care if we should be wedded or not, but that I would not be parted from him. I had tried Marriages of all Kinds, & no longer believed the State in itself to be sacred, however convenient in the Eyes of the World. Moreover, I was not, at my years, disposed to give up my financial Independence so easily, having only secured it by the Skin of my Teeth & by the continued Labour of my Profession. I was an Academician, & confident of my Ability to obtain Commissions.

Can—We shall do whatever you wish, & we may live here or in Italy, or both, as it suits you. As for the Academy, I do not believe that it can now preserve Painting from the general Decay of Taste.

Laet—Indeed, I have never thought that the Truth was to be found in any Institution, though it helps me to live.

Can—I mean, that in general the Works of Painters now are converted into Fetishes, Commodities, Adornments, Articles of Consumption. It is down to the Privatisation of Human Societies.

Laet—It revolts me.

Can—And Patronage can do no better. It is a Hot-House, & no Substitute for the Lack of Climate or genial Soil. We need a Restoration of the Public, which can alone provide an Occasion for great Works.

Laet—What should I do?

Can—My dear, how can I presume to advise you? It

was in another Age altogether that I taught you most of what I know. Liberty & Commerce have continued to level the Ranks of Society, & more equally diffusd Opulence. Private Importance has been increasd, Family Connxtions & Attachments have been more numerously formd, & thus Portrait-Painting, which formerly was the exclusive Property of Princes or a Tribute to Beauty, Prowess, Genius & distinguishd Character, is now become a kind of Family Calendar, engrossd by the mutual Charities of Parents, Children, Brothers, Nephews, Cousins & Relatives of slight nominal Claims.

Laet—I would I were in Madagascar!

Can—Come to Italy.

Laet—I do believe that in Italy, though they may have more Princes—though not so many as in Madagascar —they still may have as many Merchants. Is not Venice the commercial Capital of the World?

Can—I cannot deny it.

Laet—I think the Answer must be for me to paint not in the World at all, but out of it. I have too often made Idols of Law-Breakers, in any Case, & would rather paint the meanest Slave for no fee if the Truth shone in his Face. Do you believe, my Dearest, that the Particular, whether of the meanest Individual or the most distant Society, strikes us with the Degree of its Truth not in relation to our Expectation of the Typical but in the Element of Surprise, & the Revision of our complacent Ideas?

Can—I can only believe that I see the Truth shine out of your own Face, & that is sufficient for me.

I was in those Years divided in my Aims, though I did not see it clearly. My Head calculated for my Profession, but my Heart felt for the Oppressed. I painted for Money, but not—as in the days of Hayman—with the Pleasure of being recognised, but with the taedium of being for hire. My energy went into Committees & Petitions, & I wept not with a Canvass Niobe but for an actual Zong,★ where Interest both legal & actuarial contrivd to blind the World to murder. I worked tirelessly for the London Abolition Society, which was at last set up in 1787, but could I claim to have worked tirelessly at my Painting? Only when I painted Saka or her Brother Rafani, & recollected in their Features the Tone & Profile of Ramboasalama, did my Hand remember its true Vocation not to move only mechanically across the Canvass, but to link Head & Heart in its Movement.

Rafani was docile but sullen in Temperament, & unlike his Sister made no pretence of accepting his Situation. He allowd Mrs. Howson to teach him the heavier Occupations of the Household, which he performd without Complaint. Some of them indeed, such as raking & filling the Kitchen-Range, he eagerly undertook, for his own greater Comfort, for he sorely felt the Cold, & his Skills in the Kitchen-Garden were rightly praisd, in the digging of Trenches & tying-up of Spanish Onions. But I did not often see him smile.

When Canistrelli came to live at Croom's Hill—as more commodious than his own Apartments in Craven Buildings, Drury Lane—Rafani became resentful, for no Reason that I could see, unless it was that until then he had sufferd no other man in the House. It was not long

---

★The Zong case of 6 March 1783 was a dispute between slave merchants and the insurance company, where the captain had deliberately destroyed the insured goods (i.e. 133 of a cargo of slaves). Chief Justice Mansfield treated the issue entirely within the rules of commercial and property law: 'The case was the same as if horses had been thrown overboard.' See Seymour Drescher, *Capitalism and Antislavery: British Mobilization in Comparative Perspective* (1986), p. 60.

before he was openly surly, & taking to drinking Rum in the Taverns by the River, where according to Saka, who despaird of him, he sought voluptuous Pleasures of the most depravd Kind. Within the Year he disappeard one Day, & was never seen again.

You may imagine the Pain of this Loss, when I had brought him to Safety through such Trials & across so great a Distance. Canistrelli made many Enquiries, at some Risque to his own Safety, but could get no Information. Whether Rafani fell into Debt or a Quarrel, & met with Violence, or whether he ran away, or was taken for a Slave, I do not know. Mrs. Howson had insisted that the two of them be baptised, which was Protection of a kind, but not a Protection that I would trust. All I had left of him was his Portrait, which I took to the Academy, but it was rejected as being unfinishd. Unfinishd! I told Mr. West himself, with a great Deal of Pleasantness—though I was minded to throw his Ink-Pots about the Room—that Life itself was unfinishd & was not Art to be true to Life? I told him that the Persians leave the Design of their Carpets open at one Corner for this Reason, that the Spirit may be free. But Mr. West lookd about him uneasily, as if he wishd himself to be free of me, and said meerly, Oh, is that the reason? suggesting that he knew better. But Mr. West did not know better, & did not even know well. He was no wiser than those Divines & Magistrates who believe that Negroes may be taken for Slaves because they are Infidels, & that a Length of Parchment may be deemed finishd because it has a Crust of Wax upon it—out of which no Human Spirit may escape.

I told my Husband that he was right, & that the Admiralty Widow, being no longer a Widow, would henceforth cease to furnish Rooms with complacent Faces, for these Faces were Parchment Faces, & had made Pacts with the Law to be enslavd by it, & to become Rich, whereas I wishd only to paint Freedom & the ways of Escape. Canistrelli could not think me utterly mad to devote myself to this Wish, since he had encouragd it, but I believe that he never fully understood it as I know you will understand it, Percy. His Mind was on his Happiness, & on his Palazzo, & I do not think it could tolerate for long an uncomfortable Idea like the Unknown.

How to paint an Idea? I had had enough of the large Scenes of enacted Policy, Allegories of moral Enlightenment and crucial Choices, privileged Moments of History, & significant Personages meeting the Goddesses of their achievd Vocations. And yet I could not keep the Interests of my Life distinct from each other, as it were in stopperd Jars upon a Toilette, to be opened & applied as the Fancy dictated. Why should my Art not serve the Cause of Freedom? And why should a Marriage not—if it be not evidently for the purpose of Procreation—exist for the Service of Art? And why should a Marriage itself not be free, rather than yet another length of waxed Parchment? You, Percy, have your own Ideas upon these Subjects, which come as naturally as Leaves on a Tree. Your Season is the assured Summer of a natural Vision. Mine was a hard Seed-Time, & a stony Soil.

But in each of these stopperd vials, Art, Freedom, Marriage, & in several more, I had accumulated my own Store of Experience, & already the admixturing had begun, like a chymical Experiment fortuitously conducted. I had attached myself by Chance of Nature to three Representatives of purely masculine Exploit, a Rake, an Officer, & a Prince—and yet movd in Circles of

Protest where historical Action might itself be possible. I had painted imagind Heros. I had painted real Slaves. With the sympathetick Assistance of Canistrelli, why should I not paint the Truth of that World which exists in our Imaginaciouns for the very Purpose of being made real? Not therefore a Tableau of Manumission, but the Light in Rafani's yearning Eye, which is the Angel of Freedom? Not the Deed of Marriage, but the Angel of Love? Not the long Chronicle of Bloodshed, but the Angel of Brotherhood?

I did not believe that these Angels should be like Smagg's Angels, the Familiars of Enthusiasts, the paltry Radiances of County Town East-Windows. They must remain invisible, & unrepresented, but palpable, like that Axis of Emotion—describd to me Years ago by my dear Canistrelli—that exists between the Vision of the Painter & the Response of his Subject, & which must come alive again in the willing Participations of the Onlooker. This is a Pact every bit as difficult to contrive as a Committee for Peace after a long War, & it may be a Delusion after all, like any human Motion to transcend the Law by a Recognition of Love, to restore the Turbulence of cities to the Peace of Arcadia, or to find our First World in the poor broken Pieces which the Million have made of it.

—Why did you think, he once asked me, when Mrs. Howson had cleard the Supper-Tray & we were seated by the Firelight,—that you could portray Madagascar itself in the Figure of that Bird? Were you not in Danger of resorting to an Emblem, perhaps, something fitter for a Coin or a Flag?

At that Time I could not clearly answer the Question. I had the Notion that once believing my Father to have been transported by the Bird I could fancy flying away with it myself. Madagascar had replaced the Vision of Light, which had been my painterly Ambition, with the Vision of Colour, as a Pilgrim might take Rest & discover in the created Landscape through which he must travel a better Image, after all, of the Godhead he seeks. Now that I had returned to the familiar World, desolate in its Greed & Criminality, from what had seemd in its Plenitude to be a kind of Eden, I was less sure. The Bird itself, in existing, became a lesser Thing than itself unseen, like the grey Relicts of Ashmole's Dodo at Oxford, meer Evidence to be exhibited. Even before I had left on my quest, with Saka & Rafani, the King had given orders for Crindo's Egg to be mounted in silver. I had no doubt that it might become his Pleasure to bore a Hole in it and fill drinking-Vessels from it at Entertainments, & that it might keep his whole Court deep in Rum, being of the Capacity of—in my confident Estimation—at least thirteen quart Wine-Bottles. In such Ways is a Creature of Legend & Destiny reducd to an Item of Table-Furniture! I knew that the dusky Nobles of my African Eden would have delighted in Corkscrews & Engines for Decanters, if they had had them, & indeed, if they had had Need of Money & the Means of coining it, they would have stamped the Bird upon it, & paid their Debts in so many Vorombes. In many Things, my Eden was no more than an unfamiliar Corner of a World I knew well, with Versions of all our Customs & Institutions—though I was confident that my own Prince-of-Wales was far above Dalliance with the many Mrs. Fitz-Herberts of the Merina Court.

No, the Roc was not the Vorombe of the Merina, nor even the Rukh of the Thousand & One Nights, but it was the Angel of my Fulfilment, ever at the Distance of my Vision, & of a Size only in my Dreams.

5

Definimus nam posse Senes, cùm scire periti
Incipimus.*

I have returnd to my Portrait, Percy, as if I feel now with
an unaccustomd Urgency that there may, after all, be too
little Time left to finish it. The Portrait of the Gallery, I
mean, which stares at me with a kind of amused Defiance
whenever I return to it. The Portrait of the Terrace,
which you urged me to write, is a different Matter. I have
done what I can with it, but I see that it is but the
roughest sketch, with sharp Dents & Corners where the
Charcoal has broke in the Speed & Carelessness of
Delineation. I will finish it after my Fashion, for one
Thing I have discoverd about Writing is that everything
may be included, or seem to be included, in a single
Phrase. A Sentence is framed for its Expediency of one
Thing coming after another, without—if needs be—any
Elaboration whatever, as to say with Caesar, I came, I
saw, I conquered. The temporal Consequence is all, & the
sore Place on Caesar's mouth on a particular Wednesday,
when his Cook burned the Leeks & left Scorch-Marks at
the side of his Tent may never be known about at all,

---

*'Our Strength fails us in our old Age, when we begin to know somewhat', Du
Fresnoy, p.497.

though it be visible—and they be visible—to any who were close to him on that Day. There are Painters who would wish to record not the suspended Stillness of a Moment, but the whole History of a Body. In their different Ways, both of my Portraits must therefore be generalised, but in the Gallery I dare guess that you will be closer to a Soul than on the terrace, for there I may make a more confident Decision to omit—so to speak—the sore Places and Scorch-Marks of my History. And yet I am not sure that I have made conscious Decisions in these, or in any Matters, but have drifted where I would upon the Lineaments of my Life like a Vagabond collecting Driftwood upon a Beach, who takes no Account of Voyages & Wrecks beyond what accidentally survives of them.

And what if I finish neither? Finishing is after all an Idea of the fallen World, rooted in Time, whereas you know that I now conceive of a Truth beyond Time—as you might pick up a veined Stone from a Beach in the timeless Afternoon without thinking, when the Tide is full & the hours run neither forward nor back. That Stone is full, too, of all that there is. You may look at it, as I do now, adding it to the frailer Trophys of dried Herbs on my Table, & think that there is no Thing further to be said. And with all these material Objects of the World it is so. They come into their very Existence in the looking, which is why I have my near-sighted Glass hanging to my neck for the Purpose. Think of the Years when I did not look upon my Luigi, nor perhaps so often thought of him. Think of the Years since his Death, when no-one at all could look upon him, whether they would or no. What does this signify? I have lovd him in the Fullness of his Being, at Moments when the Hours ran neither forward nor back. For him, all is finishd, but not for me. When I shall decide to set a Finis to this Account, Percy, nothing will be truly finishd, though I were to die in the following Minute. On the Terrace, all goes on. In the Gallery, the Exhibit itself is suspended. The Portrait is in the continual State of becoming itself.

I am reminded here of some Thing that Northcote said about Reynolds, that there is scarcely a Picture that he painted that was not better at some Stage during its Progress, than when he left off. Is this not a salutary Reminder of what is so often true of Life itself? We struggle to complete ourselves & to outdo our earliest Achievements, when what we should rather realise is the essential Imperfectibility of our Attempts. All that we perform is only what it is—like the Stone—& it were futile to attempt to improve upon it.

So, why do I return to the Gallery? I lift the Brush, tippd with a Pigment ready to absorb the Light that it does not wish to reflect, angled for a Thrust like that of an opportunistick Infantryman forcd to a fatal Charge in a Battle he knows must be lost, & I apply it to the Surface that my Judgement has told me requires it. The Illusion is improvd, is it not? Or is it a secondary Illusion that this is so?

And what happens when I return to the Terrace?—I am there at this Moment—What shall I add? I could dab the improving Brush in a score of Places, say the sudden Death of Mrs. Howson & my Shame at not relieving her Suffering with sufficient Expediency; say my Delineation of the Female Parts, a Thing scarcely to my Knowledge ever accomplishd in Art & first done by me in the year 1757 with the Aid of a looking-Glass set before my spread Legs in Jermyn Street; say the Trouble of Saka being with

Child & refusing to name the Father; say my Hatred of the ingratiating Mrs. Angelica* & Shame at that Hatred for knowing it to be partly inspird by Jealousy of her as a successful Woman—which is the Reason why there is no Thing about her in these Memoirs; say the intermittent Attempts to communicate with Ramboasalama, not least in the Matter of profitable Trade in manufacturd Cloth —of which there is more to be written; say my Relationship with Mary Watkins, which did not last beyond my Dublin Days, but which is still rememberd; say the Trouble with my left Leg, with the calcified Growth upon the Bone where it was broken, the Shame at its Appearance & Pain from walking; say, as I say, a Score or more Points of substantive Interest, & perhaps not all of them shameful. There are Incidents, Habits & Practices which you might be fascinated to read of, Percy, but which I have not written down, nor will, now. Unless Life could be readily summond up as a complete Thing, as it is said of a drowning Man, the whole Life appearing in an Instant before his Eyes, then of Necessity what we choose to remember is but a Selection of prejudiced Details.

All Death is a kind of Drowning, as I know who have seen some Deaths in my time, when the Struggle for the Breath of Life is of no Avail & the Air is hostile, breeding like Water in the Lungs. That is the Breath I fear, the one that would have come after the last we take, but which for the Weakness of our Motions never comes. I fear it as a Judgement upon the Profligacy of our Breathing when we are well, for what might we not accomplish in the few Seconds of renewd Life that it would bring us? What new

---

*Angelica Kauffmann.

Thought might not occur to us in the Space of that precious Breath that we never entertaind in all our wasted Hours? What hoarded Word might we not send out in its Exhalation, that we barely knew we had in us to say, or had never dared to say, before? That Word might be the Recognition of God for all I know, that we put from us in our Days of easy Breathing, or the Delivery of some Secret that would bring Peace to the Teller or the Told. I thought this when my dear Luigi fell from the Scaffolding in the grand Saloon of the Palazzo, & in his Seizure could say no Thing but the great Moaning that came from his rigid Lips. He never spoke a Thing more in his Life, who had a moment before been speaking at Length & with Irritation about the Quality of the Mouldings on the Ceiling. I pass beneath those Mouldings every other Day of my Life, but I cannot think them in their Splendour equal to half a dozen Words from my stricken Husband, were they meerly, I pray you undo this Button. And really, the great Stage of our Lives is all of it so much pressd Plaster giving itself Airs, & all the Sequins ever received for his Design of the Palazzo was so much Ore digged out of the Earth & itself put into curious Shapes to allow us our Self-Importance. I dare say that he would have given them all back to Chiavari in exchange for his Faculty of Speech. Nay, Percy, how many of them do you think he would have parted with in exchange for another Day, another Hour of Life at the Moment of Death? That next Breath that you cannot take, Percy, what would it be worth to you?

The Mouldings are of a Silenus, grinning in flowers, & I hate them.

Where am I, Percy, with my History? I thank God I must only write it once, for in one Sett of prejudiced

Details before Breakfast may be read a very different Spirit from another Sett of prejudiced Details after Dinner. And in certain Moods you might have had much Material that I have scarcely dared to touch upon here. What? you will say. Have you met again the drawing-Master of your Childhood, the wise Mentor whom you have never ceasd to love, only to turn the Page and send him to his Death upon a marble Floor in a Country I did not think you had yet visited? You have disposd of all your Husbands with a Suddenness that begins to look like Ill-Will. You are as careless with them as some Women are with their Handkerchiefs.

But, Percy, if I pass lightly over a Liaison of a dozen Years so lightly, it is because I am freighted with a ballancing Pain of Loss, & our Life together, being happy, contained few Incidents to distinguish one Hour of Content from the next. Be assured that I lovd him. It is as though when I view the Events of my Life I lift the Eyeglass & find myself looking through the wrong End. I see not the Days but the Years, not the Catch spilling out of the Net but the Boat only, tinier than ever & at the Mercy of the gathering Clouds on the Horizon. It is as though Life became a Game playd upon a Table by a Child, & the Boat must sink because it is in her Fingers & herself the Squall which humms & whistles between her Milk-Teeth as it advances. From such a Familiarity with Chance comes a Belief in the Gods & the Reckonings they are pleasd to draw up, like Innkeepers.

God—Now then my Lady, if I may just check these Details. Above two thousand two hundred Dinners with mutual & entertaining Conversation?

Laet—I suppose so.

God—The Readiness of Lips & Fingers, at any Time,

169

would you say, for the taking? So many cubic Yards of Skin?

Laet—Yes.

God—An agreeable View? An accommodating Set of Opinions?

Laet—Yes, yes.

God—Well over three hundred—but let us settle for three hundred—Friday Evenings, with free Bottles for the rubbing? And the Genies freely arriving?

Laet—Not always.

God—(Noting down) Not—always—Genies. You should have said. But Beauty of Form? And Reciprocation of Feeling? I thought so. We do try to please. It will not take me a Moment to add all this up, my Lady, if you will be patient. Let me see—that will be—

Laet—Yes, yes?

God—Death. That comes to precisely Death, my Lady. In round Figures.

Laet—But what about all the missing Years?

God—The missing Years? They are not down here, my Lady. There is no charge. Nor for your own wasted Moments, neither. I never take unfair Advantage, is what I always say. But for what you've had the use of, of course, that's different. Death it is. But I tell you what I'll do. I will accept a promissory Note dated the first of next Month. There you are. I can't be fairer than that.

In that Month following his Fall from the Scaffolding, Luigi could give no Account of himself or of his Ideas or Feelings more than could a new-born Child. The Count had him attended Night & Day with his every Need satisfied, except the Need to move and to speak, which left him in a Desperation of frustrated Desire. He lay like a Figure of himself on his own Monument, like Marble struggling to breathe, & when I dismissed the Count's Servants & washed him myself, his Limbs were clenched & his Fingers curld like a victim of Enchantment in a Fable where Trees are Men for their natural Failings, & must be releasd by the Hero. But in his Case there was no Hero to come, nor, as I dared to think, any God neither, and so he died.

He did not know, when he brought me to this glittering Coast to see his great Work, that it was to see his Life at an End, & the Palazzo his Mausolæum. Neither did I myself know at that Time that I would never see England again, nor keep my Name alive there by my Work. When my Portrait of Bonaparte was refusd, I decided never again to send my Canvasses to the Academy. My Letter to West, explaining that the Truth of Painting must be above the trivial Issues of Politicks, I tore up on reflecting that his Understanding was limited & his Prejudices not to be dislodged by Reason. The Greatness of a Painting is not to be decided by the Whims of a Committee nor even by the Readiness of a Publick to pay the Price of Admission to it, for what is a Committee in any case but the convenient Representation of the commonest Elements of Publick Taste? The Painter must explore new Territories, & report his Conquests faithfully. His Canvasses are the Flags of his own Empire, which owes no Allegiance to any temporal Power.

In any Case, his Models are already in Nature, & should have nothing to do with human Arrogance, for Flowers are the Flags of the Fields they grow in, which therefore march only under those Banners. This very Terrace is under the Rule of the Orange Lily, & I am a sort of

Viceroy to the living Power of the Earth that was here before the first Stones of the Palazzo Chiavari were laid.

The Count was more like a Brother to my Husband than a Patron, & when he died treated me more like a Relative than a Dependant. He had seemed more amused by the planning of his little Kingdom than eager to see it achieved, & was in the Habit of changing his Mind about some central Feature precisely at that Moment when all was ready to go ahead in putting it into Effect, & then, far from regretting the consequent Delay, would be all the happier for the fresh Opportunity of drawing up a Schedule, or emending a Plan.

It was this very Uncertainty of Outcome that had led to my going out to Genoa in the first Place, for the Work could neither be settled nor delegated, & Luigi was a Slave to an Agreement which his Patron's vacillating Taste seemed likely never to bring to a Conclusion. The central Parts of the Palazzo were eventually completed in 1803 but the Wings remaind a Subject of Debate, the Designs advanced each Spring, but revised each Summer as the great Heat & consequent Torpor descended on this amiable Region. The Count was as great a Master of Delay as was the Queen of Ithaca in her Day, though his Motives—so far as I could discern any Motive at all—not the same. My best Guess at the Reason for his Uncertainty was that when all was finishd, his Master of Works departed, & the hammering & whistling stopped, he knew that he would find himself quite as lonely as he was before, & quite possibly much lonelier.

The Count was a proud & private Man, & like enough in some Particulars to Canistrelli, who was, after all, his Countryman. Their being in the same Room together brought out the Similarities & Differences in each. Both were dark of Complexion & aquiline of Feature, but the fetching Dimple of Amusement in Canistrelli showd in the Count as a grave Furrow that gave his Mouth the Air of a perpetual Suspicion of what he saw & the Readiness to pronounce in Judgement upon it. In Canistrelli the eye might twinkle—in the Count it had a Tendency to look abstracted. Both possessed a fine Brow. In Canistrelli it was lower, indicating Gravity & Power of Concentration —in the Count is was accompanied by Eye-Brows tufted & unbrushd to a Degree that they seemed more vertical than horizontal, & made him seem always surprised to see you. I have seen Clowns in the Commedia with Features like his, who sufferd Outrages with sad Patience.

I thought both of them handsome Men of their kind, & to be in a Room with them, playing at Cards, without other female Company, was a Novelty to me that conveyd a polite Excitement of animal Attraction. As a Guest at the Palazzo, and of uncertain Status, with little Recourse to my private Affairs & no Direction of the Servants, I felt myself to be continually exposd & perhaps under Scrutiny. It was natural for the Count to behave as though he had in Reserve some kind of Claim upon me, & though I had met before with such Presumptions among the higher Classes of Society, I had never before had any pressing Reason to be much obligated to them. We were given the Villa, where the changing Moods of the Sea, & the relative Seclusion, were congenial to me. The whole Extent of this wild Shore, & the Emptiness of the Horizon, had an Effect on me as of the Melancholy that urges a Departure when none may be made. The Sea ever sounds like a casting off for a Voyage that must be postponed, inducing an inappeasable Restlessness.

Here I thought more than ever of my red Island, & of my faild Attempts to establish Contact for the Purpose of importing Cloth. Whetton had correctly prophesied before he died the Difficultys to be encountered by the House of Crowther in the Competition with Manufactory & the new Machines which powerd its Production. Cottons of cheap Design rowled from the Mills of Cheshire & Lancashire to the Degree that—said Whetton, gazing in his great Ledger like a Jeremiah—we would be at great Pains to shift our Imports at any Price, let alone a Price at which we could maintain our Profit. When Benyowsky's ugly & opportunist Account of his Exploits in Madagascar was publishd,★ I thought that beautiful Country must be in as great a State of perpetual Warfare as it had ever been in the Years that I was there, & put from my mind the Idea of any free & mutually beneficial Trade with the Merina. The French, who had long been our Enemy, clearly sought to take the Island. Though they could not easily do so without great Cruelty & Bloodshed, it would not be a Place in which I could lightly—or for any Reason of Sentiment or old Affection—send the Crowther Fleet, which was now in any case diminished. Whetton had taken what he wanted from the Establishment, & had regularly maintained my own Annuity, about which I took little Interest beyond the spending of it, so that without the necessary Re-investment, the Trade had fallen off.

Within the Sound of that Sea which tirelessly attends the Rocks & stony Inlets even now with its breaking Tide, like the laving & intoning of some Priest of antient Ritual, I had at that Time a strong Dream of Ramboasalama.

★*Memoirs and Travels of Mauritius, Augustus Count de Benyowsky,* 2 vols (1790).

He appeard in the Count's Apartments at the Palazzo, not in his usual Cloak & Lamba, but in European Dress, a blue frogged Coat, white Breeches & high Kid Boots, his ruffld Shirt closed with a starchd Cravat, & his Hair powderd. There was Company, such as I had never seen there, attentive at his Presence & expectant of some Speech or Performance. I was nervous of what he might say or do, and feard that he might be laughed at as a bizarre Impostor of our Customs & Manners. But Ramboasalama walked quietly to the Fortepiano in the Centre of the Room, & seating himself at it, & taking his Leisure, he proceeded to perform a little Bagatelle of Herr Haydn, a Piece of great Charm & some technical Difficulty. I knew the Musick to be Haydn, but in fact in the Dream it was a Melody that I had well remembered Ramboasalama to play on his little Sody at Times of Contemplacioun, the Melody that seemed to have no Resolution or resting-Place, but in its continuing Sadness to encompass the Totality of Creation, & to give back its Image to the Understanding. I woke to the Lapping of the Sea, & to my own Sobbing, which I thought might go on for ever since there was nothing to explain to me why it should not.

The Count was, as I say, a Solitary. I could not conceive the Purpose of the great publick Rooms of the Palazzo, the Ballroom with its Side-Arcades, the Vestibule of Reception from which ascended the great double Staircase, the Grand Saloon, the Gallery & the two smaller Saloons above, the Pavilion, the Water Garden, & what-not, since I could not imagine any of the publick Occasions that might take place there or that the Count might take Pleasure in. He had no Family, & no Heirs that I could discover, for his Brothers were in the Church

& his only Aunt without Issue. He rarely attended the Receptions of his Neighbours & was disinclined to fetch out his Carriage for a Distance of less than twenty Miles. He had been at Court for Politeness only, & at official Functions solely when Government Affairs required it. In England I was told with Certainty that he was a Spy. In Italy he was rumourd a Libertine.

Certainly he was a man of wayward Taste & a Patron of difficult Temperament. Luigi would say to me, in Despair sometimes, but as a Jest, that he sometimes believed that he would be long dead before the Palazzo could be finishd, & that the Count, though younger than himself, had better think now of designing his own Tomb concurrent with the Palazzo, or there would be no time to do it. We would all be dead, he said, and the Works unfinishd, left standing like designd Ruins for the World to marvel at.

True enough in his Case, & though now a complete Dado of achievd Nymphs flee from Silenus beneath the Ceiling, I ever consider it a kind of Ruin. And whether it is to the Credit of the Count's Forethought or to his gloomy Vanity I cannot rightly say, but he indeed ordered his Tomb to be builded here in the Chapel & he paid Canova 500 Sequins for a pair of Angels like amorous Doves to lift him half up to Heaven in his marble Draperies. Now is the Tomb full, & the Grand Saloon empty still.

You may wonder what was my Opinion of Canova, whose present Fame has made of him the most expensive Sculptor in the World. He is a wondrous sour & clever Man, with the greatest Confidence in the classical Ideal that I ever came across, but I thought our Nollekens had more of the matter in him. Canova has a faultless

technique, which I cannot help but admire in any A
When the Tomb was deliverd to the Palazzo, &
Placing to be supervisd by him, he was calld twice to
Dinner but did not come, & was found attending to the
Finger-Nails of the lower Angel that clutchd the greater
Weight of Drapery. These fine Details are a second
Nature to him, though the Ideal has blinded him to the
commonest Level of Observation, for the Marble Count
is carried in his Bed-Sheets like an Odalisque upon an
Ottoman, with crossd Ancles & hanging Wrists, whereas
in Nature he would sagg like a Side of Beef. Carracci
could have taught him the real Appearance of such
angelick Haulage—or the Airing of the bundled Corpses
from the Merina Tombs, for the matter of that—but
Canova had made no such Study. His Beauties are
without Blemish, & attended by the most scrupulous
Manicurist.

The Fashion in Italy is still Greek, & of heroick
Proportions. In England, Luigi might have dressd his
Designs for the Palazzo in both Classick & Gothick Style,
& his Patron be likely to choose the Gothick, as suiting a
modern Country Life of pious Rectitude distinct from the
Epicureanism of the former Age. The Count made no
such Withdrawal from the Light of his Climate, but
admitted the Sun into his Chambers & decorated them
with the antient tutelary Deities of Mediterranean Belief.
This was purely unthinking Habit, for the Man was rather
made for the Contemplation of a Cloister than the
Conversation of a banqueting-Couch. His Brother the
Cardinal was twice as worldly a Man as he.

The Count's one Indulgence in the Architecture of
private Philosophy was neither classical nor Gothick, but
oriental, for he had erected at the End of an Avenue of

Cypress a kind of Pagoda in white Marble, its Tiers of decreasing Size markd with Pillars & scrolld Decoration, & surmounted by a Cupola in the Shape of an inverted Lily. Although from a Distance these Tiers appeard distinct, the Inside of the Pagoda was a continuous inclind Plane whereby the solitary Visitor might ascend at a steady Pace without knowing himself at any particular Level, until he had reachd the Top. It was the Count's Place of Contemplation, as he said, a Wedding of Greece & China, from whose Pinnacle the distant Perspective put his Mind to its largest Thoughts, not limited by Doctrine or Tradition. For myself, whenever I climb up there I feel giddy, & must straightway come down. If I do sit for a Moment on the little stone Chair, more like a sacrificial Altar than a Surface of Comfort, all I can think about is my own Mortality, or perhaps my Dinner, for it is the Place on the Estate furthest from all that is familiar or sustaining to Life.

Now that I possess this Sense of having lived for ever, which is to say, of having outlasted every One else, perhaps I should climb up there once more to be properly philosophical, or to communicate with my Maker, for He may as well be there as in the Scents of the Chapel or the Echoes of the Duomo, where I have never yet found Him. But it is now too steep for my Legs. And I dare to say that I do not need to be up there in Trances to feel removed from the World, since what is the World but all those who are familiar to me & whom I have loved, & this living for ever is seeing them all die? In my Heart the World is therefore dead to me, & there are Times when I catch myself unable to distinguish between the Tomb of Canistrelli & the Tomb of Chiavari, since both are Images of the deadest Part of this dead World to me, though one is stone Flowers falling from a stone Slab & the other the triumphant Booty of Angels.

Although, as you have come to learn, the State of Widowhood was not unknown to me, & had come almost to seem more natural to me than the being married, I was now not meerly once more a Widow, but I was perhaps for the first Time a decidedly old Widow, somewhat in the Appearance of the Widow of Nursery-Tales with her Cat & Simples. My Limp, which when I was young & in the Vigour of my blood, I might use to assist my Comportment with a kind of Swagger, was on occasion reduced to a Hobble, & I had had some Teeth pulled.

But it was only when I took the Effort to think of myself as I appeard to others that I was at all aware of myself in such a Role. Within, I felt much as I did when I was out riding in the Park & would meet with Cronies of Crowther's who would take off their Hats & make insinuating Compliments, or when I was grappled & nearly boarded by Rear-Admiral Portland & for Protection painted him in earnest with a Stroke of Yellow Ochre across his Cheek, or when I would feel that fat Forefinger of the King of the Merina assume the Licence to touch me in Places that I reservd for his second Son. To be still a Woman, but to look meerly like an old Woman, is eventually the greatest Burden of our Sex, for though many may pretend that it is a Relief to receive no longer those Attentions which so define our Difference from Men, most I believe cannot understand that they will be forthcoming no longer, & continue to expect them, & so simper unnaturally beneath their powderd Wrinkles & flirt into Senility. I had observd such Attitudes in my Seniors when I was young, & now had come to understand them better.

What was to become of me? We had stayed so long in Italy that I had come to expect that we would never return to England & that I would now end my Days on foreign Soil, which after all was not foreign to Luigi & might the more naturally offer him further Employment when the long-enduring Birth-Pangs of the Palazzo Chiavari were finally ended. I was disinclined to return alone to England, to prevail upon Robert to again turn out the Lessee of Croom's Hill, or to impose myself as a retired Person, almost a piece of Furniture, to be taken in by my Bristol Relatives out of Charity. Besides, the Wars forbade it. If my Aunt Kate had been still alive I had been tempted to stow a Passage in the Invasion from Brest,* and revisit the Dublin of my Childhood to commune with the Shade of my dear Grandfather, but I knew that I should find nothing of mine there. He was no Anchises, & I now no Hero with a Mission to be determind by consultation with the occult Powers.

However, in all my Grief & Uncertainty about my Future, I was given the free & unstinting Support of the Count, who treated me not as an embarrassing Relict of a deceasd Employee, of whom he now wishd to be rid, with perhaps a grudging Pension, but as a Friend whose Loss he freely shared & who would, if she allowd it, perhaps in time feel the Benefit of what small Comfort he could offer her. His Attentions could not have been more considerate if he & Luigi had been Brothers, & once the Obsequies were over we sat down to Cards together as if our Lives were to go on exactly as before.

It took me some time to discover that this was not an Act of Christian Kindliness only, or of Obligation, but

---

*Such an invasion was mounted by the French in 1798.

that he really admird me. For myself, I so much took my Painting as a Matter of Course, & in Italy above all as a private Occupation, and not so frequently engagd in, after all, that I did not view it quite as the Count did, which was, I believe, as an Ornament to his Estate, & Evidence of his Taste & Magnanimity. He might, I thought, be happy to mention it carelessly in Company, as he might boast of some Breed of racing-Horses or a well-run Vineyard, saying to his Brother the Cardinal as he crumbled some Bread into his Soup,

—You should see my Yellow Saloon now that the Decorations are completed. There is nowhere in Europe where you may see in one place all the Flora & Fauna of Madagascar, life-size & in their very Colours.

The Thing would soon be known well enough, but as a Mystery, & he need not be put to the Trouble of sending Invitations.

I know that it is said that Men are drawn to Women as Moths to Candle-Flames, & when I have sate long on the Terrace I have seen them sputtering in their Wax, or walking up & down the Candle in the Terrour of their fatal Desire. From my own Experience of being driven to my own Errands, I might think this to be generally true of both Sexes, & there is in this Compulsion of Opposites a like Recklessness, for though the Aim may be a divine Union, the Result is a kind of bodily Death. And what is the Likelihood of Union, after all, in things so dissimilar?

And if a Man die upon a Woman, he may thereafter vow to attend her for Eternity, or at least until her natural Term, which were Dame Nature's Reckoning for the Settlement of the Errand. But if a Man die upon a Man, or a Woman upon a Woman for the Matter of that, I cannot see where is the Flame, or the Terrour, & Eternity has closed her ever-watchful Eye upon such a Relationship.

It may be a Wonder to you, Percy, that I should have been inducd to marry the Count, as though for a Moment I could have believd that I had anything of the Flame about me. But I do not flatter myself that this was his Motive, even though mine may well have been the Inclination thereby to retain my Standing in the Annals of animal Experience, like an Actor who has livd only for the Stage who will take any Part be it never so small or ridiculous compard with his passed Glories, & enter a Fig-Seller when his Voice is too crackd for an Antony.

I knew from some Incidents about the Palazzo, & from common Rumour about the Count, that he was in the Habit of abusing his Servants & other your Persons from the Villages. He was discreet enough in these Activities while Luigi was alive, & perhaps ashamd to let them be suspected by another Man who would think ill of them, but something in the Nature of these Activities in themselves seemd to compel him to reveal them to me in a Manner designd to be accidental, so that if needs be I might consent to ignore them.

You will not, I trust, think ill of me, Percy, when you discover that I by no means ignored them. Your Friend the lame Lord once said to me that a Woman was by Design ill-fitted to be a General in the Field of Love, & that her Conquests were better achievd in the Surrender than the full Charge. My reply, which brought him closer to a Blush than I had ever seen the brazen Fellow come, was that a Woman was frequently put to it to work secretly in the Field, and moreover in advance, like a Sapper, so that the Weapon might discharge to the greatest Effect. And so I believe it, but do not yourself be shockd by this Story, for I am myself no Libertine.

The Count's Manner of revealing these Performances to me was, to be sure, an Invitation to me to share in them, for I had at his Insistence movd my private Apartments from the Villa to the Palazzo, for the Ease of Working at the Frescos—which indeed I liked to do at first Light—& my Bedroom was not twenty Paces from a Room that the Count began to use soon after my Arrival, though I was not to know then that it had not always been his dressing-Room. How petty are the Stratagems of Desire! And how devious the human Mind, that can pay attention to a Dish of butterd Artichokes or a Trick at Cards, while planning a quite different Entertainment for the Hours of Darkness! And why indeed should he think that I might share them, or that any Woman would? He later let it be known that from certain Freedoms in my Conversation, unknown among Italian Women, whose Delicacy of Appetite confines them to little Talking & little Cakes, he bclievd me to be a Free-Thinker in Venereal Devotions, as perhaps all Englishwomen were, a Race natural to produce Governesses, Châtelaines, Keepers of Houses of Correction, and what not else. For myself, as I say, I had no inclination to put on my Widow's Capp for good, & relinquish those tender Sports which a lively Husband can provide. Besides this, I was curious as to the private Life of the Count, whose publick Character I had not fathomd, nor perhaps ever fully did.

But there are no ready Explanations of those strange Incidents & Passages of our Lives where we find ourselves acting upon our Instincts. Mr. Coleridge would say that the Effects are what in former Ages & in primitive societys would have been thought of as Witchcraft, but now we may understand as his Science of Psycho-Somatology, or the strange Influence of the Mind upon Bodily Events.

My first Entry into the Count's private World, as if by a strange Compulsion not manifest to Reason, was on a Night when I was awakend by a strange Knocking from a neighbour Room, as of some Creature that ran about & heeded not the Furnishings. I raisd myself on one Elbow & listend. I heard dimly the Voice of the Count, which seemd to reprehend this Creature, but mildly, & then perhaps to encourage it, as though it were—as I first conceivd it, thinking of no other possible Explanation—a Bat that had flown into the Room in Error, which would not go towards the Window opend for it, but persisted in fluttering above some tall Cupboard, & would not listen to the friendly Voice of human Reason, nor could be chastened like a Dog to any Profit.

I came to the Count's Door—which had been left ajar—& gave a slight Knock before entering, for though there was a Candle burning in the Room & the Count making no Concealment of being heard, the Hour was late & the Privacy of Retirement to be respected. There was no Bat, but a Scene of human Activity; no cajoling down from a Cupboard, but the Urgency of Instruction & the Moans of Desire.

The Actors in this Night-Scene were a Footman I recognisd, calld Paolo, & a Girl I did not, who lay upon the Bed beside the Count in a silent Fright, while he, with the Assistance of Paolo, made an attempt upon her which I could see at once—since they were all three of them stark naked—would get nowhere. I was minded of nothing so much as the famous Sculpture of the Priest Laocoön and his two sons wrestling with the Serpent, an heroick Incident of sublime Suffering turnd, as so often, into the Artist's Excuse for admiring the Musculature of the human Body. Here was not much heroick

Musculature, but the robust Flesh of indoor Servants with the heavy Peasant Frame of the Tuscan Country-Side juxtaposed with the Pallor & Plumpness of the Count & with the Hairiness of Arms, Chest and Shoulders which classical Antiquity had no means of representing in their Statuary. And here was no Serpent, either, though what in their Despair they wrestled with was like enough to it in its way, & its Owner would have wishd it a Dart or a Javelin instead.

Paolo was startled to see me come in, & seemd torn between conflicting Emotions, that I might effect a Rescue of himself & his Sister—as I later discoverd it was—which gave him Hope; and that I might incur his Master's Displeasure thereby, which increasd his Fear. But as I quickly perceivd—putting down my Candle on a Chest at the Foot of the Bed—the best Course to secure the Peace of all Parties was to bring Matters to a Head & thus to a Conclusion. It is true of Venery as it is of Politicks, that more are harmd by those that seek Power than by those who have gaind it. In War, the besieged City suffers the longer she resists, & it is only when she yields that the disturbd Inhabitants may again go about their Business.

Yet in the convenient Contract of Psycho-Somatology there are Clauses which allow our every mortal Action a moral Excuse. In helping the Count to the Accomplishment of his Errand I had the Justification of bringing the whole Party the closer to a good Night's Sleep, but at the same Time I was the better enabled to satisfy my aforesaid Curiosity & to pursue an opportune Errand of my own. Ever since my Trials upon the lewd but sluggish Crowther in my Youth, I had ample Opportunity to observe the male generative Organ & to judge its Needs & Discipline. I have always thought it an overweening

185

Thing, that must swagger to conceal its Shame at having been turnd inside-out & draggd out from the Body—as to all Women it must appear so. Being in the Air it must attempt to become a little Body of itself, so that it might speak, and once it is a Body it thrusts all aside in this Desperation to speak, though it have but little in the End to say. And when it is allowd to have spoken, it is once again ashamd, like a Child that is acknowledged ignorant & sent into the Corner. It will hang its Head, & pretend that it is not there.

Only with Ramboasalama did I feel that this fleeting Body had acquird a Power over itself, to know itself, & to grow itself from a Child into a Man, which had nothing to prove because it has nothing to learn, & is therefore without Restlessness. For in its Hour of Fullness, it came into me slowly & lay still as the Plum-Stone in a Plum, & said nothing, nor needed to say any Thing, & we would lie so the whole Night long until the Fullness broke, & the Pleasure draind out of me in Shivers, as though I found that I were riding a Ghost, & all this Time Ramboasalama as still & tender with me as at first Touch.

By comparison with this, & with many Trysts & Errands with my other Husbands, the little Scene in the Count's dressing-Room was not a serious Drama at all, but a farcical After-Piece that an Audience might have hooted at. And yet it was a serious Matter for Paolo & his Sister, who for Shame would have wept to see each other naked, were they not in fear of the Count & the Cruelties he threatend them, indeed on previous Occasions may have performd. And so I enterd upon the Stage, & extemporisd my Role. If there is a God, I am sure He may forgive me.

God—And yet, as you well know, I designd you for

Despair only. Your Expectations must not be to be forgiven but to be damnd, if my Forgiveness is to have any true Effect.

Laet—But what if I know you to be forgiving?

God—You may put on that winning Smile of yours as you will, Madam, for as you must realise, the Knowledge quite undoes its Effect.

Laet—Like most Knowledge, I suppose, in your View, who never intended Mankind to reach Enlightenment?

God—I intended that Mankind should be happy.

Laet—And yet Mankind is continually seeking for Knowledge, in the course of which, whatever else he might discover, he discovers that he is not happy.

God—You shall not play Aunt Sallys with me, like any £100 Curate. Go to your Room immediately.

Laet—I shall not. I would like to know what Harm there was in assisting the Count to his Pleasure, with the least Discomfort to his Servants.

God—You took the Count's Pleasure to yourself, in place of Paolo's Sister, in a Manner forbid by the Church, *a tergo*.

Laet—But that was precisely the manner he requird, for the Girl was there among the hurt Sheets, Buttocks spread like the little O'Murphy, but without the Complaisance.*

God—You took Pleasure in Paolo also. Yea verily, you took Paolo's Pleasure unto yourself.

Laet—Would you have had me waste it? The Boy scarcely knew what to do with himself, for the Incense was ready, & no Altar to receive it. He was like a Grandson to me.

God—You had better let him escape at the same time

---

*She refers to Boucher's painting of the King's mistress, 'La Petite Mourphil'.

as his Sister. It was your Selfishness & Licentiousness that hinderd you.

Laet—If you had ever taken Joy in a stiff Prick—which I much doubt—you would better understand. Besides, his Departure would have displeasd the Count, who would not be fobbed off without his Orgy. My Conduct was the Height of Diplomacy, & concluded in the Darkness, for my own Candle was used in the Performance, & the Count's went out.

God—Go to, Madam. You are a veritable Jesuit of the Bedchamber.

It was true that I had negociated a brilliant Truce between all Parties, for the Count had not the Strength of Desire nor Recklessness of Will to force himself with much Hope of Success upon these Innocents. In his Mind were Pictures from Aretino, but in his dressing-Room only the Awkwardness & unhelpful Weight of real, rather than imagind Bodies, with little constructive Complicity from his youthful Victims. As in the World of Taste he fancied himself a Medici, so in the World of Intrigue he fancied himself a Borgia, but truly in neither was he anything more than a Chiavari.

From assuming the Role of Mistress of Ceremonies in his dressing-Room it was but a short Step to become Mistress of the entire Palazzo, & I made sure that this was put on a permanent Footing, accompanied by all the Legality & Absurdity of Nuptials. These Rituals, especially in the Sensuousness & Splendour of Catholick Observance, are designd to exalt & solemnise the Fecundity of Youth, & to regulate its Passions. Applied to an elderly Roué & his pimping Crone, they cannot but appear a Travestie of sorts, & I believe that God absented himself on that Occasion, with polite Apologies.

The Cardinal, however, was perfectly obliging, having no fear that I might disoblige his Expectations with an Heir, & at the end of a lengthy Mass, at which he presided, arranged for the Organist to perform some pretty Toccatas of the Earl of Kelly, as a Tribute to my exotick Origins. I would have skippd down the Aisle to the Sound of them, had my left Leg let me, not so much for Love of the Count himself, but for the Thought of the pleasing Body of the faithful if puzzled Paolo, for my latest Marriage was not a Wedding of like Minds or even of mutually agreeable Bodies, but a Passport to Adventure, & a front for Profligacy.

My Writing down Aretino calls to Mind an interesting Idea with which it occurred to me to amuse the Count. I transcribd some of Aretino's Figures on to a Card no more than a few inches square & repeated the Drawings on some two-score Cards of the same Size, yet altering their Position & Attitudes little by little on each one, so that when the Cards were viewed the one after another, but as quickly as possible, through the release of the Thumb— they being held together as One might deal them at Whisk—the tiny Figures went through the visible Motions & completed those Lewd Intentions which were ever in the Original suspended in the Pursuit, without Animation.*

The Count was as pleasd with this Device as a Child is with a Hobby-Horse, & clappd his Hands. He was like a Child, too, in his Couplings, expecting Chastisement for Transgression, but unlike a Child in taking Pleasure in it. I made other Sets of Cards, one of a Design of Satyrs from a Greek Vase, & another of the Czar of Russia bestowing

---

*Animated drawings employed in optical toys, such as the phenakistoscope or the zoetrope, do not seem to have been recorded before the 1830s.

upon Bonaparte the same Indignity that the Count had intended upon Paolo. The latter gave me the most Trouble, for lack of Models, yet borrowing the free Style of a Cartoon by Gillray I made the Motions vigorous enough, if crude. It occurred to me that some Machine might be constructed both to store & to present in like Manner some hundreds, perhaps thousands, of such cards & that there would be much Money to be made of it, but the Extent of the Labour involvd in the drawing of the Cards forbade it.

Now that I am alone again & more truly nearer Death than I ever thought myself, save after the Ship-Wreck, I know that I shall never again live with a Man. What is it to have done so, & to be so strangely left without Issue or Family? Whenever I come into a Family, & perceive the Bustle & Negociation, the common & conflicting Interests laid up daily as for a Kitchen Committee, the Provisions, the Resentments, the Concern, & all of it, the Good, Bad and Indifferent, never to be forgot for one Hour, I marvel at the Life I have steered through. Myself being barren I have long lived with, & now it stirs in me no more than a distant sort of Curiosity, as it might be that I was a Man who in Idleness tried to imagine what it would be like to bear a Child. But that with five Husbands I have collected so little Family! To have been such a Pilgrim to the Shrine of Venus & to have met with so few Blessings from Juno on the Way! One Step-Son, & he a Port-cheeked Celibate dozing his Days away in a pretty Vicarage in Grantchester! I often wonder if Daisy had livd whether she would have had Children. I might even now be entertaining her Grandchildren with Sugar-Plums at the Fireside, & stories of the Arabian Nights. There was a Time when I even stirrd myself to make

Enquiries of a Bastard Child of Crowther's that I had known of, though I had pretended Ignorance out of Rage. I baited my Hook with mention of an Interest in Silks & Cottons, but heard Nothing, & was content to have heard Nothing, for I could not have in all Honesty had much feeling for the Creature had she been found. In my few Day-Dreams of the future World I find myself populating it with the little naked Offspring of the Merina, some of them Ramboasalama's, & with their Offspring, & their Offspring's Offspring, the precocious Generations multiplying each dozen Years all over that teeming Island.

And what of the Men themselves, how may I compare them? I have often thought that if Men in their publick Persons manifested the same Variation of Shape & Stature as they do in their private Member, then one would hardly know them to belong to the same Species. And yet it is their Scents & Faces that I remember, where Individuation acquires its Essence beyond all Category. If Man had truly been made in the Image of God, then the Generalisation would have rendered meaningless all that seems God-like in a Person, which at the Moment of apprehending it appears unique. Every Man in the Light of being loved is the God of himself, & of the World he draws into himself, & the same is true of every Woman. It is in the publick Sphear, of course, that the Character is formd, but here the Differences may be perceivd by any common Observer. You yourself, Percy, from this inadequate & brief Account, may easily conclude—as you would, Wealth being your Hatred & ever the encumbering Dross that keeps us from soaring into the Empyrean—that my two husbands who labourd to earn their Money were very different from the two who inherited it. But were they wholly better? When I look back upon my Life, as this Writing has compelld me to do, I can see that there may be something dull to a Career or a Vocation which the surprising Diversions provided by a Rake—however half-hearted—or a Roué—however theoretical—do something to alleviate. A Man will always be chearful in the squandering of Money, but sober in the gaining of it. A Wife will like something of both Moods, but not a preponderance of either. Yet truly I believe I was happiest with the Man who had never heard of Money at all.

But what is it that draws us to one Man, & not another? Morality would have it that in our Minds is a perpetual little Theatre of rational Argument & considerd Choice. But I cannot think from my own Mistakes that this can be true, or Life would be as comforting as a painted Roundel on an Alcove,—Beauty Directed by Prudence Rejects with Scorn the Sollicitations of Folly. The Forces directing our Actions are more wayward, & leave us more to our own Devices, than we would like. I sometimes think of it as a natural Attraction or Repulsion as is found in Nature in the Poles of a Magnet, or as is well-known in the Case of Colours.

Some Colours will not be reconcild & are incompatible, which we discover by mingling them, as in a Marriage. If in the Mixture we find nothing disagreeable to the Sight, then they have a Sympathy, viz. Green is an agreeable Colour, which may be made by Blue and Yellow mixt, therefore there is a Sympathy between them; Blue and Vermilion produce a nigre Colour, therefore there is an Antipathy between them. Men show themselves in that dangerous Refraction between Yellow and Vermilion. Think of me as Blue.

The Comforting Fallacies of the Count Chiavari. On his Death-Bed, when he lookd no more despondent than he did in Bed on any Day of his Life, the Count said,—Since I am better to-day, I will go on getting better.

This was so much like himself that I nearly smiled. I certainly did not have the Hardness of Heart to argue the Point with him. His Philosophy ever consisted of the simplest of Conclusions from inappropriate Premisses, without even the Interposition of an undistributed Middle. Many of his Sayings arose from his Fear of bodily Discomfort or his Desire to avoid Trouble, & all of them dismissed the Need to think or to act with the slenderest of Excuses. The first I heard him pronounce, though I did not think it significant, was on the matter of some Niches for Statues:—I have not yet decided, he said, to make a Decision.

And in the early days of our Understanding:—Paolo has never said any thing about it, so his Sister must be all right.

And in parallel with this:—If I don't hear what you say, it can't really matter.

Or sometimes:—I don't remember anything about it, so it is no longer important.

In his social Life, such as it was, his Philosophy was designed to leave him unscathd by Dangers:—More Brandy will surely do me no harm; I have drunk three Glasses already.

Or:—I will make no Reply to his Challenge; he is only an Innkeeper.

Or:—I am a Count, & therefore I am of account.

Truly, on occasion he thought himself absolutely immortal. After Canova's Angels had been in place a Year or two, he remarked one Morning:—They are so beautiful. It would be a pity if they were never put to use.

The Manner is catching. There are Times when I find my Thinking not in my Stoick Blue, but shot through with a Contagion of Chiavari Vermilion. As I shuffled to the Terrace this Morning, with my Basket of Paper, I began to mutter defiantly:—My painful Leg is giving me no trouble, so I might as well live for ever.

And why is it giving me no Trouble? Yesterday Admiral Parker sent his Carriage for me, as promised, to take me to his Experiment with the Scafandro at Genoa & to Dine on his Ship. I expected to be tird, & nearly refusd him, but the Expedition did me good, even though the Entertainment was disappointing.

The Admiral's Men had Cauldrons placed over their Heads, with Eye-Holes, and Tubes protruding from the Front like the Trump of an Elephant. Their Fellows pumpd in relay on Deck, while the poor Monsters, weighd down with Cannisters at the Waist, were lowerd into the Harbour. The Purpose is said to be for the readier repair of Ships without being put to the Expense of a dry-Dock, but from the Equipment handled I would have guessd them Nautical Engineers, or Sea-Sappers, ready to attach Bombs and lay Fuses to the Hulls of unsuspecting Vessels. I cannot think that the Attempt would meet with great Success, for the poor Monsters movd slowly enough on board & must have been immobilised when entombed in Water. They were eager enough, by the Signs given, to be hauled up again, & I remarked to Lady Parker that my Giovanni's Hyacinth could stay much longer under water, naked & quite unencumberd. It was not breathing-Cauldrons the Sailors needed, but Finns to move quickly, & practised Lungs not coarsend by Rum & tobacco. I offered Hyacinth to Lady Parker as a Demonstration in return, & for a Moment she almost thought me serious.

But I have returnd refreshd from this nautical Charade, & conclude from it that Man has some way to go before he may easily explore the Elements alien to his Nature. In truth, although we may freely partake of these Elements to which many of our Fellow-Creatures are more closely confind, we are ourselves limited in our essential Beings to one Element only, and that is the Element of Time. Unlike the Beasts, who are not conscious of it, we may travel back & forth within it, visiting in our Minds the Beings that we once were. Yet in no suffocating Scafandro of Prophecy can we trespass into the Future,—only we gaze upon it, as upon the level and unbroken surface of the Sea, in an agony of Hope & Fear. What will become of us? What will be the manner of our dying?

There is a Bird out there upon the Water, flying fast over its Surface which is calm in the windless Air & glittering in the Sun, the last perhaps of the warm Autumn Days. The Sea itself has a quality of Expectation, for always it unrolls before the Sight & leads the Eye to its own Invisibility. There have been Storms, & there will be Storms again. The burned & salted Plants have not recovered, & to-day Angelo had to cut down my favourite Bush of Rosemary. The Bird still flies, confident in its Purposes. But its Flight is melancholy, as across the dusty Floor of a deserted Ballroom.

The Portrait of the Terrace has been the brief Passage of a Summer, wingd by Memory. Where it originated is now forgotten in the Haze of Distance. Its Destination is unknown. It ever betrays the regular Motions which propel it within its Element of Recall, yet this produces a Flight or Trajectory within the vast Accumulation of experienced Life which at every Point must ignore most of the Events that lie around it. It therefore must mirrour the Subject's very Adventures which it intended to portray, as a Sequence of lost Alternatives & Paths not taken. I feel lost in it.

But the Portrait of the Gallery, to which I more & more return, gives me the greater Confidence of Truth, which you shall judge for yourself, Percy, when you shall see it. For a written Narrative must of Necessity be constructed upon the consecutive Details which have by Chance really occurrd, whereas a Portrait is entirely concerned with the accumulated Effect of that Experience in Emblems, if you will. The Narrative is, like Time itself, a kind of Mapp wherein we only know the single Carriageway that runs between the Places whose Names we have charted, but the Painting is of the Terrain itself, recognisd like a beloved Patria in its Wholeness, where we are everywhere welcome & all Journeying is done.

When I shall have finishd my Portrait of the Gallery, then you shall see me as I am, not all I have been, but all I have become. At my Age, there is nothing left to be done. I have run through all my Possibilities, like a Chest of Cloaths, each of which I have put on & acted out its Part, as though a Bequest of theatrical Costume. These are now the meer Ghosts of me, left in the Darkness like Attitudes without an Audience.

I thought something of this when I went last Week into the Count's Apartments, & found yet again his own Cloaths, as I expected to, for I have not yet disposd of any of them. These sad Habiliments & folded Wrappings, not unclean, & yet with the Scent of the Man still upon them in spite of fragrance in Sprigs laid with them, are the veriest Apparitions of his vain Hope of Life, & therefore like Hauntings.

Gold Shoes, with the Heel that lent Height; the Turkish Slippers; the riding-Boots; the cream silk Stockings, patched at the Toe where the Nail caught them; Linnen Drawers; white Breeches; Flanders Shirts;

green Waistcoats; black Waistcoats; blue Coats with silver Buttons; scarlet Coats with gold Frogging; Night-Shirts, with large Sleeves ready to flapp; Cravats to choke; the Japanese dressing-Gown; the Japanese Sword; the Japanese hat, never worn; other Hats, looking unhappy at not riding five and a half Feet above the ground.

These were his Disguises, or rather the necessary Forms in which his invisible Self decided to meet the World, which he always feard. Behind these empty Tubes, Girdles & half-Containers, so troubling to me for their Indication of what was now eternally missing from them, was the Idea of the naked Man who tried to become himself by putting them on. But he was not happily himself when naked, either, so that I do not know what he was, or what he thought he was, certainly not a Japanese Count, by putting on the Blade of a Samurai, nor yet a Husband by putting on a Night-Cap. Perhaps he was simply the Ghost of himself, putting on visible Shape as Fashion, or the Idea of the Moment, dictated.

Are we all created by some Idea of what we might be, which first our Parents impose upon us? Do we ever escape from such Expectations, and if we do, is it only into the equally constricting Roles which our Imaginacion makes available to us? What happiness did the Count claim for himself as a Samurai ascending his Pagoda, to exclaim with the Sunset all about him & his whole Life uncreated in his hands:

—Once I have climbd to the Top, where can I look but down?

In the Descent, to the Clink of the Sword, & the Slap of the Sandals on the Stone, did he hear about him in the Stillness of the Evening the dry Summons of the Crickets, & imagine it to be Laughter?

I hear the Crickets myself, & would wish them Anthems. Their Sound enters the Gallery through the open Windows at Night, where I paint by the Light of fifteen or twenty Candles that sputter & fizz with their Sacrifice of Insects. In the green Mirrour I might be a Demon in my Hair, staring so hard at myself that I almost might tear the Skin away, Layer by Layer, as the Sea-Wind burns the Flowers of the Summer. Behind these Layers is not the Bone, but the Spirit. The Painter of her own Self looks into the Eyes not to see what Image the hesitant Sitter desires or fears, but only to see her Inquisition returnd upon herself by the Glass. There is that sudden Infinity between the multiplied Reflections in those sentient Spheres of Jelly that dizzies the conception, as in the mutual Recognition of Love. There the Spirit dances, & might be caught if she would be for a moment still.

I can never find the Colours fast enough, & work in Tones of the same Pigment to save Time, so that I appear a Creature of the Shadows, like a moonlit Vision, or one of Smagg's Angels. I am in a kind of Fury to catch this Spirit, & to see in the unfortunate Appearances of my corporeal Being some fleeting Evidence of a permanent Truth about me. The Dressings to my Calfs have come adrift, like a Grenadier's Puttees in the heat of Conflict, & the Growth on my Leg protrudes like another Joint. Here I must find some Carmine, & yet again some sort of blue for the Bone. Quick, Quick! It stands jutted out, an heroick Pose but turning into a kind of a Claw. We often fancy we might extend our Parts, do we not, Percy, as that little Tenderness—like an Absence—beneath the Bone of the Ancle that might become a sixth & grasping Toe, or Shoulder-Blades Wings? And at the Base of our Spine, the Sense of a Tail? Perhaps I have lived so long, not to die, but to change into my next Shape, neither a wise Methuselah nor a dull Struldbrugg, but some Thing never before seen, about to break from its wrinkled Pupa, with streaming Hair.

My ground Colour was a new Device, for it is not the Darkness of an interior Space, as in Tradition to concentrate the Light on the Figure, but an open Blue, to expose the Figure in its proper Element, which is the Air of this rocky Coast. Yet I wish, after all, that I had made it to be Night, & that I could paint into it the Sound of the Crickets, for look, here comes the promisd Storm as well, with a Wind that flattens the Candle-Flames.

The Thunder announces itself quietly at first, like Maria beating out the Carpets in the Kitchen Yard. I remember now that Angelo used to help her, but gave up with his Head-Ake, for he woke from his Dreams of the Prognosticacion of Death—I told you he was a Mazzere—in a Daze of such Pain. He had been gathering Asphodel, hunting over the Hills all Night, & knew that his Quarry would die in Truth, & would not say who it was he had killed in his Dream. Perhaps it was myself he intended, & could not bring himself to say so, for Maria has been strange with me ever since.

Well, perhaps I am to die, after all. But if Angelo can become a wild Animal in his Phantasy, & hunt me down, as these Corsicans believe, why should I not think myself into a Prey fleet enough to elude him? If I so dream to-night, and will myself to it by thinking hard upon my Bolster that I am a Vorombe, I shall undo his guilty Dream,—for why should he dream me, or any One, killed unless he wished it so?

The Thunder comes again, & nearer, like a Barrel rowling into a Cellar. What shall I do to defy this Storm? I need a Charm to protect me. On the Island Ramboasalama told me that I would be safe in the Forest if I placed an Egg upon the Ground to be picked up later on my way out, & if I did not forget myself so far as to whistle there. But Children will whistle to keep their Courage up.

My Portrait shall defy all Storms. I will turn these eyes into lucky Eggs, and outstare Cataracts. My Leg is like the Thigh-Bone of the Vorombe, & my Body is a Throne to bear the Spirit like a King. Now the Lightning. At first it is a Flicker, darting through the Clouds like a Shiver on the Skin.

Is a Storm male or female? Is it the Seed or the Blood? Is it the Bone or the Flesh? Is it Death or Birth? The Islanders said it was neither, but the wooing of the Earth by the Sky, and therefore both. Here is the Lightning again, & I feel it between my Legs like a Memory of Passion there, its wet Flint-and-Tinder. The Sky descends upon the Earth to bring it alive, though it break itself in the Process like Crockery. Listen to the Thunder, in Pieces! The Lightning is a Crack in a Plate, like my Chinaman's Head-Ake. It strikes the Count's Pagoda, which stands there in the Darkness, suddenly lit like a Man's Yard with its Energy to speak & die.

I have heard this Voice all my Life, and have sometimes spoken to it. The Portrait will be my Voice, speaking, and I will give it Beads & Feathers like an Oli of the Spirit. This is the true Terrour which the Lightning illuminates. There is no Bird unless I myself am the Bird. I will speak through the Thunder and see Visions. I will paint my Eyes as the Eyes of the Scafandro. The Earth will leap up to the Sky, and carry my Life with it. I shall escape the fevered barking of the Mazzere, & I shall again see my Father, Percy, & there shall never be an End to this

200

Appendix A
Swift's 'To Letty Connell, on her Pictures'

Swift's verses to the six-year-old Letty were among the last that he wrote. There is a transcript among the Harley Papers in the possession of the Duke of Portland, Welbeck Abbey [Ref. W] and a transcript in the John Rylands Library, English MS. 659. The poem appeared in Faulkner's edition of 1746, VIII, p. 320 [Ref. F] and in Hawkesworth's *Works*, 1755, 4to edn. IV, p. 288. The following text, and apparatus, is taken with permission from *The Poems of Jonathan Swift*, ed. Harold Williams, 2nd edn (1958), II, p. 682.

Darling Letty, well you please us
With little Pictures of Diseases.
At your Pencills grave command
The Likeness grows beneath your Hand
Of what was never seen before,
The Shapes that ailing Men abhor.
Fevers like the Fates are spinning
Infirmities from dirty Linnen;
Feathered Spasms, scaly Shivers,
Swarming on our Lungs and Livers,   10
Flocking Dropseys, flying Agues,
Winged as is ye Winter Sea-Goose;
As Fallen Angels take ye shape
Of a First Minister or Ape,
So Fevers to ye human Eye
Grow Feathers & appear to fly,

So Geographers in *Afric*-Maps
With Savage-Pictures fill their Gaps
And so a myriad Chinese
Are found alike like Mites in Cheese.   20
     More like a Dreamer than a Medick
You trace yᵉ flapping of a Head-Ake.
We wonder how it is you show
A Scurvy or a Vertigo,
And innocent can raise a Pox
As did Pandora from her Box.
Little Rogue, we'll not forget ye,
For who will not remember Letty?

———————
I well] will 1755
21 Dreamer] W, F. Prophet 1755
25 innocent] innocent, W, F.

Appendix B
The Cancelled Stanzas of Shelley's
'The Witch of Atlas'

Shelley's fantasy in ottava rima, 'The Witch of Atlas', was composed in 1820. The following stanzas exist only in a fair-copy (without title or ascription) belonging to Magdalen College, Oxford (MS 6742) and have never been incorporated into a published text of the poem. Since Shelley was already drafting the poem on 14 August, and this seems too early for him to have seen any of the Horsepole Memoirs, the stanzas may well have been an unusable afterthought suggested by a reading of the Memoirs, where she hopes, by painting the Roc, to 'bring it to Birth in the Womb of [her] own reflecting Eyes' (see p. 132). Of course, it is possible that Horsepole may simply have spoken of the Roc in similar terms to Shelley while he was staying at the Villa Chiavari.

Mary Shelley was settled at the Casa Prinni at the Bagni San Giuliano, four miles from Pisa. She mentions Shelley's first visit to the Palazzo Chiavari in her journal for Thursday 27 July: 'Greek—S. goes to Genoa, at the call of the mad paintress. Finish 4th book of Lucretius' (*Journals of Mary Shelley, 1814-44*, ed. Paula Feldman and Diana Scott-Kilvert, 1995, I. p. 328). Shelley was ostensibly looking for a house for the rest of the summer for his family.

To what other poets did Shelley show his draft, or talk to about the fabulous bird? There was a curious fashion

for introducing the Roc into poems in the 1820s, e.g.
Bryan Proctor in 'The Flood of Thessaly' (1823) and
Mary Howitt in 'The Desolation of Eyam' (1827).

There in the Cavern light had never been
The very dark knew not that it was dark
As that which hath been lit by tapers green
And lifted flaming torches does whose spark
Dashed to the flinty floor is barely seen—
Like Meteors that make their fiery mark
Faint messengers that hasten through the sky
To tell of what has wounded them and die.

This darkness told no news nor lent a hand
Of air to guide the stumbling venturer
Towards a passageway, it was a land
Where Sight was dumb and sound could make no stir
Where Mind found nothing it could understand
And every sense rebelled into a blur
The very Womb of all forgetfulness
Like letters sent to a last known address.

Yet in this darkness she alone could see
Whatever grew there all that stirred and spawned
In lightlessness and struggled to be free
All that having slept an Age now yawned
And woke or having not been wished to be
Strange clots of feathers, little jellies horned
And eager to be walking, puddles with legs
Embodied groans and soft enormous eggs.

Of these none greater than the ivory home
Of that strange creature called the Eastern Roc,

Its surface dimpled like the Ocean's foam
Seen from a mountain might withstand the shock
Of earthquakes, duly at her behest the dome
Cracks open when the bird begins to knock
Its giant legs as thick as crocodiles
Its infant cries rough as the rasp of files.

It came to birth reflected in her eyes
Which fill with liquid looking like a sea
Wherein a willing Madagascar lies
All-shadowed by the white Immensity
Of its unfolding wings before it flies
To other islands, and this bird is she
Who called it into being and no other
She is its sticky self and her own Mother.

Appendix C
Extracts from Joseph Farington's Diary

The following extracts, which provide the only detailed reference to Laetitia Horsepole (other than that of the Shelleys) that I have been able so far to find, are taken from *The Diary of Joseph Farington*, ed. Kenneth Garlick and Angus Macintyre (1978), II, pp. 415, 449 and III, p. 501.

Friday Novr. 27th, 1795
Soanes I dined at, Miss Archibald,—Fuseli, Dance, Lawrence, Canistrelli, Smirke & Tyler there.

Fuseli was in Italy 8 years, which he said was much too long. Ramsay, the painter, said, "Rome was a noble Theatre for an Artist; but it was dull playing to an empty pit." Canistrelli said that idleness is owing only to an insufficient stimulus to urge an Artist on, and that the decline of patronage could not be wholly blamed.

We left Soanes abt. Eleven o'clock.—Smirke and Fuseli came home with me & sat till near one o'clock.—Fuseli remarked on the admirable choice of words, and the arrangement of his sentences, when Lawrence spoke about Grants speech on the Sedition Bills in the House of Commons on Wednesday last. He told us that Canistrelli, though now supposed to be married to Laetitia Horsepole, is more often in Genoa than London, where he wastes Carrera marble by the ton on Italian Bath-houses of ill design, which might account for his views on patronage. He said that Signora Canistrelli is even dirtier than her husband and though a woman of striking appearance was now a lunatic Jacobin who talked of nothing but her visions. Her laugh, it is said, can be heard across the river at Vauxhall, and bears a resemblance indeed to the ascent of a rocket. She shewed paintings in the Academy thirty years ago, but had since wasted her talents on sea Captains & merchants. Her former husband Horsepole was a dull dog, and died in Madagascar where they were ship-wrecked.—Fuseli being in spirits had after tea paid much attention to Miss Archibald & we laughed much on our return at his sudden & extravagant admiration of her, as she is a very tall woman, though not so tall, he said, nor as lame, as Laetitia Horsepole.

Saturday Decr. 19th, 1795
Dance said that Johnson had intervened ten years ago on behalf of Mrs. Horsepole (Canistrelli) when her portrait of her slave had been refused, but he had not been successful as he had been in the case of Mr. Lowe. He did not know if the reason for the refusal was political. She frightened the Porter at the Academy, who said that she sailed in like the figurehead of a Frigate under fire, and took the painting away in her own arms.

Monday March 3rd, 1806
Fuseli said that Signora Canistrelli's large portrait of Bonaparte brooding after the Peace of Amiens was the greatest work of genius he had ever seen but that it was refused because (he said) the public would not stand for it. He thought her a sad case of illimitable talents wanting Judgement, & blamed her decline on her feud with West, who had once ill-advisedly made advances to her. Kauffmann, Moser, &c, her inferiors.

Appendix D
The Paintings of Laetitia Horsepole

Apart from two of the four works in the National Gallery, London (see nos 12, 13, 17 and 18 below) and the late paintings and drawings in the Galleria di Palazzo Bianco, Genoa (see nos 26–34) Horsepole's paintings have attracted little comment, and there has been no separate study of her work, nor any attempt at a catalogue. The most interesting modern criticism is to be found in Gustave Soulier, *Les Influences étrangères dans la peinture Toscane romantique* (1924) and Alberto Ragazzacci, 'Il "rossor di mattina" di Laetitia Horsepole', *Rivista storica dell'arte Toscani* (1935), xxv. 3, pp. 85-94. There are, of course, passing comments on the 'slave' paintings by Ruskin, Berenson and others. The portraits of Mrs Howson and her brother have never, to my knowledge, been on public display, and the relatively substantial number of portraits at the Admiralty, the National Maritime Museum and elsewhere has not attracted much attention. There must be many works which I have not been able to locate, and many more which will not have survived. Nothing of her work in Madagascar has been found, while the extensive repainting of Madagascan wildlife in fresco at the Palazzo Chiavari was entirely destroyed by Allied bombing in 1944. Her sketch of the Roc in the Natural History Museum (no. 16) is dismissed by Erroll Fuller, *Extinct Birds* (1987), p. 19, as an amateur fantasy. Nothing is known about the fate of the contents of her studio after her death, nor of the self-portrait she was working on.

1 *Katherine Connell*, oil [1761], National Gallery of Ireland.
2 Illustrations to *Pharmakopion Okeanikon* (1762).
3 *Mr and Mrs Francis Hayman with their Children*, oil, 1762, National Portrait Gallery, London.
4 *Captain Gifford*, oil, 1764, National Maritime Museum, Greenwich.
5 *Lord Osborne*, oil, 1764, National Maritime Museum, Greenwich.
6 *The Fleet at Portsmouth Point*, oil, ?1765, Barnstaple Athenaeum.
7 *Piping aboard*, The Maid of Kent, oil, ?1766, Royal Navy Museum, Portsmouth.
8 *James Horsepole*, oil, 1767, Admiralty House, Whitehall.
9 *Admiral Browning*, oil, 1767, Admiralty House, Whitehall.
10 *Captain Lodge*, oil, 1768, National Maritime Museum, Greenwich.
11 *Abraham Entertaining the Angels*, drawing with sepia wash, ?1768, Sion House.
12 *Mrs Howson*, oil, ?1768, National Gallery, London.
13 *Elkanah Howson in the Garden*, oil, ?1768, National Gallery, London.
14 *Commander Warre*, oil, 1769, National Maritime Museum, Greenwich.
15 *Samuel Johnson*, oil, 1769, the Garrick Club, London.
16 *Rukh*, drawing, early 1780s, Natural History Museum, South Kensington.
17 *The Untrusting Slave*, oil, ?1786, National Gallery, London.
18 *Freedom*, oil, ?1786, National Gallery, London.
19 *Robert Horsepole, M.A.,* oil, ?1788, Jesus College, Cambridge.

20 *John Thelwall*, ink drawing, ?1797-8, National Portrait Gallery, London.

21 *Samuel Coleridge*, drawing, ?1797-8, National Portrait Gallery, London.

22 *Sir George Parker*, oil, 1798, Admiralty Office, Whitehall.

23 *Lord and Lady Brock*, oil, ?1798, Spelhampton House, Essex.

24 *Sir Harry Burrard*, oil, ?1798, Southampton University Library.

25 *The Eagle*, oil, 1802, Musée Fesch, Ajaccio, Corsica.

26 *Conte Chiavari*, oil, 1814, Galleria di Palazzo Bianco, Genoa.

27 *Lord Bentinck*, oil, 1814, Galleria di Palazzo Reale, Genoa.

28 *The Lark*, oil, after 1815, Galleria di Palazzo Bianco, Genoa.

29 *Horse Terrified by a Storm*, oil, after 1815, Galleria di Palazzo Bianco, Genoa.

30 *Blue*, oil, after 1815, Galleria di Palazzo Bianco, Genoa.

31 *Bathers*, oil, after 1815, Galleria di Palazzo Bianco, Genoa.

32 *Bat and Fruit*, drawing, after 1815, Galleria di Palazzo Bianco, Genoa.

33 *Shepherd's Warning*, oil, after 1815, Galleria di Palazzo Bianco, Genoa.

34 [sketches of the Ligurian Coast], drawings with coloured washes, after 1815, Galleria di Palazzo Bianco, Genoa.

Appendix E
Æpyornis maximus

Laetitia Horsepole's Roc is a ratite of the order Æpyornithiformes. The *Æpyornis maximus* of Madagascar, the 'elephant bird', was a flightless bird with a dark body and a white neck, reaching ten feet in height and laying eggs over a foot in length. Although Marco Polo's account of it dates from 1294, the rukh, or roc, or *vorombe*, is often reckoned to have died out in the twelfth century. This creates a twin problem with Horsepole's account in the *Memoirs* of seeing a vorombe 'larger than' a house (see p. 136). The bird was the largest species recorded, three times the size of the ostrich and weighing half a ton, but it was hardly that big. Nor could she have seen one if it was extinct.

Supposing, however, that she may have seen a surviving specimen, the dramatic and abbreviated circumstances of its sighting were very likely to have led to an exaggeration of its size. Her earlier computation of its dimensions (see p. 132) need not be unreasonable if we presume the King's palace to be a single-storey building, and a 'house' in her mind to be a Merina and not a European one. Always in her mind, too, I take it, is the mythic size of the bird in *The Thousand and One Nights*, where Sindbad walks all round the great dome of the egg that he finds, and later unwinds his turban and ties himself by the waist to one of the talons of the creature. Which of course flies away with him.

But could she have seen one at all? There is some

suggestion that the bird may have survived after 1642, when the French claimed Madagascar. The latest reported sighting (in Flacourt's account) in 1658 contradicts the medieval date of extinction of *Æpyornis maximus*, but was, of course, uncorroborated in any way. Nonetheless, the Oxford Museum (which possesses gizzard stones and sub-fossil bones and shell) claims only that it was 'extinct by the end of the seventeenth century'. Victor Sganzin, a French naval officer, acquired a complete egg in the 1830s, and sold it to the natural history dealers, Verreaux. Unfortunately the ship bringing it back to France ran aground at La Rochelle. Three eggs were found in 1851 by a Captain Abadie, and enough bone to articulate a skeleton. Multiple dating of surviving egg fragments (radiocarbon, electron spin resonance, and optically stimulated luminescence) is still at too early a stage to establish limits, but a comparatively late date is thought not to be absolutely impossible for the survival of individual groups of birds. A comparison may be made with the Moa of New Zealand: it was mostly extinct before 1600, but George Pauley claimed to have seen one in the 1820s. Madagascar is a large island, two and a half times the size of the UK. The Roc may have been killed to obtain the eggs as containers, but they were not hunted to extinction for food as ruthlessly as the Dutch eliminated the Dodo in Mauritius. It is just conceivable that Horsepole saw one of an isolated pocket of survivors.